A SECO[illegible] DEATH

Josef Slonský Investigations
Book Five

Graham Brack

Also in the Josef Slonský Series

Lying and Dying

Slaughter and Forgetting

Death on Duty

Field of Death

Laid in Earth

A SECOND DEATH

Published by Sapere Books.

20 Windermere Drive, Leeds, England, LS17 7UZ,
United Kingdom

saperebooks.com

ISBN: 978-1-913028-83-1

Chapter 1

The dark water bubbled white as it skipped across the rocks. While the centre of the river flowed serenely on, all the energy appeared to be concentrated near the banks, but here and there the water became still where obstructions narrowed the channel.

The late September sun skittered across the surface as the river turned to head towards the sunrise, illuminating the overhanging tree branches and the scattered debris, a shattered plank of wood, an empty plastic milk carton and a girl's body, the head wedged against a protruding tree root and the blonde hair streaming behind like weed on a rock as it clung to her sodden back.

The two young hikers who had spotted her sat shivering against a tree, their wet boots and socks drying on the path. The paramedics had wrapped them in foil blankets, but how much of their tremor was due to the cold was hard to assess. One had taken a photograph before they waded in to retrieve her and a technician was busy transferring it to a spare memory card. The pathologist, Dr Novák, was examining the body on the bank and supervising the paramedics who were to take her to the mortuary. At length he stood up, nodded to them to take her away and walked over to the car where Captain Josef Slonský was leaning with both arms on the roof, talking into his mobile phone.

'Can we cut the bit where I ask you lots of questions and you pull a face and tell me it's far too early to say?' he asked Novák.

'If you like, but that's one of the best bits for me. Keeping you on tenterhooks is what makes this job worthwhile.'

Slonský broke off to end the call before resuming his attempt to wheedle useful information out of the pathologist.

'Time of death?'

'Too early to say.'

'But, if pushed…?'

'Let's tell you what I can say. I think she's probably been in the water about thirty-six hours but it could be twelve hours either way. It's very difficult to estimate until you get significant wrinkling.'

'Cause of death?'

'No visible wounds, but the fact that she is well dressed but wearing no underwear is suggestive.'

Slonský grimaced. He hated child murders at any time, but ones in which the victim had been molested first were especially difficult for him. Like most police, he could never understand why people did these things.

'Was she raped?'

'Too soon… I think so, but I can't be sure. There was certainly vaginal penetration with something. I suspect the water has washed a lot of blood away but I'll be looking to see if the penetration may have been the cause of death.'

'Any idea of her age?'

'Based purely on dentition, somewhere between ten and twelve, probably nearer the lower end.'

'Let me know what you can as soon as you can,' Slonský said, and patted Novák encouragingly on the back before striding off to see what Officer Jan Navrátil was doing.

'Nothing in the pockets, sir,' Navrátil anticipated the first question.

'Labels in the clothes?'

'Not in the jacket. We couldn't see inside the dress and Dr Novák didn't want to disturb it here.'

'It's a shame schools don't have uniforms any longer.'

'I've asked for details of any lost girls aged eight to thirteen just to make sure we don't miss her.'

Slonský nodded and stood gazing out over the Vltava river.

'We know where she ended up, lad, but who knows where she was heaved in?'

'It's a busy river that flows through some populated areas, sir. Surely the fact that she wasn't discovered before now suggests she was thrown in somewhere quite near?'

Slonský consulted his map. 'We need to talk to somebody who knows this water well. One of the boat owners, for example. I'd have thought that once the body was caught in the mainstream it would be dragged away from the banks. It's a wide river. That makes me think you're right. Or it reached the Vltava from a tributary.'

'Dr Novák said he'll get one of the technicians to mock up a photograph of her as she would have appeared in life.'

Slonský nodded to show that he had heard, but did not say anything.

'I've got statements from the hikers, sir. Can we let them go now?' Navrátil continued.

'Contact details checked?'

'Their identity cards check out, sir.'

'Then let them go, though I suspect this has spoiled their day out a bit.'

Slonský was not the big, boisterous figure he had long been. Part of the reason for that was that Officer Kristýna Peiperová was not there. After a little over a year of working for Slonský she had been seconded to the Director of Criminal Police to act as his Personal Assistant for a year. This was a great opportunity for her and Slonský had encouraged her to take it, but in practice it had proved mind-crushingly boring. The Director spent a lot of time in meetings so the chatter and frequent coffee breaks that had characterised her time with Slonský had disappeared and her inclination was to visit her old office at every opportunity where things were always livelier.

Against this, she had to recognise that frequent visits provoked enquiries about her motives, because she and Navrátil were engaged, a circumstance which accounted for Navrátil's general lack of spark since she had been separated from him during working hours. He still worked diligently and well, but things had been different since Slonský's promotion, an elevation that Slonský had resisted for so long but which Captain Lukas had engineered by the simple expedient of retiring and threatening to recommend either of the other lieutenants, Dvorník or Doležal, if Slonský did not accept his job. Knowing that Slonský would sooner pull out his own teeth with pliers than work under either of those, he had correctly calculated that this would spur an application from Slonský, whatever his feelings about becoming a captain and taking on responsibility for the team.

No sooner had Slonský done so than they had lost Doležal. The murder of a policeman in Pardubice left the criminal team there short of numbers so Doležal had been loaned to them. The subsequent arrest and suspension of two senior officers from the team for impeding the investigation had left the department in disarray, so Doležal had been appointed as the new captain there. Sadly the injuries that he had received at the hands of those colleagues had meant that four months later Doležal was only just taking up his new role, and had been given his former assistant Rada to help staff his team. This left Slonský with a very depleted squad of his own. The old team of a captain, three lieutenants and four other officers had suddenly become Slonský, Navrátil, Dvorník and Hauzer, and finding some replacements was testing Slonský to the utmost, depressing his spirits and making him less exuberant than was normally the case.

Over the succeeding weeks Slonský had read a number of files relating to officers who thought that they would like to work in crime but none of the folders he had ploughed through encouraged him to believe that the answer lay within their covers.

Chapter 2

Navrátil disliked going to the mortuary, whilst completely understanding that it was a necessary part of his job. It was not that he was particularly squeamish, but he felt that the activities there were too impersonal. He therefore attempted to redress the balance a little by silently reciting prayers for the dead as he watched Novák and his team at work.

On this occasion he felt hindered by his inability to insert a name where the prayer called for one. He appreciated the gentle way in which Novák dealt with the young girl, particularly the fact that he kept covering her with a sheet to preserve her modesty so far as he could while he worked, but it was still horrible.

'Do you want to come over and see what I'm doing?' asked Novák.

'Only if it's necessary, doctor. I'm content to let you work in peace.'

Novák nodded slowly. 'It's painful, isn't it? If it's any consolation, I hate it too. It has to be done, but I regret that it's necessary. And the best that I can do for her is to collect as much evidence as I can so that you can bring her killer or killers to justice.'

'I understand that.'

'Unfortunately, to do that I have had to open her up, but I'll do my utmost to ensure that when she's dressed for burial you won't be able to tell.'

Navrátil could feel a burning tear in his eye. He did not want to cry, but the sorrow was so profound that he could not resist.

'Why don't you get a coffee and I'll come and find you when I've finished?' Novák said kindly.

'Thank you, but my place is here.'

'Yes, it is, but that doesn't mean you have to watch every move I make.'

'Am I disturbing you?'

'No, not at all. She disturbs me; you don't. Or, more precisely, whoever did this to her disturbs me.' Novák passed a metal dish to an assistant, drew the sheet back up to her neck and peeled off his gloves. 'I think she was about ten years old. I don't think she had reached puberty yet. She had been maltreated sexually, and not for the first time. There were old scars and tears.'

'Was she raped?'

'There are some abraded skin cells there which I don't think are hers, but we'll have to get some tests done. I've taken DNA swabs from her and if this DNA is different it will be an indication that she was raped.'

'Cause of death?'

'Asphyxiation. She has a few fibres under her nails which may come from a woollen jumper. Whether she was deliberately killed or simply suffocated under the weight of a heavy man, I'm not sure. She certainly tried to get him off, so she wasn't unconscious. I've taken samples to see if she was drugged.'

'I almost hope she was,' said Navrátil, 'for her sake.'

Slonský was taking a walk along the riverside in the centre of Prague. To the observer, he looked as if was simply strolling, but actually he was looking for a man, and this was where he believed he might find him, if he could be patient enough.

He bought himself a sausage and sat chewing listlessly as he watched the public going about their business. By the law of averages some of those who passed him must have been criminals, but he was not looking for a criminal today. Rather the opposite; he was looking for a policeman.

He could, of course, have made an appointment through the normal channels. The problem with that approach was that if he was refused he could do nothing about it, because this particular policeman did not work for the national police, but for the municipal police, over whom he had no power.

A little over half an hour had passed when a pair of policemen ambled into view. The shorter one, tubby enough to make his jacket look short as a result of its detour over his belly on the way towards the ground, was of no interest. That was Officer Vacha. Slonský's interest was in Officer Krob.

Around sixteen months earlier Krob had caught Slonský's eye when he used his initiative to stop witnesses to a hit and run accident from sloping off by giving them free coffee and biscuits. Their paths had crossed a few times since and Slonský had become convinced that Krob was wasting his life writing parking tickets and subduing British stag parties who had contributed disproportionately to the profits of the Czech brewing industry (as had Slonský himself over the years). If he had anything to do with it Krob was going to be the newest member of his crime team. All he had to do was to persuade him to apply. Ideally, the application would be backdated ten days so that it could be included in the batch he had been reading, where it would shine, once he had applied some judicious lustre to it himself. He would then tell Human Resources that he had selected Officer Krob and they need never know that Krob had not applied before the closing date.

'Good afternoon, Lieutenant Slonský,' said Krob, echoed a few moments later by Vacha.

'Good afternoon, Officers — though it's Captain Slonský now.'

'Oh — congratulations,' said Krob.

'Yes, congratulations,' added Vacha.

'Thank you.'

Slonský was pondering how to detach Vacha from Krob so he could have that little private chat he was planning, and decided that only the direct approach would do.

'Vacha, would you do me a favour?'

'Certainly, Captain.'

'Good. Push off and let me have a word with Krob in private, would you? I'll return him in sound working order within ten minutes.'

Vacha removed his cap and scratched his head as if to stimulate the thinking part of his brain. 'Right. Yes. Of course.'

Observing Krob's quizzical look Slonský continued. 'Do you like your job, Krob?'

'Yes, sir.'

'You don't feel you'd like to be stretched more? Face a tougher challenge?'

'This part of town is challenging enough, sir.'

'I wasn't thinking of the city police, Krob. I have a vacancy in the criminal police and I thought it would suit you very nicely.'

'Working for you, sir?'

'Yes. Have you got a problem with that?'

'No!' replied Krob, just a little too quickly to be entirely convincing. 'No, not at all. It's just a bit sudden. Won't I have to fill in some forms and stuff first?'

'There are always forms, Krob. There is no part of the police service that is free of forms, or I would be working in it. But I think I can guarantee that if you apply you have a very good chance of getting the job.'

'Well, if you think I'm up to it, sir, I'll come by and get the forms.'

'No need, lad. It just so happens I have a set in my coat pocket here.' Slonský unfolded some pages and attempted to smooth out the worst of the many creases in them. 'I also have a pen here. If you'd like to fill in the personal details at the top, I'll tell you what to write in those big boxes further down the page to maximise your chances of success.'

Nobody could begrudge Navrátil and Peiperová meeting at their permitted breaks, though both knew that they were not in full control of their respective timetables. At 15:32 Navrátil glanced up to see Peiperová gliding into the seat opposite.

'Is he in today?' he asked.

Peiperová shook her head. 'Yours?'

'No. He's gone to liaise with the city police, whatever that means.'

'It sounds like it means he doesn't want people to know what he's really doing.'

'No news on your boss's promotion?'

Peiperová shook her head again. At the time when she accepted the secondment it was widely believed, not least by her new boss Colonel Urban himself, that he was likely to get the job of Director of Police for the Czech Republic when the current national director, Major General Musil, retired in September. However, here they were in September and the incumbent was still there, to the evident frustration of Urban.

Even Sergeant Mucha on the front desk, normally the nerve centre of all internal evidence gathering about the police force, had no idea what was going on. He had tried asking around his network of contacts and the most he could discover was that Musil had been asked to stay on by the Minister of the Interior himself. This in itself was unusual because, as Slonský pointed out, the natural run of things was for ministers to spend much of their time trying to get rid of high ranking police officers, especially the efficient ones, in favour of nonentities who looked good in photographs.

'Any sign of new people?' Peiperová enquired, not without a little residual concern that a place would not be kept vacant in anticipation of her return on 31st May which, in her eyes, could not come soon enough.

'No, and we're really stretched. We've got a murder to investigate on top of the usual stuff and only the Captain and me to do it.'

Peiperová squeezed his hand. 'The Captain and you are enough,' she said encouragingly.

Krob's application form had been slipped into the bundle, four from the top. Slonský and Mucha had each attached an unsigned handwritten sticky note endorsing his candidature and Slonský had laboriously typed a covering letter giving the opinion of himself and the senior colleagues whom he had consulted that the post should be offered to Ivo Krob, currently of the Prague Metropolitan Police. He dropped the bundle in at the Human Resources reception desk and then set upon part two of his plan by cornering the building superintendent and inviting him to inspect the offices his team used.

'What's wrong with them?' the superintendent asked.

'I sit there, and the rest sit here. And there's a wall between,' Slonský replied.

'That's because senior officers get an office to themselves so they can work in private.'

'I don't want to work in private. I want to be able to supervise my team. I want them to have unfettered access to me. I want the wall down.'

The superintendent goggled. 'The wall?'

'Yes. That thing there covered in drab paint. It is separating me from my colleagues. This is my President Reagan moment. Tear down this wall!'

'The difference is,' said the superintendent, 'that in Berlin you couldn't just walk round the wall by going out into the corridor.'

Slonský put an arm round the man's shoulder. 'Think what demolishing that wall did for the world,' he said. 'Democracy flourished, more or less, the dead hand of Communism was lifted, a new era of liberty was ushered in. You could do that here.'

'That's a weight-bearing wall,' said the superintendent. 'If I knock it down you'll have Major Klinger and the fraud squad in your office.'

Slonský flinched a little. 'Yes, well, we don't want that, do we? Just go away and think of a solution, okay?'

Navrátil returned from the archives with a suspiciously thin folder.

'All the young girls who have gone missing this year so far, aged between eight and thirteen. The snag is that none of them look like our girl.'

Slonský accepted the proffered folder unenthusiastically. 'No matches at all?'

'Our victim has long blonde hair. None of these do. There is a blonde girl, but she has short curly hair.'

Slonský found the relevant sheet. 'Went missing in April. How quickly does hair grow?'

'Not four centimetres a month, that's for sure.'

Slonský grunted an acknowledgement of the truth of the proposition, then lobbed the folder into his in-tray. 'What news did Peiperová have today?'

'How did you know I'd been meeting…?'

'Because it's between Monday and Friday. And Colonel Urban is at a meeting which, I have learned by skilful interrogation of one of the drivers, is at the Ministry of the Interior and is being attended by a significant amount of top brass.'

'Do we know what they're discussing?'

'Well, it won't be about Bohemians' chances of winning the football league this year.'

'Do you have any idea why the Major General delayed his retirement, sir?'

'No. And, unusually, Sergeant Mucha doesn't know either. I don't know what we do next when even Mucha doesn't know something. I don't think it's happened before.'

'What about Major Rajka?'

Slonský leaped from his chair with an athleticism that Navrátil had never suspected was concealed within him.

'Brilliant! Rajka is just the sort of person who would know.'

Major Rajka led the Office of Internal Inspection, a sort of police for the police. A former Olympic wrestler who kept himself in trim by tearing telephone directories in half and crushing drinks cans in the crook of his elbow, Rajka had once worked for Lukas who had given him unofficial time off to enable him to win his place for the Olympics. As a result, Rajka would do anything he could for Lukas, and now that Lukas had retired Slonský hoped that this goodwill had been transferred to the new incumbent, namely himself.

Slonský found Rajka's number in Lukas' address book and gave it a call. After an exchange of pleasantries Slonský got to the point.

'There is a body of opinion which holds that if anyone knows why the Director of Police hasn't retired yet, it will be you.'

'That's very flattering,' replied Rajka, 'and highly inaccurate.'

'You don't know?'

'I don't know, but I can guess. And, by the way, I think they call it President of the Police Presidium now.'

'I bow to your superior knowledge. So, spill the beans.'

'Between us?' Rajka confirmed.

'Shall we say not for general circulation? And definitely unattributable.'

'Good enough for me. Do you remember Colonel Dostál?'

'Dostál? The one who ran the SWAT teams?'

'That's him. Have you wondered where he has been for the past three years?'

'I can honestly say it has never crossed my mind,' said Slonský, 'but no doubt you're going to tell me.'

'He's been attached to Interpol managing their Incident Response Teams. But his tour of duty is up in October and he'll be back here looking for a job.'

Slonský's heart sank. Dostál had some depressingly weird ideas about doing things by the book, by which he meant a book that he got to write and revise at will. He was also very much a "hands-on manager" as he kept telling people. Slonský's life under Dostál could be much more difficult, particularly because Urban would have a chip on his shoulder for years to come.

'And the Minister is behind this?' Slonský asked.

'Dr Pilik thinks Dostál is just what the police service needs to shake them up.'

'We're a law enforcement agency, not a cocktail.'

'I agree. Dostál would depress morale and cramp the senior managers' style.'

'You mean your style.'

'No, way above me. I am but a humble major. It's colonels and upwards that don't like this idea.'

'Can it be stopped?'

'Two options, I suppose. Urban has a big success, or Pilik is removed from the Ministry. Come to think of it, you have form when it comes to removing Ministers of the Interior, don't you?'

This was a reference to Pilik's predecessor, Dr Banda, whose career had taken a bit of a jolt when he was arrested by Slonský and charged, quite wrongly, with murder. In the event, Banda had done quite well out of it, because he had been compensated with a job in Brussels that he really wanted and which came with a salary that Ministers of the Interior could only dream about. Nevertheless, Slonský and Banda did not exchange Christmas cards.

'A misunderstanding, that's all,' Slonský answered.

'Isn't there anything you can pin on Pilik?' Rajka asked.

'He was a pretty lousy defence lawyer in a case thirty years ago,' Slonský said, 'but I can't bang him up for that or the cells would be full of lawyers. We'd have no room for criminals.'

'Well, there's your problem. If I can do anything to help, remember that I draw the line at anything illegal. After all, I'm supposed to be safeguarding police ethics.'

Slonský dropped the receiver and collected his coat.

'I'll explain all that on the way, lad,' he said to Navrátil.

'The way, sir? To where?'

'To a place where my brain can be lubricated and tuned to perfection.'

'Oh — we're going to a bar.'

'Correct. I need to do some of my best thinking. Probably about two litres' worth, I'd say.'

To nobody's surprise, Valentin was already in the bar when they arrived. Navrátil occasionally wondered when and where Valentin ever wrote anything for the newspaper since he seemed to spend most of his time in the bar and rarely had a notepad with him.

'Getting rid of a Minister of the Interior?' Valentin mused. 'That's a new one. They don't usually hang around long enough to get people plotting against them.'

'This one has been around nineteen months,' said Slonský. 'He's probably done any good he's going to do.'

'He came when you arrested that other one, didn't he?' said Valentin.

'No need to drag that up. It was a perfectly reasonable response to the evidence available at the time.'

'But he was innocent,' teased Valentin.

'No, he was guilty,' Slonský protested. 'He just didn't do what we charged him with. But he did loads of other stuff, which is why he didn't sue us when he got out. He didn't want to face charges of obstructing a police enquiry given that he supposed to be in charge of us.'

'I suppose you can see his point of view.'

'Look, I bought you a drink in the hope that you would lend your brain to the common cause and all you can do is drag up ancient history.'

'From last year.'

'Nitpicker.'

'So what do you want from me?' Valentin asked.

'Anything that might persuade the Prime Minister that Pilik needs a change of scene. He doesn't have secret mistresses or any disgusting habits he wouldn't want to see plastered all over the gutter press?'

'I don't think so. He's depressingly dull. He wants to lower income taxes for the wealth creators, which is shorthand for "his mates", I think.'

'And how does he think the country is going to afford that?'

'He's in favour of increasing the duty on beer.'

There was a shocked silence.

'Isn't that treason or something?' asked Slonský.

Chapter 3

The image of the murdered girl stared up at Slonský from his desk. There were two versions; one was a photograph of the girl's face which had been doctored to give the impression of continued animation, and the other was an artist's interpretation which seemed to Slonský to offer a better glimpse of what she had been like in life. The artist had given her a smile and a faint rosiness to the cheeks. Her hair was brushed and had a central parting and her dry clothes exhibited more vibrant colours.

'Pretty little thing,' Slonský commented.

'Maybe that's why she's dead now,' Navrátil replied.

'We'd better get it in the papers. I hate doing it because I don't think any parent should learn that their child is dead by seeing her picture on the front page, but if she hasn't been reported missing I don't know how else we can find out who she is.'

'I'll take it to the press office, sir.'

'Thanks. Any other ideas we can follow up?' Slonský asked.

'She looks well kept. She's not a street child.'

'Too blonde to be a Roma girl. Not that I'm stereotyping,' Slonský added quickly.

'Could she be a foreigner?'

'Her top is Czech. I doubt you can buy it abroad. But it might explain why we haven't heard anything. Ask for the photo to be shared with the Slovak and Austrian police just in case and get them to check their missing children's lists.'

'Could she be on a school trip?'

'She'd have been missed, surely! What kind of school doesn't notice a child has gone missing? Anyway, whoever she is and however she got here, there's a pattern of long term abuse in Novák's report that we have to look into. I'm going to go down to the river and talk to a couple of the cruise boat captains.'

'What shall I do, sir?'

'Use your initiative. You're not a new trainee any more. You should be coming up with ideas of your own. Which is another way of saying I haven't got a clue. Just keep busy, lad, and something may turn up.'

Slonský sat on the wall and listened as the two river boat captains debated what might have happened.

'The thing is, you really have three rivers in one here,' one of them explained.

'Is this going to turn religious on me?' Slonský asked.

'No, it's simpler than the Holy Trinity,' replied the older man. 'The central part of the river flows fast. To each side there's a zone that moves slower. As a result, anything that joins from the side is likely to be kept near the bank, at least until it reaches a bend where it might get swept towards the centre. So if your girl was found where you've marked it on the map, I'd say she went in not too far away. Perhaps a couple of kilometres, but if it was much further she'd have been seen from the riverside villages, especially wearing a red top.'

His colleague was quick to agree. 'There's less boat traffic here than further along the river, but it's hard to imagine nobody saw her for a couple of days. She was probably put in the river at night by someone who didn't know the water and thought she'd be well clear by morning.'

'And it would have to be from the right bank?' asked Slonský.

'Couldn't have been the other because she'd have had to cross that faster current in the centre that would push her forward.'

Slonský thanked them and walked away deep in thought. While he lacked the social skills that many others prized he had never had any difficulty in persuading ordinary Czechs to speak to him. Of course, the fact that he encountered many of them in bars and cafés may have helped.

Slonský was Prague born and bred. It was his city. Aside from a few months during his national service in the army, he had never lived anywhere else, nor could he imagine doing so. It was overlaid with memories for him, many of which would have been utterly unknown to any of the umbrella-wielding tour guides who made the Old Town Square such a misery these days.

He gazed from the tram window and reflected that they were only two blocks from the flat where a jealous music teacher murdered one of his best pupils, having castrated him first in the hope of ruining that beautiful baritone voice. They turned the corner and Slonský could see the ornate building that had once housed a bank, the one that the idiot Klimek had tried to rob all those years ago when the police payroll was being collected. If it had been after 1989 he would probably have served a few years before being released into the community to fend, albeit unsuccessfully, for himself, but in 1975 that sort of thing got you put up against a wall while a gang of recruits attempted to shoot you with a rifle from ten metres. Slonský could remember such an execution where the officer had been compelled to administer the coup de grâce with his pistol to a startled prisoner still trying to come to terms with the fact that the entire firing squad had missed him. That may have been deliberate, of course; nobody likes shooting a man in cold blood, and they tell themselves that no-one will ever know they deliberately fired a little to one side, which is fine so long as they don't all think that way.

Slonský believed that he understood Praguers. If pressed, he would admit that Czechs from elsewhere were harder to read, and as for Slovaks, well, they were just different. But the inhabitants of Prague thought like he thought, he believed.

There was a balance within each of them between a fervent desire that nobody should poke their nose into their business and their clear right to investigate everyone else's. Couple this with an innate sense of justice that would, on occasion, cause them to embellish evidence to ensure that the right person was convicted, regardless of the facts of the case, and you ought to have had a policeman's nightmare; but Slonský could gently tease them round to giving him the facts without the extras, and was very tolerant of attempts at perjury so long as they were not too blatant.

It was this sympathetic sense that Slonský had detected in Krob. Faced with an indignant crowd who had been present at a hit and run that had killed a retired policeman, Krob and Slonský had been offered detailed eye-witness accounts by people who, by their own evidence, could not possibly have seen what they claimed unless they had x-ray vision that could penetrate the tram from which the policeman had alighted. But whereas many policemen would have recited portions of the law code to explain why passers-by should tell the truth, Krob had simply kept them there for expert questioning by Slonský and Peiperová, meeting their grumbling with good humour, free coffee, and pleas to "help me out here, mate."

The faces turned towards him alerted Slonský to the ringing of his mobile phone. He did not recognise the number but answered it anyway.

'Velner. I work in Human Resources.'

'Good for you. I'm glad somebody does,' Slonský replied.

'I've read the folders that you dropped in to us. I just need to check the equality and diversity aspects.'

'What, exactly, are "equality and diversity" aspects?' asked Slonský, easing his collar away from his jugular vein to allow the blood to escape from his head.

'You know — race, gender, background, disabilities. So far as I can see, all your department are white, male and Czech.'

'We have a female — whom I was personally responsible for appointing — but she has been snaffled on secondment by the top brass.'

'I see. You don't think the post should go to another female?'

'I think the post should go to the best person for the job, male, female or somewhere in-between,' Slonský asserted.

'A female would give you more balance.'

'This is a police department, not a damn trapeze act.' Slonský could feel the headache starting again. Novák had warned him about his blood pressure before. He was about to add a few well-chosen phrases of street Czech when an idea came to him. 'However,' he smoothly added, 'there is more than one vacancy. In fact, there are three, and if you were to approve Krob and let me fill the others I would be very happy to give due consideration to any woman officer you might suggest. Send me a Vietnamese lesbian if it helps with your quotas; just give me Krob to be going on with.'

'We couldn't possibly propose an officer for a post,' protested Velner. 'That would be most irregular.'

'Then I will find one. Or even two, if they're good. Just approve the filling of the vacancies so I can get on with it.'

'We would be very happy to search our records to find officers who fitted your requirements, of course,' Velner added.

'That would be welcome,' Slonský agreed, inwardly vowing to disregard anyone put forward by such a route.

'I don't know if I can get approval for both posts,' Velner retorted, 'due to the current budgetary pressures.'

'That's because you don't let criminal gangs sponsor police officers any more. The days when drug dealers could slip a million or two to high ranking officers to ensure that complete idiots were appointed to posts have gone now.'

'That would be completely improper!' Velner spluttered.

'One new post?' Slonský pressed in his sweetest tones.

'For now. I'll confirm with a memo this afternoon.'

'And I can appoint Krob?'

'Of course. He's clearly the best man for the job.'

'I think you mean "best person".'

'Yes, person. It was just a figure of speech.'

The tram pulled up and decanted Slonský whose sixth sense had detected a bar round the first corner on the left. It was some time since he had been there, but after speaking to Human Resources he felt in need of a little something. Once refreshed, he stepped outside to discover that it had gone dark in the interim, so he decided to head home.

He mounted the stairs to his flat and was surprised to find his front door was not locked and the lights were on — or, at least, those of the lights that possessed working bulbs. There was an unusual smell emanating from the kitchen.

'I was beginning to give up on you,' said his ex-wife Věra, emerging from the small kitchen area with a saucepan in her hand.

'Was I expecting you?' Slonský asked.

'No, but I had the afternoon off so I thought if you were free it would be nice to cook for you. If you hadn't come in I'd have left it for later. It'll re-warm very well.'

She produced a tablecloth from her bag and laid the table before dispensing two portions of stew into the bowls which she had also brought. In fact, it was likely that everything necessary for the manufacture of the stew had been brought in her bag, though Slonský vaguely recognised one of the serving spoons as his.

'This is all very … unexpected,' he began.

'I've got you a beer as well. Unless you've had enough,' Věra interrupted.

The concept of having had enough stunned Slonský sufficiently to rob him of independence of action, and before he knew it he was sitting at the table and scooping up gravy with a slab of bread.

'Good day?' Věra asked.

'Not really. We've found a dead girl.'

'Do you mean a young woman or a female child?'

'A child, about ten.'

'Oh, dear. Accident?'

'Murder.'

'Did you have to break it to her parents?'

'We don't know who she is. And there doesn't appear to be a missing child on our register who fits the description.'

'Goodness! How awful! So how will you find who she is?'

'She's well dressed and groomed, so she hasn't been living rough. Someone cares for her. I suppose we'll have to wait until they report her missing.'

'And if they don't?'

'Why wouldn't they?'

'Well, if the whole family has been murdered, for example.'

'If they have, why throw one in the river and not the others?'

'You're the detective. You tell me.'

Slonský ate in silence for a while, debating whether he could justify the expense of sending police boats along the river looking for the bodies of the girl's parents. The mode of death would tell him more. It is hard for one man to suffocate or strangle three people, so that would point to a team of criminals.

'I suppose the parents could be the killers,' he remarked at length.

'How appalling!' said Věra. 'It doesn't bear thinking about.'

Slonský felt the same way, which was why he was trying not to think about it.

Chapter 4

Slonský pushed open the office door the next morning and was surprised to find Navrátil already scribbling notes on a report he was reading.

'You're in early,' he said.

'Ten to seven,' Navrátil replied. 'About the same as usual. Dr Novák's preliminary report came through, but there's a bit extra he's added that you'll find interesting.'

'Say on, young sage,' Slonský replied, flopping into his chair.

'Basically, everything he said about the death seems to be right. A girl of around ten, and she'd been raped, probably not for the first time. The DNA retrieved is male but not known to our records.'

'Interesting.'

'Not as interesting as the next bit. The victim's DNA *is* known to our records. She is Viktorie Dlasková, reported missing seven years ago and presumed dead.'

Not too many things rendered Slonský speechless, but that intelligence came very close.

'She's a missing person we never found?'

'That's the sum of it.'

'We thought she was dead, and now she is?'

'That's right.'

Slonský rubbed his face vigorously to enliven himself.

'We'd better dig out her file and find her parents' details so we can communicate the sad news.'

'I've put in a request, sir. Should be with us in an hour or so.'

'Good. You seem to have everything in hand, lad. I suppose our next step is obvious.'

'Sir?'

'We may as well get some breakfast while we're waiting.'

There was no avoiding the matter, thought Slonský. He could fill his day with activity, if you were prepared to define the term to include the occasional snack and a beer or two, but at some point he had to think about what he was going to do about Věra.

Nearly forty years before they had been married, but after a little over two years she disappeared with a long-haired poet in a leather jacket. The next contact was a letter from Věra asking for a divorce, so he signed the papers and returned them to her forwarding address. There must then have followed the mother of all alcohol binges, because very little of 1971 to 1973 still existed in Slonský's memory, and the next life event of which he had clear recollection was being carpeted by his boss for his attitude, his insubordination and being drunk on duty. It could not, in all honesty, be claimed that his attitude or his insubordination issues had been fully conquered, so his personnel file was littered with further appearances over the years, and that was even allowing for the pages he had managed to abstract and shred when he copied Mucha's key to the personnel department's file store, but he had reduced his drinking. Reasoning that he was on call twenty-four hours a day, seven days a week, it was plainly impossible not to drink on duty, but he had avoided being drunk on duty since then. More or less.

Then, a little over a year ago, Věra reappeared, having sought him out to explain that she had never actually got around to lodging the signed divorce papers, so they were still legally married. She thought he ought to know, in case he had found someone else. Slonský's initial reaction was that waiting thirty-six years to tell him he could be an accidental bigamist did not earn her many merit points, but over the succeeding year they had begun to tolerate each other a little better.

This meant that occasionally they visited each other's flats. Věra liked to make herself useful by doing some cooking and cleaning, and occasionally Slonský thought he detected a hint that she envisaged a future where they were back together. There were attractions to not growing old on your own. On the other hand, he had managed without her for almost all his life, and the hurt was still there. Not to mention the distinct possibility that she would expect him to go home after work rather than having a beer and sausage with friends like Valentin.

It was potentially the most difficult problem he had ever faced.

Mucha never knocked on Slonský's door. Slonský would not have expected the desk sergeant to do so, given their long association and the utter certainty that if Slonský had insisted on it Mucha would have found some way of embarrassing him in completing the task. Instead, Mucha entered bearing a manila folder on a clipboard, bowed respectfully, and extended the clipboard so that Slonský could retrieve the file.

'Some mail for you, sir,' said Mucha.

'Thank you, my man,' responded Slonský. 'But who is minding the desk in your absence?'

'Sergeant Vyhnal, who is a fine officer, if a little touchy about being called a bastard by our unwilling guests, on account of actually being one.'

'It is an unwise detainee who annoys Sergeant Vyhnal,' observed Slonský.

‘Less so since they’ve moved the cells up from the basement so they don’t have to descend that flight of concrete steps.’

‘That’s true. Mind you, we solved crimes a lot faster when we had them. Well, don’t let me detain you.’

‘I’ll stay a minute. You’ll be asking for my help again.’

‘Oh, cocky, aren’t we? Let’s see.’ Slonský opened the folder and scanned the first page. ‘Do we have a telephone number for the Dlasks’ address?’ he asked.

‘No, because they don’t live there any longer,’ Mucha replied. ‘And now you’re going to ask me to track their ID cards, which I beg to report I have already done. And, joy of joys, they’ve separated, so you’ll need to make two trips.’

Slonský emitted a low growl of disappointment. It was going to be a difficult interview anyway, let alone having to go through it a second time.

‘Do you remember anything about the case?’‘Not really,’ said Mucha. ‘I scanned the first couple of pages before I brought it up to check it was the right file, but it didn’t really involve the Prague police too much because she went missing near Most.’

‘So our friends in Ústí nad Labem would have dealt with it.’

‘One would think,’ Mucha replied.

‘You sound doubtful.’

‘I can’t put my finger on it, but the file is very thin for an enquiry that ultimately wasn’t concluded satisfactorily. I’ve asked for anything more that they might have at Ústí.’

Slonský nodded. Mucha was a connoisseur of bureaucracy, and if he judged that the file was scanty, that was not an opinion to be discarded lightly. ‘Give me a few minutes to read this through and I’ll come and find you so we can discuss what was involved.’

‘You know where I’ll be,’ agreed Mucha.

Slonský slowly read the pages, handing each to Navrátil as he finished with it so that the younger man could read it too. In this way they passed around half an hour in silence, before Slonský closed the file with a decisive slap, stood up and had a good scratch of his numb rear end.

'What do you think?' he asked.

'I can see why Sergeant Mucha thought it looked thin. There are quite a few statements collected at the time from people who ought to have witnessed something but didn't, then they seem to have jumped to a conclusion about who was responsible, though they don't say clearly who that was. They collect some more information about the family and then it's just a string of negative reports.'

Slonský grimaced. 'Can we find somewhere better to sit? Let's collect Mucha and get some coffees. And maybe a pastry or two. I'm feeling deficient in sugar.'

Dumpy Anna at the canteen counter frowned when she saw the plate.

'I thought you were meant to be watching your weight?' she said.

'I am,' said Slonský. 'One of these pastries is for Navrátil.'

That this was news to his assistant was clear from the look on Navrátil's face.

'Suppose he doesn't want it?' asked Anna.

'I'll have to find room for it,' Slonský replied. 'Can't waste good food. Or this.'

Anna nodded her head towards a corner of the room and lowered her voice. 'Love's Young Dream is over there.'

Following her gaze he saw Peiperová cradling a cup of coffee and looking about as fed up as he had ever seen her.

'I suppose I'd better let him sit with her. Have you got a cloth in case he dribbles again?' Slonský marched over with the tray and perched himself opposite his former assistant. 'Since you've been good, I'm letting Navrátil come out to play for twenty minutes. You can hold hands if you like. But that's all you're to hold under the table.'

'Sir!'

Navrátil sat beside her and smiled. That their fingers were intertwining out of sight was apparent from the way her face relaxed and almost seemed to become rosier. Sergeant Mucha took the remaining chair.

'Well, now we're sitting comfortably, we can begin,' Slonský said. 'Peiperová, you can join in because I need all the brainpower I can muster for this case, and a woman's perspective might be helpful. Or possibly not, I really don't know.'

'What case, sir?' Peiperová asked.

'We pulled the body of a young girl from the river just south of the city, lass. She's about ten years old and she's been horribly abused over a period of time. But she's not uncared for. The snag was that no such child had been reported missing.'

'I checked that,' Navrátil chipped in.

'Thank you for reminding me that you're not completely useless, Navrátil. Now, for various reasons Dr Novák sent material for DNA testing. It doesn't identify the man who molested her, but it told us something surprising. The victim is a girl who was reported missing seven years ago. Věra something-or-other.'

'Not Věra, sir,' said Navrátil. 'Viktorie.'

'Quite right. Věra was a girl reported missing thirty-six years ago. I can't think why that name came to mind. Anyway, this Viktorie…'

'Dlasková,' Navrátil supplied.

'Thank you — Viktorie Dlasková disappeared aged three some years ago, so we sent for the file on her disappearance.'

'Excuse me, sir,' Peiperová interrupted. 'How did they identify her as the victim?'

'Because if we can we secure a sample of known material from the girl so that if an unrecognisable body is found later we may be able to identify her from DNA, so in this case the officers who visited the Dlasks' house secured some blonde hairs of hers from her hairbrush.'

'Thank you, sir, I understand now.'

'Good. So we have the conundrum that somebody, presumably not her parents, who have separated, has been looking after this girl for some years but hasn't apparently felt the need to report her missing. Of course, her new family may have been killed in the same attack and are waiting to be discovered somewhere.'

'How awful,' said Peiperová.

'The abduction was near Most, up in the north of the country, and nowhere near the place where she was put in the river after death, so there's one problem. Where has she been living in the interim? Second problem, who has been looking after her? Third problem, why haven't they come forward to report her missing?'

'Then there's her case report,' Mucha observed.

'Yes, and that's a bit of a puzzle too. There are several statements from people who were apparently in the vicinity of the place where the girl went missing, mostly parents of other children of a similar age.'

'Where did she go missing from?' asked Peiperová.

'From a nursery school. Without seeing the place it's hard to picture, but it seems that the children were being collected by their parents and it was all very confused. Lots of little ones and lots of parents, and when the dust cleared Mrs Dlasková was left standing but there were no children left. She was adamant that she didn't even see Viktorie. The nursery superintendent was equally clear that Viktorie was one of the first to leave, as she always was.'

'The trouble with that is that when something *always* happens there's a tendency for witnesses to convince themselves that it must have happened on a particular day,' said Mucha.

'Correct. Let's park that a moment. There are some photos in the files that explain a little more. The nursery school consisted of two buildings like corrugated iron sided huts which formed a straight line, like a short train, and their doors faced each other with a small porch at the end of each building. So the parents waiting at the gate couldn't see the doors clearly because there was a sort of small alleyway between the buildings that the children had to come down. The superintendent claimed that she opened the door and watched the children leave and she saw them all go into the yard where the fence and gate was where their parents were waiting. The officer in charge, whose signature I can't decipher, proved to his satisfaction that in fact she couldn't see what she said she saw from where she must have been standing. He didn't think she was involved in the disappearance, but he thought she was trying to prove it couldn't have been the nursery staff's fault. You take over, Navrátil. My coffee's getting cold.'

'Yes, sir. The next bit I find troublesome is that all this is supposed to have happened a little after four o'clock, but it's nearly five before the police are called. Questioned about this, Mrs Dlasková says she insisted on it because the superintendent didn't want to call until they'd finished searching the buildings and grounds and was convinced Viktorie would turn up. They thought perhaps she'd gone to the toilet and locked herself in or something like that.'

'But she didn't shout?' asked Mucha. 'When my niece was that age she could make herself heard across three fields if she got separated from Mummy.'

'She doesn't seem to have shouted at any time, or at least not so it was heard over a class of little kids running to their mums and dads,' Navrátil answered.

'Would you hear one squeal among so many?' posed Slonský.

'A mother would,' Peiperová affirmed. 'They tune in to their child's sounds. When a child cries out a mother always knows if it's her child or not.'

'Is that fact or folklore?' Slonský enquired.

'Widely believed but possibly true despite that,' Mucha told him.

'I'm not so sure. Anyway, the statements collected seem to indicate that none of the mothers heard a child cry out in distress, so true or not it's probably an irrelevance. So, to recap, after the first day they've got a statement from all the parents present and all the nursery staff. They take Mrs Dlasková home and while they're there they search the house in case she's made her own way home — bit unlikely for a three-year-old, I'd have thought, but anyway — and they quietly take some hairs from her hairbrush for DNA testing in case a body is found later. That's how we know this body is hers.'

'But then it gets really weird,' Navrátil said. 'You'd have thought they'd have checked out any known child molesters in the district, but if they did, they didn't provide a list. They simply say that they don't think that's likely.'

'That's about five days later, so they had time to conduct some enquiries. And maybe they did, but their record keeping is rubbish,' added Slonský.

Mucha tutted loudly.

'Then the next thing we find in the folder is a report from a social worker who has been asked to work with the parents,' Navrátil continued. 'She describes their home and that Viktorie is an only child, that she hasn't exhibited any unusual behavioural problems, that her father works as an engineer and her mother has a job as a shop assistant. And that's it! I don't know what to make of it.'

Mucha looked meaningfully at Slonský. 'I do,' he said.

'Yes,' Slonský agreed, 'I think I do too. They thought the parents staged it.'

'What?' chorused Navrátil and Peiperová.

'They didn't believe she'd really been abducted. There is a sentence in there that Mrs Dlasková had complained about the superintendent's attitude to the children and that she didn't exercise enough care. I think the police thought they staged this to make the nursery look bad.'

'That's a bit extreme, isn't it?' asked Navrátil.

'I'm not saying it's sensible, just that, for whatever reason, the police jumped to that conclusion.'

'But surely when the child didn't reappear that must have shaken their complacency?' Peiperová insisted.

'Maybe they thought she'd died in an accident, or of shock at being snatched. They seem to have spent some time trying to assess whether Mrs Dlasková's distress was just clever acting. They comment that the father just went back to work and wouldn't talk about it, which didn't seem natural to them.'

'I'm sorry, sir,' said Peiperová, 'but is there an approved way parents are supposed to react to having their daughter kidnapped?'

Slonský took a bite of pastry before answering. 'I hope we'd do it differently. They don't seem to have had a senior woman officer at Ústí, but that shouldn't surprise us, because we'd have trouble rustling one up here. The sooner you get yourself promoted to Lieutenant the better off we'll all be, lass. Without a woman's viewpoint, they jumped to a conclusion that was probably wrong but they tested any evidence they had against that incorrect theory. I suspect what we'll need to do is to try to tease a theory out of whatever evidence the statements give us, but I have to admit I don't see anything in them to give me much hope at first glance. Anyway, it's plain where we have to start. We have to tell the parents we've found Viktorie, but unfortunately not in the way they'd want.' He pushed his chair back and stood wearily. 'Are you busy, Peiperová? It would be good to take a woman officer.'

'The Colonel's in his office, sir. I could ask.'

'Better if I ask. We don't want to give the impression you're itching to get out and about.'

Colonel Urban responded to the knock with his usual brisk "Come!", then 'Good morning, Slonský.'

'Good morning, sir. Nice to see you able to spend some time here. All those meetings must be tedious by now.'

'No, they were tedious from day one. What can I do for you?'

Slonský outlined the case to his superior.

'I see. And no doubt you want Peiperová back.'

'Only for the purpose of being present while I break the news to the parents, sir. In time, of course…'

'Yes, yes,' Urban responded testily. 'You'll get her back at the end of the year like I promised.'

'Thank you, sir. I just wanted to check nothing had changed.'

'You mean because I'm still here?'

'Well, yes, sir. We're all surprised that you haven't already been given the job, sir. You're clearly the outstanding candidate.'

'Thank you, Slonský. No doubt the Minister has his reasons, but I'm hanged if I know what they are.'

Slonský had never been one for letting his brain curb his tongue. 'Colonel Dostál, sir.'

The look on Urban's face clearly demonstrated that this was news to him. 'Dostál? He's abroad somewhere.'

'His tour is up soon, sir, and my sources tell me he wants to come back to Prague. Plainly there are very few vacancies at his rank, so perhaps Dr Pilik is holding this one open with a view to giving it to Dostál.'

'Dostál! Over my dead body! I'd resign.'

'I think a number of your colleagues feel the same way, sir.'

'I'd no sooner put Dostál in charge than I would Dvorník. They're birds of a feather, Slonský.'

'So I understand, sir.'

Lieutenant Dvorník, formerly Slonský's colleague and now his subordinate, was a gun fiend, far too ready to resort to firepower and possessor of a personal home armoury that would not have disgraced a decent-sized hunting lodge.

'How do we stop him, Slonský?'

'Perhaps if you and your colleagues made your views clear to the Minister, sir…'

'That would be counter-productive. He'd appoint him just to prove he wasn't going to be leant on.'

'Then we need to boost your popularity, sir. We have to excite sympathy for your candidacy.'

'And how do we do that?'

Slonský thought furiously, and an idea came to him. 'Have you ever thought of being shot, sir? Officers who are shot on duty always excite great public sympathy.'

'Do you see a possible flaw in that plan, Slonský?'

'Not seriously shot, sir. Not fatally. Just … winged a bit.'

'Winged?'

'Flesh wound. Top of the thigh is good. Big muscle, bleeds a lot, not a lot of chance of hitting anything important underneath. It would make for dramatic pictures.'

'And who do you propose to entrust with the job of shooting me? You can't just "arrange" with criminals to be shot.'

'Dvorník could do it! He's a crack shot. Hitting a stationary target at fifty metres would be a doddle for him. He can shoot the conkers off a running squirrel at that distance.'

'Don't I recall that Lieutenant Dvorník shot the wife of a suspect by mistake during an arrest a while back?'

'Ah, yes, technically. But he shot the suspect too. Sedláček just failed to stop the bullet, that's all.'

'I don't think you can blame the person who has been shot for "failing to stop the bullet", Slonský.'

'And his wife made a full recovery. Eventually.'

'If you overlook the hole in her shoulder blade.'

'He was going to cut her throat, sir. I'm sure if you ask her she'd say she got off lightly.'

'Enough of this tomfoolery, Slonský. I am not going to get myself shot just to get sympathy.'

'How about being shot at, rather than shot? You know, a close miss.'

'No.'

'Well, it was just an idea.'

'And not your best. Take Peiperová with my blessing. I can manage without her for the rest of the day, But I want her back in one piece, so I hope you have no plans to let Dvorník use her for target practice too?'

'Certainly not, sir.'

'And if you do have any better ideas, I'll be pleased to hear of them, Slonský. I appreciate your loyalty and effort.'

'I'll just get on with trying to solve this crime, sir, and hope something turns up on the other front.'

When Slonský returned to his office he was aware of a dark and sinister presence. It was standing in the middle of the room avoiding all contact with any germ-ridden surfaces.

'I wish you wouldn't do that,' said Slonský. 'Beaming down from upstairs. I must renew the garlic on the door frame.'

'Very droll,' said the head of the Fraud Squad, Major Klinger. 'I find myself in the unusual position of wanting a favour from you, rather than the other way round for once, so as the supplicant I have come to you.'

Opinion was divided as to how Klinger got to work on the floor above, since nobody ever saw him on the stairs, nor did he usually come down during the day, preferring his highly controlled surroundings. He had his own coffee machine and his personal cups, and kept his office spotless by liberal use of antiseptic wipes.

Slonský invited him to sit, which Klinger did once he had brushed the seat with his handkerchief.

'You want something,' Slonský stated boldly.

'You will be aware, because you keep reminding me unkindly, that my former assistant Kobr was jailed for three years for corrupt practices.'

'Oh, yes, that does ring a bell. I seem to remember the headline in the newspaper: "Fraud Officer jailed for Fraud".'

'Well, his sentence ends this week and he will have to pick up his life. The snag is that although he was convicted we never found the money.'

'Didn't he trust banks?'

'I think even an amateur like Kobr realised that banking stolen money might be problematical. The thing is that now that he is out he'll need some of that to live on until he can get a job.'

'And?'

'We'd like him followed to see where he goes to get it.'

'Well, you're a police officer and it's a fraud case.'

'Indeed it is, but you will be aware that there are only two of us in the Fraud Squad, so we cannot provide the cover needed. Besides which, he knows both of us by sight. I hoped that you might be able to help out.'

'I would love to, if I had unlimited officers, but there are only four of us, and it takes at least three to follow a man round the clock. Plus we've got a murder on.'

'Only four?'

'Lukas retired and Peiperová has been seconded to the Director of Criminal Police. Doležal and Rada have been sent to Pardubice. That leaves four. And Human Resources have been slow to approve the advertising of the vacancies. I've only just got permission to advertise two officer jobs.'

Klinger stood. 'You have my sympathy. I haven't been permitted to replace Kobr either.'

Slonský experienced an unusual feeling. He was feeling sorry for Klinger. 'I can't follow him, but we can make some spot checks on him. And if we catch him with unexplained money on him we can invite him to spend a night in the guest wing here while we obtain an explanation. Just let us know when he's being released.'

'Tomorrow afternoon, it seems.'

'Then I'll send Navrátil to offer him a lift home. That should remind him that his old colleagues haven't forgotten him.'

'Believe me, after the grief I had dumped on me from above there is absolutely no danger of that,' answered Klinger bitterly.

Slonský and Peiperová drove north-west out of Prague along highway 7; or, more accurately, Peiperová drove while Slonský took the opportunity to catch up on his sleep.

'It's a mark of my trust in your driving that I'm prepared to close my eyes and catch forty winks,' he explained, 'confident that you won't kill me in my sleep by driving into the back of a truck. I don't sleep with just anyone, you know.' Realising that this last sentence was a little ambiguous, he felt the need to expand a bit. 'And I mean sleep. As in zzzz.'

'I understood that, sir.'

'Good. Didn't want any misunderstanding. Now, if you can point the car in the general direction of Most we have to turn right to get to Bilina where Mrs Dlasková lives now. Put your foot down, lass, and we'll make it in time for a late lunch.'

They drove in silence, apart from Slonský's irregular snoring, until Peiperová turned off and pulled up by the side of the road to get the exact address.

'Sir?'

'I'm not asleep. Just resting my eyes.'

'So who was snoring, then?'

'It wasn't me, because I wasn't asleep, so it must have been you. I've warned you before about cat-napping at the wheel.'

'Have you got the address, sir?'

'Address? What address?'

'Mrs Dlasková's house.'

'It's on the photocopy of the ID card application Mucha gave us.'

'Yes, sir, but have you got it?'

Slonský patted his pockets. 'I thought I gave it to you.'

With anyone else Peiperová would have offered some judgemental comment about the fact that she had just driven eighty kilometres in the belief that the person beside her knew where they were going.

'No problem,' said Slonský. 'I'll ring Mucha and he can tell us.'

Mucha obliged with both addresses, assuming that if Slonský had left one behind he would undoubtedly have forgotten the other too.

'Ah, no,' said Slonský, 'because I copied Mr Dlask's into my notebook. Here it is … right under Mrs Dlasková's.'

Peiperová could not prevent the escape of a deep sigh.

'It's because I'm short of calories,' Slonský explained. 'Let's grab something at the first bakery you see.'

Mrs Dlasková answered the door. She was a slight woman in her mid-thirties, though she looked older. Slonský offered his identification and asked if they could come inside. Mrs Dlasková nodded. She seemed very nervous, as if she thought that some great crime of hers may have been uncovered.

'This is very difficult,' Slonský began. 'I'm afraid I have to bring you some bad news. We have found the body of your daughter Viktorie.'

Mrs Dlasková's covered her face with her hands and emitted a horrible, intense low groan before erupting into deep, urgent sobs. Peiperová wrapped her in an arm and held her tightly for a while. This was the part of the job that Slonský hated most, largely because he knew he was no good at it. There was, simply, nothing he could do that would make a bereaved mother feel any better, and he knew it. Maybe he could learn something from Peiperová who was holding the back of Mrs Dlasková's head, partly so that the grieving woman could not see that she was crying herself; and seeing Peiperová cry was threatening to unman Slonský. He decided all he could do was carry on as usual.

'Would you like to see her?' he asked.

Mrs Dlasková opened her eyes wide. 'I'm not sure … after so long…'

Slonský could have kicked himself. 'I should have told you that she died only a few days ago. We're trying to find out where she has been in the intervening period.'

'She was still alive last week?'

'So it seems.'

If Slonský supposed that this was in any way better than having been killed seven years ago, he could now see that Mrs Dlasková drew no comfort from it.

'I owe it to her,' Mrs Dlasková said at length. 'I suppose you're certain it's her?'

'The DNA sample you gave us matches,' said Slonský quietly. 'I'm afraid it's quite certain.'

Mrs Dlasková nodded and wiped her eyes with her sleeve. 'I'll get my coat,' she said.

Peiperová took the opportunity to repair her make-up which, though discreet, was ravaged by the tears.

'There are some things I can't teach you,' Slonský murmured, 'except by giving you a bad example and telling you not to copy it.'

Mrs Dlasková reappeared. She must have lost weight lately, because the coat was too large for her frame.

'We ought to tell your husband on the way and invite him to join you,' Slonský explained. 'I realise that could be difficult…'

'Yes — yes, of course. He's entitled,' Mrs Dlasková interrupted.

'I've got his home address but he's probably at work now. Do you know where that is?'

'Yes. It's not far from our old house. I can give you directions.'

Mr Dlask was called by his foreman and rolled out from the underside of a tractor. He continued to cradle a large wrench, which Slonský would have preferred him to put down.

'What is it?' he asked, closely followed by, 'And why is she here?'

Mrs Dlasková got in first. 'They've found Viktorie's body, Václav.'

'Viktorie? Where?'

Slonský decided to be vague. 'South of Prague. We've taken her to Prague now. It seems that after she was abducted she was looked after, because she only died in the past few days, but we've identified her from a hair sample. We're taking Mrs Dlasková to see Viktorie now. If you'd like to come we'd be happy to take you too.'

Mr Dlask glanced at the foreman, who nodded his agreement, then he dropped the wrench on the floor and went to the washroom.

'She can't see me in this state,' he said.

It was a very long drive. Slonský feared that the Dlasks would not speak to each other in the back, but after a while Mrs Dlasková asked her husband about funeral arrangements and they began talking sporadically.

Peiperová dropped them at the mortuary's door and drove off to park the car. Slonský held the door open and directed them to Novák's office, following behind them. He knocked on the door, explained his business to Novák and the pathologist came out to meet the parents and conduct them to a waiting room, excusing himself at the entrance to go ahead and prepare things in the mortuary.

In less solemn times Slonský had been heard to wonder where Novák put all the other stiffs when the relatives were paying their respects, because there was no sign that the mortuary had any other occupants, but on this occasion he kept his mouth firmly shut, removing his hat respectfully and standing back to let the parents take all the time they wanted.

Novák turned back the sheet and Mrs Dlasková's legs buckled. Her husband grabbed her and kept her upright.

'That's her,' Dlask said. 'She's older than when we last saw her, but there's no mistaking her. She'd grown up into such a pretty girl.'

If he intended to say anything else, it was lost as his face crumpled and his head dropped across his wife's shoulder. At length his wife detached herself and gently adjusted Viktorie's hair before planting a kiss on her forehead. Dlask followed suit.

'Could we have a photograph of her?' he asked. 'She looks so peaceful. And we don't have any taken since…'

Novák promised to arrange it. 'The prosecutor's office will have to agree to release Viktorie's body,' he explained, 'then we'll bring it to the funeral home you've chosen. I can't promise when that will be but we won't keep her any longer than is necessary.'

The parents nodded mutely.

He gently steered them towards the door. Mrs Dlasková looked back longingly but allowed herself to be conducted into the corridor.

'If you feel up to it,' said Slonský, 'I need to ask you some questions. Let's go to my office and then we'll drive you back home.'

Mrs Dlasková stuck doggedly to the story she had told seven years earlier.

'It was the third of February, a Thursday. They had predicted snow but only little wisps of it were falling when I walked up to the kindergarten to collect her.'

'This was after work?' asked Slonský.

'Yes. I worked in a small supermarket on the tills from 7.30 to 2.30. I didn't like doing so many hours but if I didn't we couldn't afford to pay for child care for her.'

'So you walked up around 2.30?'

'No, it would have been nearer to 3 o'clock when I set out. I had to do some shopping myself first. So I arrived at the kindergarten around 3.15.'

'And what was the drill there? I mean, what should have happened when you got there?'

'We weren't allowed into the buildings. The parents used to stand by the low fence around the playground. The staff could see us there and would bring our children out to us. But there were quite a few who always came at this time, so they would start getting those children ready in advance. I suppose there were about six of us waiting when they started bringing children out. It was just so very normal. The parents collected their children and started taking them home, and I was still there.'

Mrs Dlasková took a drink of her coffee, holding the cup with both hands because she was aware that she was trembling.

'There was a young assistant, Katja. I don't know her surname now. She was training to be a kindergarten teacher. She saw me and said "Haven't you got Viktorie?" I said I hadn't seen her, and Katja ran inside. When she came out again I could see that there was something wrong. She ran straight across to the Director's office and I could see her burst in. The office had a big window looking out on the yard. The Director stood up and seemed to be arguing with her, but eventually she came out and marched over to me. "There'll be a perfectly simple explanation for this," she said, and told Katja she was a silly girl. I climbed over the fence and ran across to join the search. Viktorie's teacher told us she'd gone for Viktorie's coat but when she came back Viktorie wasn't there. Her first thought was that Katja had left the door open and Viktorie had run out to me. They searched the buildings but I insisted that they had to call the police. The Director didn't want to do that but I made her.'

Slonský passed a pencil and notepad to her. 'Can you draw a plan of the school so I can understand the geography?'

Mrs Dlasková drew, occasionally stopping to discuss something with her husband.

'So,' said Slonský, 'we've got two long buildings with a short gap between them and a little porch on the end opening onto the gap. Viktorie's classroom was the first one in the building to the left, the one nearest the gap. The Director's office was in the near corner of the other building. Then there was a playground around the whole building with a low fence. Could Viktorie have climbed it?'

'No,' Dlask insisted. 'It was well made and the horizontal struts were too high for her to climb on. It was sound as a bell. No gaps, no broken planks.'

'And you're standing on this side of the building. What's at the back of it?'

'There were some bushes at the two ends, but in the middle there was a flat area where the Director used to park her car. You could maybe get another couple of cars there.'

'And presumably there was a gate?'

'Not there. The Director used to go out of the main gate and walk all the way round.'

'What was Viktorie wearing, Mrs Dlasková?'

'A red skirt, red tights and a white jumper. And she had a white jacket. I've still got that — the teacher kept waving it at me as proof that Viktorie couldn't have left because her coat was still there.'

'Did she always wear that jacket?'

'I think so. She had one we kept for best, but white goes with everything. And we couldn't afford a lot of clothes for her when she was growing so fast.'

'When the police came, what did they do?'

'Next to nothing,' snapped Mr Dlask. 'I got there before they did, and they kept trying to persuade Natalka — my wife — that she must be mistaken and that Viktorie had come out to us but we'd somehow missed her.'

'But I saw every child who left,' insisted Mrs Dlasková, 'and Viktorie wasn't among them.'

'Did they interview all the staff?' Slonský asked next.

'Yes, nobody was allowed to leave until the police had spoken to them, even the teachers in the other room. It was nearly eight o'clock before they let the teachers leave,' said Mrs Dlasková.

'And what about the other parents?'

'I don't know if they spoke to them all, but quite a few told me they'd been visited by the police. They were all concerned. Nobody wanted to believe that someone was going round kidnapping our babies.'

Slonský asked for the names of the other mothers who had been there and wrote down those the Dlasks could remember.

'Let's get you home,' he said kindly. 'Peiperová, your shift has finished. You're stood down.'

'I'm happy to drive, sir.'

'Good girl. Mr Dlask, Mrs Dlasková, I'm sorry the police didn't do a good job seven years ago. But I will find out what happened to your daughter and I will see someone prosecuted for it.'

They murmured their thanks and followed him to the car.

When they reached her house Mrs Dlasková held her husband's hand and told him she didn't want to be alone. He nodded, and they got out together.

'That was sweet,' said Peiperová.

'We don't know what drove them apart, but losing their child can't have helped.'

'Do you think he blames her?'

'Yes.'

'But that's not fair!'

'I didn't say it was fair. You asked what he thought, and I told you. He knows he wasn't to blame, and somebody must be, so he takes it out on those around him. It's a common enough story. But when we went through the detail he realised she did exactly what she should have done. Maybe he needed to be seven years away to see that.'

'What now, sir?'

'Swing by the kindergarten, lass, and let's get our bearings.'

'It's probably changed in seven years, sir.'

'Not if it's relying on public money, Peiperová. A lick of paint if they're lucky.'

Peiperová had no trouble finding it and it was soon clear that the Dlasks' drawing was very accurate. Slonský climbed out of the car and stepped over the fence.

'Do you need a torch, sir?'

'No, it's light enough for my purposes. I just want to test an idea I had.' He returned to the car. 'Drive round the back so we can see how the Director gets to work each day.'

Peiperová turned at the next left turn, then found the lane that led to the car park, a patch of gravel and concrete. She turned round as instructed.

'Go back to the end of this road, but don't turn right. I want to see where we can go.'

Peiperová turned left, and the road curved slightly to join up with the main road to Most.

'Turn left here and let's see how far we are from the kindergarten.'

They drove around three hundred metres before they saw the turning to the kindergarten down which they had driven in the first place.

'Satisfied, sir?'

'Yes, thank you. What a bunch of blithering idiots!'

'Who, sir?'

'Mankind in general, but the local police in particular. Let's pay our colleagues a visit and see if we can find any relevant files.'

'It's quite late, sir. The archives staff will have gone home.'

'Then we'll get them to come back. And don't pull that face. The Director said I could have you for today. He didn't say anything about tomorrow, and you're as keen to get to the bottom of this as I am.'

'Yes, sir.'

'So, pedal to the metal, my girl, and let's go to Ústí and kick some bottom.'

The duty sergeant at Ústí was as accommodating as he could be, given that nobody connected with the case was in the building. He did not personally remember the incident, but he was confident that the local crime inspector would because he had been there for over ten years.

'And he'll be in tomorrow morning?'

'Certainly.'

'Excellent. I'll wait. Peiperová, you may as well take the car back to Prague and I'll catch the train back.'

'As you wish, sir.'

'Now, don't pull that face. The Director let me have you for the rest of today. He'll need you in the morning.'

'He has a meeting at the Ministry of the Interior until lunchtime, sir.'

'Meaning?'

'Meaning I wouldn't be missed if we were finished here by eleven o'clock.'

'And where do you propose to sleep? You plainly can't stretch out on a couple of chairs like I planned to do.'

'There may be a hotel in town with cheap rooms, sir. You've said yourself in the past that if they haven't let them by this time of night they'll be glad of anything we're prepared to pay.'

'Meaning that the police service is prepared to pay?' Slonský sighed and turned to the desk sergeant. 'Is there anywhere you would recommend?'

'Actually,' the sergeant said, 'there's a brewery that has a few rooms. You get a free beer if you're booked there.'

Slonský brightened at once.

'And where is this demi-paradise?'

An hour later, Slonský was having an animated discussion with a couple of locals about prospects for the hockey season, while Peiperová excused herself after dinner and retired to her room, but not before collecting her free beer and giving it to Slonský.

It was not quite too late to call Navrátil to update him, so she hung up her uniform so the creases would fall out and lay on the bed.

'Good evening, Officer Navrátil,' she began.

'Good evening, Officer Peiperová. And where are you?'

'I'm in a hotel room in Ústí nad Labem. Don't worry, I'm alone.'

'I never doubted it.'

'We need to talk to the crime team here about the abduction so Captain Slonský agreed we should stay over rather than come back another day. But I need you to do me a favour.'

'Of course.'

'Will you write a note to my boss telling him where I've gone and stick it on tomorrow's page of the big diary on my desk?'

'You mean you haven't asked him?'

'He's in a meeting in the morning but just in case we don't get back as quickly as we expect…'

Navrátil was resigned to doing her bidding. 'All right. Did you get anywhere?'

'We viewed the kindergarten. I think Captain Slonský thinks the child was abducted over the back fence where a car was waiting.'

'I didn't need to go there to deduce the same. But who handed her over the fence? And who was waiting on the other side to receive her?'

'Ah, not much progress there yet. But we'll keep at it.'

A thought crossed Navrátil's mind. 'Have you got a change of clothes with you?'

'No. I've taken my uniform off to keep it smart. If you must know, I'm lying here on the bed in my underwear.'

'Kristýna!'

'I feel like one of those girls in the chat line advertisements you see. Shall I talk dirty to you?'

'No, thank you,' Navrátil replied briskly.

Chapter 5

Slonský regretfully declined the offer of more beer with breakfast, feeling that it might provoke comment when he arrived at the police station, but he gleefully accepted a business card for the hotel and tucked it securely in his wallet. If you had to go somewhere on holiday this was as good a reason for choosing a place as any, he thought.

The colonel who directed the regional criminal police left them in the company of Captain Velek. Velek was in his early fifties, and although not a local man, he had been there for over a decade and recalled the investigation quite well, though taking pains to stress that he had not led it.

'Meaning you'd have done things differently?' asked Slonský.

Velek strolled along with his hands in his pockets and shrugged.

'There wasn't much scope for doing things differently. We did what we had to do. I might have shown a bit more urgency and I certainly would have given the Director of the Kindergarten a harder time.'

'What for?'

'Basically for being a heartless bitch. All she wanted to prove was that it wasn't her fault, and Captain Matuský left her alone once he'd determined that she wasn't implicated. But their systems were archaic and inadequate and I'd have thrown the book at them because it was just asking to happen again.'

'Do you think whoever snatched the child knew that?'

Velek scratched a pattern in the dirt with his toecap while he thought.

'There were other kindergartens they could have targeted. On the other hand, this one was made for a getaway. You only have to drive a few hundred metres and you're on the main road.'

'We drove around it last night and established that,' Slonský confirmed.

'The only good thing was that they operated a rule that parents couldn't just wander in past the fence. The children were brought out to them, so if all the witnesses were telling the truth the parents at the gate couldn't have been implicated. In particular, Mrs Dlasková was in sight the whole time. Captain Matuský thought that was suspicious, as if she was trying to draw attention to herself.'

'You didn't?'

'I think a mother whose daughter has been snatched is entitled to be an attention-seeker. But it wasn't so much what happened on the day. It was the fact that nobody reported any sightings in the succeeding weeks. Captain Matuský thought that either the child was killed at once — and how many children are abducted and immediately killed? — or she was with people she knew where she wouldn't be thought out of the ordinary if spotted. She wasn't a little baby. She knew her parents and grandparents. Why wouldn't she kick up a fuss?'

'Silver Blaze,' murmured Slonský.

'Come again?'

'It's a story by the British writer Conan Doyle. A horse is stolen from a stables where there is a guard dog and the dog doesn't bark.'

'So the dog knows the thief?'

'That's right. But if not the family, what about the workers?'

'We checked out the movements of all of them but they were all in sight the whole time.'

'So if I summarise this correctly,' Slonský said, 'you concluded that the child was kidnapped, but it couldn't be anyone from outside because they would have been seen, or anyone inside because everyone was in view of somebody else the whole time.'

Velek shrugged again. 'That's about the sum of it.'

'I see,' said Slonský. 'The difficulty with that conclusion is, of course, the small ugly fact that someone got the child, however impossible that should have been.'

'It's a puzzle,' agreed Velek. 'The little one didn't seem to scream or shout out, but neither was there time to render her unconscious unless she was smothered.'

'And there's a further puzzle,' commented Slonský, 'because if she was smothered in 2000 what's she doing turning up newly dead in 2007?'

Velek's eyes widened to the point that Slonský wondered whether they would close again. 'Newly dead?' he asked.

'Found in a river a few days ago and identified by DNA.'

'Ten years old?'

'Well, we didn't saw her in half and count the rings, but if she was three when she went missing seven years ago, ten would be a pretty good bet.'

'But I don't understand…'

'Neither do I. But the difference is that I'm going to do something about it.'

Velek shut the door to his office and indicated that they should sit in the chairs beside his desk.

'Look,' he began, 'I'm not saying there weren't deficiencies in the initial investigation. I've already said that I didn't trust the Director's testimony.'

'Yes, you did,' agreed Slonský. 'But what did you actually do, because it seems to me that Matuský was convinced the parents staged it all?'

Velek waved away the information impatiently. 'That was all that woman's fault. It was all a mistake.'

'A mistake?'

'Matuský's first report certainly hinted at the parents being the culprits but he withdrew it later once it became clear that the Director hadn't been entirely honest with us.'

'In what way?'

'She gave us the impression that the parents had only reported the girl missing around five o'clock, long after she should have been collected. It was only later that it became clear that they had been begging her to ring the police for over an hour. That time was critical, because you can get to the border with Germany in around forty minutes. Matuský became convinced that the reason he wasn't getting any leads locally was that she had been taken out of the district and the likeliest direction was north to the border.'

'There's no request to the German police for help in the file.'

'He probably telephoned and didn't bother to note it.'

'And is there anything else you can remember Matuský doing and not noting?' growled Slonský.

Velek shook his head sadly. 'He didn't do much, so I shouldn't think so.'

'He didn't, for example, haul the Director over the coals for deliberately misleading us?'

'Not that I know of.'

Slonský grabbed his hat and strode to the door. 'Better late than never,' he snapped.

The Director was surprised to find her office invaded by a large and indignant Prague detective and a tall, blonde haired policewoman. She prided herself on her reading of body language, but little expertise in that area would have been required to detect that Slonský was very angry.

'At least the parents can think about closure now,' she suggested.

'Very like this kindergarten then,' Slonský responded.

'You seem unreasonably aggressive,' she tried next. It took mere moments for her to realise that perhaps that was not the thing to say to a raging Slonský.

'I am aggressive,' he explained, 'because I think it's the job of a kindergarten director and her staff to ensure that the children in their care are returned safely to their parents. In the circumstances I don't think that my aggression is unreasonable.'

The Director had the grace to look rather sheepish.

'Is this about that young girl who went missing some years ago?'

'Why? Have you had any others you haven't told us about?'

'There was a full enquiry at the time,' she protested, 'and our procedures were declared acceptable.'

'This would be the report conducted by the Head of Children's Services for the District?'

'That's right.'

'Who happens to be your brother-in-law,' said Slonský, using information provided by Velek.

'That's quite beside the point. He was the person whose responsibility it was to oversee our services.'

'Well, he failed there, didn't he? Peiperová, make a note that we may need to speak to him later. However, the deficiencies in the care of children are not our interest. We are much more concerned about the fact that you seriously misled the police at the time by giving the impression that Mrs Dlasková only noticed her child was missing at five o'clock.'

The Director felt the need to interject. 'I'm sure I gave an accurate account. The police simply jumped to the wrong conclusion, that's all.'

'Well, let's examine what happened that day and you can give your testimony again, without any risk of misunderstanding. When did you become aware that Viktorie Dlasková had gone missing?'

'I must protest! This is most unfair. I can't be expected to recall these events at a moment's notice.'

'Oddly, that's the way the police work. We tend to find that if we give witnesses notice of our questions their answers tend to be less useful than we are entitled to expect. So, I repeat, when did you become aware that she had gone missing?'

'It must have been around a quarter past three. A group of mothers used to come around that time to collect their little ones.'

'Who told you?'

'I don't remember. One of my staff.'

'We understand it was a woman called Katja.'

'Yes, that's right. She was an assistant then.'

'And what did Katja tell you?'

'She said that Mrs Dlasková was complaining that her daughter had not been returned to her and Katja could not find her anywhere in her classroom or in the classroom behind which was used for the older children.'

'I understand there are two classrooms in that building.'

'Yes, the little ones go in the one nearer the door and the older children go through that to reach their room.'

'So what did you do when Katja told you this?'

'I immediately left my office to speak to Mrs Dlasková. The poor woman was extremely distressed and I gave immediate orders to search the buildings and grounds.'

'Who did you have to carry out your orders?'

'Each classroom has a teacher and an assistant at all times. Then there was me, the cook and the handyman.'

'Seven of you?'

'Yes. I asked the cook to check the kitchen and the dining area, and the handyman to search the grounds and the toilets. Then each teacher and her assistant looked round their own room, though, of course, they had also to mind the remaining children who were becoming aware that something was wrong.'

'Did anyone find any clues?'

'Katja produced Viktorie's coat which was still on her hook, though her outdoor shoes were gone.'

'Did she have gloves or a hat?'

'It was a cold day so she must have come with gloves. Her coat had a hood attached so she did not need a hat.'

'But she didn't have her coat, so she would have been cold if she had gone outside?'

'I assume so.'

'Can the children open the doors themselves?'

The Director looked uneasy. 'Since then we've replaced the doors. You now need to hold two handles at once to open the doors, but then it was just one handle. But it was quite high up for a little one. I don't think Viktorie could have reached it unless she stood on something.'

'Could she have slipped out when the other children left?'

'That was my first thought. When they are collected the drill is that one of the staff goes to fetch the coat and shoes of the child and dresses them to go home while the other walks them to the gate. That way one is always in the room with the children. No child leaves unless he or she is holding an adult's hand, so a couple can leave at a time. I was worried that Viktorie had followed other children out when the door was open.'

'But she had been coming to the nursery for a while. Surely she would have known where her mother would be and have headed straight for her if that were the case?'

'You would expect so. When we couldn't find Viktorie that seemed the likeliest explanation — she had run to the gate and her mother had missed her.'

'A mother who never left the gate area?'

'I know it sounds unlikely but excitable children can move very quickly. She might not have been noticed.'

'The police report says there were no children's footprints in the snow off the path, though of course there were plenty on the path to the gate.'

The Director played nervously with a retractable ballpoint pen, flicking the button repeatedly to the great annoyance of Peiperová.

'Did you come to work by car that day?' asked Slonský.

'Yes, as usual.'

'Who else uses a car to get here?'

'Then, nobody. Katja has a car now, but everybody else works within walking distance of home.'

'I'll need a complete list of all your staff then.'

'We don't keep records that far back.'

Slonský stood up and bent over her as if addressing a particularly recalcitrant toddler. 'Then perhaps you and your colleagues could put your heads together and recreate one. Today would be good. Peiperová can give you our fax number because I can never remember it.'

'We'll try.'

'No, you'll succeed. It would be very much in your best interests to do so. Is Katja around?'

'She only works three days a week. Most of our staff are part-time. I can give you her home address if you like.'

'Yes, I'd like that very much,' smiled Slonský sweetly.

Peiperová sat in the driver's seat and waited for the coming storm. Slonský had suggested that she might like to start the engine while he "finished things off" with the Director, which she took to mean that some street Czech was going to be used which might be unsuitable for her delicate sensibilities.

Finally the passenger door was flung open and Slonský threw his hat in the back seat as he climbed in. Peiperová decided to wait until she had instructions before starting the engine, partly because she was concerned about the colour of Slonský's face and the force with which he was grinding his teeth.

'Is everything all right, sir?'

'No, Peiperová, as you well know everything is not all right. It's very far from being all right.' Slonský slammed his hand on the top of the dashboard. 'If I do nothing else in this case, lass, I'm going to see to it that that woman is never allowed a position of responsibility again. By the time I finish with her she'll be damn lucky if she gets a job hosing down a school bus.'

'She seemed mainly concerned with defending her actions, sir.'

'No, she wasn't mainly concerned with that; she was entirely concerned with that. I hope she goes to Viktorie's funeral so I can drag her to the graveside and tell everyone it was her fault.'

'She didn't kill her, sir.'

Slonský pinched the bridge of his nose with his fingers.

'No, she didn't. But if she'd done her job Viktorie would have been here with her parents instead of getting herself killed a hundred kilometres away. Come on, Peiperová, let's go and see what this Katja woman has to tell us.'

The drive was quite short, but Slonský had recovered himself by the time they arrived outside a concrete block of flats. While the apartment blocks in much of the town were quite neat affairs with red tiled roofs, this row of blocks stood like children's bricks. Graffiti disfigured the entry way and the space under the stairs smelled of urine. Slonský checked the address he had been given.

'Third floor. Let's take the elevator.'

After a couple of minutes it became clear that the elevator was purely decorative and was going to take them nowhere, so the two detectives began to climb the stairs. Although Peiperová could have mounted them much faster, she felt that she should stay behind Slonský in case the unaccustomed effort proved too much for him. As it happened, the adrenaline released by the case, topped up by the interview with the Director, lifted Slonský to the third floor with relatively little effort, though he paused with his arm against the wall when they reached the door.

'Shall I ring the bell, sir?'

‘Unless you can magic us inside some other way, that would be good,’ he wheezed.

Katja proved to be a small, dark-haired woman with a neat figure. She wore a chunky wool sweater and jeans, and quickly invited them in when they produced their badges and identified themselves.

‘Come in and sit down,’ she insisted. ‘Sorry about the mess.’

Slonský looked around for any sign of disorder but saw nothing. His own flat had not been this tidy since around fifteen minutes after he moved in, so he felt that the apology was unnecessary.

‘You might want to sit down,’ he began. ‘I’m afraid we’re here because we have some sad news.’

Katja did as she was bidden, pulling a handkerchief from her sleeve as she did so in case it might be needed.

‘You’ll recall that seven years ago a little girl called Viktorie Dlasková was abducted from the kindergarten where you work.’

Katja nodded.

‘I’m afraid we’ve found her body. This is now a murder enquiry.’

Katja’s eyes opened wide and her hands jerked involuntarily towards her face.

‘She’s dead?’

‘I’m afraid so.’

‘And it’s definitely her. I mean, after all this time…’

‘She only died in the last few days,’ Slonský explained. ‘Perhaps a week or so.’

‘But I don’t understand. Where has she been for the last seven years?’

‘That’s what we need to establish, Mrs…’

'Švandová. Katja Švandová.'

'Well, Viktorie's body was found outside Prague. But in the process of trying to solve that crime, we've become aware of some — lack of clarity, shall we say? — about the original abduction. And since you were there, I hoped you could answer some questions.'

'Of course.'

'I think we've established the timeline. Let's start when Mrs Dlasková tells you that she hasn't got Viktorie.'

Katja closed her eyes and frowned in concentration. 'I'd taken two children out, one on each hand. I think they were probably the fifth and sixth children I'd delivered. Mrs Dlasková asked if Viktorie was ready, so I said I'd bring her next. I went back into the classroom where Petra was putting their coats on.'

'Petra?'

'Petra Vesecká. She was the class teacher. I was just an assistant.'

'Do you know where she is now?'

'She gave up work soon after. I've lost touch with her, I'm afraid.'

'Never mind. We can check national records. Please continue.'

Katja paused as if internally repeating what she had already said. 'I asked Petra if Viktorie was ready. She looked around the room and said she hadn't seen her, but the girl wasn't there. At Petra's suggestion I went through to the back room to see if Viktorie had sneaked into the older children's class, but she wasn't there either. By the time I came back, Petra was holding Viktorie's coat, a white one with a little hood.'

‘And it was a cold day.’

‘It had snowed earlier but there was only little bits of snow falling by that time. But if she had gone out without a coat she would have been freezing. That’s what I’ve always thought must have happened to her; she had somehow got outside without her coat and been overcome by the cold. And — I hate to say this — her body had been eaten by animals in the woods.’

‘No, she lived to be ten years old, but it involved a lot of abuse, I’m afraid.’

Katja’s eyes filled with tears. ‘Oh, my God,’ she gasped. ‘How horrible!’

‘You see now why I’m so keen to find out exactly what happened. You didn’t hear a car leaving?’

‘There were a few cars leaving, because the other parents were going.’

‘But not one in the car park where the Director parked?’

Katja looked at each of them in turn.

‘I don’t know! I didn’t think…’

‘No reason why you should,’ said Slonský gently. ‘Let’s carry on. So you had a coat but no girl. What did you do next?’

‘Petra stayed with the remaining children while I ran to fetch the Director.’

‘She was quite abrupt with you, I believe.’

‘She called me a silly girl and told me to stop panicking. But a toddler isn’t like a ring or a key. They’re not easy to lose. I was already convinced something terrible had happened.’

‘So you searched the rooms again?’

‘We were told that one of us had to mind the children while the other searched the room, then we should switch over and do it again. Meanwhile the cook and the handyman searched the grounds.’

'Were there footprints in the snow that might have helped?'

'The children had run everywhere during their playtime. It would have been hard to pick out any particular prints.'

Slonský knew what she meant, but it was disappointing.

'And they found no clues of any kind?'

'Not a thing. By this time Mrs Dlasková was nearly hysterical. She was screaming at us to fetch the police.'

'Was she still outside the gate?'

'Yes. That was the rule.'

'You might have thought it would have been relaxed in the circumstances.'

'I don't think anyone would have told her off if she had come in, but from there she could see along the paths and a bit of the main road. She could just about see that back car park too, or at least a part of it. We brought her inside and tried to calm her down but she said that if we didn't call the police at once she would run round there herself. The city police station was about six hundred metres away. The Director rang the police and explained what had happened and they were there in about five minutes. We had to repeat the search with an officer, and then we had to give statements, but to be honest I was so shocked I don't think I could remember anything very useful.'

Slonský could be brutal with uncooperative witnesses, but he was certain that Katja was being as helpful as she could be, so he just picked up his hat and thanked her.

'We may need to talk to you again, but you've been a big help,' he assured her.

As they walked back to the car Peiperová's curiosity got the better of her.

'Was that really any help, sir?'

'Well, I think I know how it was done. And I think I know who took her. But apart from that, not much.'

Peiperová held her tongue all the way back to the driver's seat, but then felt compelled to ask a question. 'So are you going to tell me what happened, sir?'

Slonský chewed his lip for a moment before replying. 'I wish we hadn't asked for the file to be sent to Prague. If it was still here I could have settled my last doubts on the spot. As it is, I want to read that file before I say anything. But don't fret; with luck it'll be waiting for us when we get back. Especially if we stop on the way for a little something to keep body and soul together. Keep an eye open for somewhere we can get coffee and a pastry or two. I tell you what — I'll treat you.'

Chapter 6

Back in Prague, Officer Krob tapped politely on the open door of Slonský's office before walking in. Navrátil glanced up at the new arrival.

'Sorry to intrude. I was looking for Captain Slonský.'

'He's out of the office, I'm afraid. Can I help?'

Krob dipped into the inside pocket of his uniform. 'I have to return this letter of acceptance.'

Navrátil accepted the envelope. He had no idea what this was all about but he was, when all was said and done, a detective, so he decided to do some detecting.

'Acceptance of what?' he asked.

'The job.'

Seeing the expression on Navrátil's face Krob realised that some further explanation might be needed.

'The captain said he had a job going. I had the job offer in the post yesterday.'

'I didn't know there was a job going,' Navrátil explained, 'but he doesn't tell me everything. Did he say who you would be replacing?'

'I'm afraid not. I can't start for another couple of weeks because the City Police are making me serve out my full term of notice, but I'm looking forward to it.' He offered his hand. 'Krob. Ivo Krob.'

'Jan Navrátil. Well, I suppose we'll be working together.'

Krob was sufficiently sensitive to realise that the atmosphere was a little strained.

'Yes. I suppose so. Well, better get back to work. Nice to meet you.'

Navrátil watched Krob depart and wondered, not for the first time since he had joined Slonský, what on earth was going on.

Colonel Urban had left his meeting and returned to his office to discover that his personal assistant was not around. The little yellow sticky note that Navrátil had left being markedly uninformative, largely because Navrátil did not know enough to make it otherwise, Urban picked up the phone and dialled Peiperová's mobile phone. If she had been driving at the time she would not have picked up the call, but since Slonský had spotted a bakery with a queue, which he said was always a good sign, they were enjoying a refreshment stop so she was able to answer.

Slonský could only hear one side of the discussion but it was very clear to him that Peiperová was getting the pointy end of the stick from her boss. She assured him that she would be back in no time at all and then noticed Slonský pointing to her phone and making a beckoning gesture.

'Captain Slonský would like a word with you, sir,' she stammered.

'Slonský! I might have known he would be involved…'

'Slonský speaking, sir. This is entirely my fault. Unfortunately we've had an unsatisfactory trip. The office at Ústí sent the file we wanted to Prague rather than keeping it here for us. It took us some time to wrap things up.'

'Like all yesterday and half of today?'

'No, sir, we were interviewing witnesses as agreed. It was just this morning that we could have done with the file. Officer Peiperová offered to catch the train back while I stayed here but I thought that it was unnecessary expenditure given that you had a meeting.'

If Slonský's former boss Lukas had heard him claim to be exercising economy he would probably have had a stroke, thought Peiperová, but she sensibly kept her mouth shut, whilst wishing she had not had her mouth full of cinnamon bun when she had answered Urban in the first place.

Urban seemed to have calmed down a little.

'You're on your way back now?'

'More than halfway, sir.'

'Good. Ask Peiperová where I can find the job applications for the interview panel this afternoon.'

Slonský posed the question and was delighted to return the phone to Peiperová so she could direct her boss to the second shelf of the letter trays on the corner of her desk and promise to be in place first thing the following morning.

'Lucky I was here to vouch for you,' said Slonský. 'He didn't sound too happy that you were out for so long.'

Peiperová bit her tongue. Anything she might have said could only make things worse. After a few minutes she felt bold enough to raise a point with Slonský.

'Sir, should you have told the Director an untruth?'

'I didn't. Show me one thing I said that wasn't true.'

'You gave the impression that we didn't know that the file was on its way to Prague.'

'No, Peiperová, I said it was. I drew no conclusions from that. I just recited some facts. If people want to incorrectly link them together that's their problem. There's a lesson there, my girl. Honesty is the best policy.'

The wicket gate opened briefly and an untidy figure stepped through, emerging to stand for a few moments blinking in the autumn sun. Wearing a suit that now seemed a little too large, with an open-necked white shirt and a navy raincoat flapping in the wind, he froze as Navrátil climbed out of the car and walked towards him displaying his badge.

'Mr Kobr?'

The middle-aged man nodded. His hair needed a cut. In fact, it needed completely restyling, because the comb-over was stretching credibility nowadays beginning, as it did, just above his left ear.

'I'm Navrátil. Would you like a lift somewhere?'

'Do I have a choice?'

'You have a choice about the lift. The conversation isn't quite so optional.'

Kobr followed to the car and eased himself into the passenger seat.

'Have you had lunch?'

Kobr nodded again.

'Coffee, then?'

'I haven't got much cash.'

'That's okay. I'm paying.' Navrátil pulled into the traffic. 'I've been asked to have an unofficial word with you. You realise, I'm sure, that your every move will be watched to see if you try to pick up the missing money?'

'They can watch as much as they like,' spat Kobr. 'There is no missing money. I never had it.'

'So you said at your trial.'

'It's true. I admit that I agreed to accept a bribe, but once they had that on tape they didn't actually need to pay it to get me to do what they wanted, so they didn't.'

Navrátil, unlike his former boss Klinger, believed him. Why would a criminal gang pay money to a police officer if they already had a hold over him?

'As far as I'm concerned,' said Navrátil, 'you've served your time and there's no more to be said if there isn't any proceeds of crime.'

Kobr was wringing his hands in his lap.

'The payroll thing — that money went at the time. But the bribe never existed. They offered it, but they never paid it. Would I be going to live in a hostel if I had half a million crowns somewhere?'

Navrátil weighed this carefully for a few seconds.

'Come on,' he said at length, 'let's get you a coffee.'

Slonský and Peiperová entered the police building together, but while she turned into what Slonský liked to call "the posh corridor" he paused at the desk to chew the fat with Sergeant Mucha.

'I have something for you,' said Mucha.

'Is it riches beyond my wildest dreams? A winning lottery ticket?'

'No, it's an old file from Ústí.'

'Ah, that. Have you opened it?'

'It's addressed to you,' protested Mucha.

'So it is. Have you opened it?'

'Naturally I flipped through it to see whether it was what it purported to be.'

'And?'

'It's a slipshod piece of work.'

'Now if Klinger said that I'd assume he'd noticed that the margins weren't the same on all the pages, but I'm guessing that's not what you're talking about.'

'You might want to look at page five, the list of witnesses interviewed.'

Slonský laid the folder on the counter top and quickly found the page in question. Running his fingers down the list he could see what Mucha meant.

'There's no continuation on page six?'

'That's the lot.'

'Imbeciles.'

'If it's so easy for me to spot, why didn't Ústí notice it at the time?'

'Who knows? Either you're unusually brilliant or the investigating officer in Ústí was astonishingly dim.'

'It'll be that, then,' murmured Mucha.

'That's where the smart money is,' agreed Slonský.

'I feel sorry for him,' Navrátil told Slonský when they had both returned to the office.

'He's a criminal,' observed Slonský. 'A disgrace to the police force.'

'Yes,' agree Navrátil, 'but on a human level I still feel sorry for him.'

'For heaven's sake, why?'

'He's got no job, no money, no reputation, nowhere to live and his wife divorced him.'

'That's all true of me, too. Except the job. And my wife hasn't actually formally divorced me.'

'He's lost it all and got nothing to show for it.'

'Permit me to observe that this is the result of bad choices he made. This is not bad luck, Navrátil. I'd have thought that as a believer you would have understood that bad things happen to you if you're naughty.'

'I know, but it's disproportionate. And he has served his time. He's paid his penalty but it's as if we're punishing him some more for the same thing.'

Slonský smiled. 'You poor young thing. If you'd been around when I started you'd have seen all this and more. Back in the day if someone got sentenced for something his family and friends fell over themselves to have nothing more to do with him. They'd often bring in extra evidence even after he'd been convicted.

'I can remember a factory manager out near Letňany who was caught dipping his fingers in the till. He got eight years, if I remember correctly, and within a month his wife had filed for divorce, his children had changed their names and two of his workmates organised a petition saying they'd always had suspicions about him and the sentence was too light. Imagine what sort of welcome he got when they let him out. Nobody would admit to having ever met him.'

Navrátil was unmoved. 'Kobr served his sentence. That pays for his crime. Anything extra is just spite.'

Slonský was often intransigent, occasionally downright stubborn, but even he was impressed by Navrátil's dogged refusal to accept things that offended against his sense of ethics.

'You really mean that, don't you?'

'Yes, sir. I'm not defending what he did, but once he's out, he should get a fair crack of the whip.'

Slonský dropped his pencil on the desktop. 'You realise you're making me question everything I've believed in for the last forty years?'

'I don't think I am. I think you think that too.'

'What makes you say that?'

'Because you can't abide injustice, and this is unjust. Once you realise that, you'll agree with me.'

The arrival of Peiperová terminated their discussion.

'Am I interrupting something?' she asked.

'No,' said Slonský. 'However, you've arrived just in time to examine this file which our colleagues in Ústí — and I use the word colleagues in its loosest and most temporary sense — have forwarded to us. We can either read it here, and die of thirst and hunger, or we can go to a bar, but we'd have to keep our voices down because this is confidential. Or, at a pinch, we could go to the canteen for a coffee, safe in the knowledge that everyone who might overhear us is a police officer.'

'So were the people you've been abusing under your breath for the last hour,' Navrátil pointed out.

'Good point. A quick conference here, then, followed by our decamping to a nearby hostelry for a little something to fortify us for the journey home.' Slonský opened the folder and turned it so that his juniors could read it. 'Cuddle up, then, and feast your eyes. Page one — mainly drivel. Tells us nothing we don't know.'

He waited for them to finish reading, then turned the page.

'Page two. Background drivel. Family tree for the child, map of the town, that sort of thing.'

They scanned it quickly and nodded to show that they had reached the end.

'Page three. Forensic drivel. Not much to say because they didn't call the experts fast enough.'

The page was mainly blank, so it did not take long for Navrátil and Peiperová to take in its contents.

'Page four. List of all the external reports requested that appear as appendices. Social worker report on parents, psychiatric reports on parents — they were, apparently, depressed, but who wouldn't be? — requests to other police forces for details of similar cases.'

Slonský pushed his chair back and had a good stretch.

'Page five. The good stuff. List of people interviewed for the enquiry, with job title and address. What do you notice?'

Navrátil and Peiperová read the list intently but offered no suggestion.

'Oh, you disappoint me!' said Slonský. 'Let's step through it slowly and we'll see if that makes a difference. It's a bit unfair to ask you, Navrátil, because you haven't visited the site, so Peiperová can take the lead. So, how was it done? How was a young child snatched in broad daylight with the minimum of fuss?'

'If it was February it wouldn't be broad daylight,' objected Navrátil.

'Sunset was at 16:58, so objection overruled, but a nice try. It was gloomy because there was snow in the air, I'll grant you that.'

'The mother must have been distracted, sir,' suggested Peiperová.

'Didn't the investigating officers think the father took her?' asked Navrátil.

'Whoa! I can only deal with one incorrect wild hypothesis at a time,' Slonský told them. 'If the father took her, where did he keep her for seven years? Or even for seven hours, because the police took the home apart that night?'

'They're divorced,' Peiperová noted, 'so perhaps this was his way of getting custody and the mother knew nothing. But it would explain why the child didn't cry out.'

'Again, where did he keep her given that he was contacted at work, and a little girl in an auto repair workshop would be noticed? There's no dispute that when they finally rang him he was at work three kilometres away.'

'But if they were so slow,' Peiperová doggedly persisted, 'he'd have time to snatch the child and then go back to work before they called.'

'Yes,' agreed Slonský, 'but he can't have known that Ústí would be so damn inefficient. They might have called within minutes. Or Mrs Dlasková might have found a public phone and called. Besides which, it's bad for our image if we build a case based upon the guaranteed ineptitude of the police, however accurate that might be.'

Navrátil rested his head on his hands and concentrated on the floor, a pose he found conducive to serious thinking. After a few moments a light dawned.

'The only piece of solid evidence we've got is the coat,' he said, 'so whatever the explanation is it must start with that.'

'Aha! We're getting somewhere. We've got her white coat. What would happen to her if she went outside without a coat on?'

'She'd freeze,' said Peiperová.

'In time. But I bet she'd complain. She'd ask for her coat. People would notice a child leaving with no coat on. Therefore I postulate that she had a coat, in which event…'

'The kidnapper brought one,' Navrátil concluded.

'Indeed they did. And it was different to the other. With a coat on, and the hood up you wouldn't see much of any particular child. So Mrs Dlasková possibly did see Viktorie leave, but she wouldn't recognise her because she was wearing a different coat. If we're right and the child left via the back fence that just strengthens the case because she would be facing away from her mother.'

'Why didn't the investigating officers work this out, sir?' Peiperová posed.

'Because they didn't have the benefit of my brains,' said Slonský, 'and they don't appear to have had any others of their own to call on. But hold hard, that's only half the story. Who did it?'

'You know that?' Navrátil enquired.

'I don't have a name yet,' said Slonský, 'but I should have in a day or so.'

'Who is it?' Peiperová asked.

'Katja gave us the clue, lass. Now look again at that list and tell me who we're looking for.'

'It all looks in order, sir. Everyone on the list was interviewed and accounted for. They either had an alibi or they were in sight, weren't they?'

'Yes, they were, young lady. Which means it isn't anyone on this list. But what about people who aren't on this list?'

'It's got the other parents and the kindergarten staff. I can't think of anyone else, sir.'

Slonský sighed. If two intelligent young people like this couldn't see it maybe he had been too hard on the numbskulls at Ústí.

'Where did we interview Katja?'

'At her house, sir.'

'Why was she at home?'

'Because it was her day off.'

'Because...'

'She only works part-time.'

'So who was there in her place?'

'Well, we don't know...'

'They didn't interview all the staff!' blurted out Navrátil.

'Of course!' Peiperová agreed. 'They only interviewed the ones who were at work. But Viktorie would have known anyone who was off duty that day and might well have gone with them without complaint.'

'Finally!' said Slonský. 'Come on — I've earned that drink.'

An hour or so later, it appeared that Slonský believed that he had earned several drinks, as a result of which he had gone to adjust his personal fluid balance. This gave Navrátil the opportunity to unburden himself of a task he had been putting off.

'Mother thinks it would be good for the two of you to spend some time together. She wants me to invite you for the weekend.'

'That's kind of her,' Peiperová replied.

'No, it isn't. It's like being brought in for questioning.'

'Are you worried she'll tell me all your little secrets?'

'Not at all. I don't have any. I just don't want her judging you.'

'If she's going to judge me she'll do it anyway, before or after the wedding. Better get it over and done with. Anyway, I want her approval. And it's not like we haven't met. We had a meal together last Christmas, remember?'

'A couple of hours in around eighteen months?'

'Is it worth reminding you that we might have known each other better if you had told her that I existed?'

This touched a raw nerve. When Navrátil first met Peiperová she was still a uniformed officer in Kladno and he had told his mother he was going to Kladno to spend a Saturday with a new friend, carefully avoiding any specification of the friend's gender. When he had started going out with her he had said nothing to his mother and when, much to his surprise, he had impulsively proposed and been accepted he decided it was time to tell his mother he was "seeing someone". Only now she would see the engagement ring and he would be on the end of her tongue for keeping it from her.

'Do you want me to take the ring off?' Peiperová asked.

'How do you do that?'

'Do what?'

'Respond to thoughts I haven't voiced.'

'I can read you like a book.'

'Well, no, certainly not. I'm not going to conceal our engagement from my mother.'

'You have so far.'

'I haven't concealed it,' Navrátil protested. 'I just haven't mentioned it yet.'

'Well, she's your mother,' said Peiperová. 'It's not for me to advise on how to handle her. But imagine the shock when she sees the ring.'

'I'll tell her tonight.'

'By phone?'

'No, I'll go round there as soon as we've finished here.'

There was a lengthy pause.

'Maybe I'd better have another beer,' said Navrátil.

Chapter 7

The list finally arrived from the kindergarten and Slonský pushed everything to one side of his desk so that he could get busy with the highlighter pen he had snaffled from Peiperová's unoccupied desk.

'Right, lad, we're up and running.'

'What are we going to do, sir?'

'Not we, Navrátil. You. It's time you flew solo. The experience will be good for you. I'm going to work my way through this list. We're going to tackle this case from both ends.'

'Sir?'

'I'm going to see if I can work out what happened to Viktorie Dlasková seven years ago. I want you to get the photo of her doctored so she looks alive, then get it to all the head teachers south of Prague. She must have gone to school somewhere and I want to find out why nobody is making a fuss about her being missing.'

'I've already had the photo done, sir. It's on the wall behind you.'

Slonský turned in surprise as if the installation of a notice board had been done in secret.

'Good work. If you speak nicely to the Ministry of Education they might have some idea where you can get a list of schools. When you get a response, go to the school and collect all the information you can. Then, with a bit of luck, somewhere we'll see a link between what you've got and what I've got and work out what's been happening the last seven years.'

Navrátil decided not to mention that he had already obtained a list of schools from the Ministry. Unfortunately, not all of them had faxes, so he had to think of an alternative.

'If the school doesn't have a fax, can I send it to the local police station and ask them to take it round?'

'Why not? It'll give them something to do besides watching daytime television. Sign the request in my name but put your details as the point of contact. This list may take me a while, so I'll just pay a visit to the canteen and see if they've got anything edible. Do you want anything while I'm there?'

This was a novel experience for Navrátil. Usually he was sent, and even if he and Slonský went together he would find that Slonský's wallet had not accompanied them. He was torn between taking full advantage and having something to eat that he did not need.

'Just a coffee, thanks,' he finally replied.

Slonský bent over his desk and made direct — and rather threatening — eye contact.

'There was a significant pause there, lad. Were you contemplating some dietary wickedness? Go on — I won't tell her.'

'No, really, I'm fine.'

'I don't want you fainting from hunger while you're watching me eating my roll.'

'I had a good breakfast, sir.'

'Well, if you die of malnutrition don't come running to me,' declared Slonský as he left the room.

Within a couple of hours Navrátil's efforts appeared to have borne fruit. A head teacher in Komořany telephoned to say that the young girl might have been one of their former pupils.

'Former?' asked Slonský.

'She left in the middle of September.'

'And we know why, don't we?'

'No, that's why they hadn't reported her missing. She says the mother came to see her on Friday, 14th September to say that she and her daughter were moving away.'

'Did she give a reason?'

'Not immediately. The teacher didn't want to pry, but then the mother said if her partner came to pick Viktorie up they weren't to hand her over because their relationship had broken down and she and her daughter were leaving town.'

'And how was the teacher supposed to stop him?'

'She's not his daughter and they weren't married, it seems, so he had no say in the matter. The teacher said she wasn't entirely surprised because Viktorie hadn't been her usual self for a while.'

'How long is a while?'

'Certainly before the summer. I thought I'd drive out there now and see if she can confirm identity from the clothes and the photograph, and I'll take a statement while I'm there.'

Slonský was studying the map and measuring distances with his thumb.

'Komořany is about four kilometres upstream from where she was found. Perhaps a bit more allowing for the bends in the river. It sounds plausible. Off you go, lad.'

Navrátil grabbed his coat and left, and Slonský returned to his list. There were four people not on duty on the day Viktorie Dlasková was snatched, but they all still lived in the district. It seemed inherently unlikely that anyone who kidnapped a child would be able to conceal her presence for seven years in a place where she was known and where the local police, inept as they were, had been looking for her, but he decided he had to go there just to check.

The small problem was that Navrátil had the car, so Slonský was compelled to ask Dlouhý for the use of a pool car.

Relationships with Dlouhý had been a little strained since Slonský took advantage of Dlouhý's poor eyesight to switch the car keys he had been allocated for those of a much better model in which he, Navrátil and Klinger had driven to Germany to interview a witness. Although that was over a year and a half earlier, Dlouhý had a long memory, largely because it had taken him several days to work out why the mileage logs on the various vehicles did not reconcile correctly.

'Would it help if I apologised? Again,' asked Slonský.

'I thought you were one of the good guys,' muttered Dlouhý. 'One of the old-timers.'

'I am an old-timer,' Slonský asserted. 'I'm older than almost everyone here.'

'I've got a 2002 Fabia over there,' Dlouhý offered.

'Nothing with a bit more leg room? I'm taller than average, you see.'

'No,' said Dlouhý firmly.

'What about that blue thing behind you?'

'Only for majors and above. They haven't made you a major yet behind my back, have they?'

'Of course not. I wouldn't accept anyway.'

'You wouldn't?'

'I didn't want to be a captain, so I sure as hell don't have any plans to become a major.'

This lack of ambition seemed to Dlouhý to speak to at least one of the old-time virtues, public service without thought of reward, so he softened a little.

'I've got a van.'

'A van?'

'You know what a van is?'

‘Yes, but it’s not exactly the thing for a drive to Most, is it?’

‘Big engine. With no load you can get it to a hundred easy as pie.’

Slonský felt in a mood to compromise. ‘Really?’

‘Goes like a greyhound. You’re going to Most, you say?’

‘That’s right.’

‘There’s more than enough fuel in the tank for the return trip. Promise me you won’t try to fill her up. It’d be like you to forget she takes diesel.’

Slonský declined to reply in case it upset the delicate negotiation, and simply held out his hand for the keys.

‘Sign here, here and here,’ said Dlouhý. ‘Your own name this time, if you please.’

The teacher was in no doubt.

‘Yes, that’s Viktorie,’ she sighed. ‘How awful!’

‘Do you have a surname for her?’

‘Viktorie Broukalová.’

Navrátil wrote it down.

‘How did she die?’ asked the teacher.

‘I can’t tell you that,’ Navrátil replied, ‘but she was found in the Vltava. And she didn’t drown.’

The teacher covered her mouth with her hand in shock.

‘She was murdered?’

‘We can’t say that for certain. It’s just possible it was an accidental death, but the fact that someone put her in the river rather than calling for help strongly suggests it wasn’t an accident.’

‘No … no, I can see that.’

‘What can you tell me about Viktorie and her family?’

‘Viktorie was a very quiet — I might almost say timid — girl. Studious, and well liked by her teachers. Never disobedient.

Her disciplinary record was excellent. So far as her grades go, she was above average until earlier this year, when they dropped quite sharply.'

'Did you wonder why?'

'Her class teacher came to see me to express her concern. She was convinced there was some problem at home. Viktorie was still cared for, so there was no hint of neglect, but it was just a few little pointers that the teacher had noticed.'

'Such as?'

'One of the things we ask them to write about after the summer is what they did on holiday. Viktorie didn't mention her parents at all. Or, should I say, her mother and her mother's partner, because I gather he wasn't Viktorie's biological father.'

'Let's talk about the parents. I'll need to find them, so if you have an address that would help.'

The teacher scribbled it on a leaf from a small notepad and gave it to Navrátil.

'If you cross the road when you leave, you go three or four blocks and turn left,' she added.

'Thank you. What do you know about Mrs Broukalová?'

'She seemed a very pleasant woman. She doted on Viktorie. Viktorie spent her entire school life with us, so we saw her grow up. Her parents were very proud of her. That is, her stepfather…'

'I understand.'

'Though you wouldn't know she wasn't his. He was very gentle and affectionate with her. She called him Daddy. I don't think she remembered her birth father. I gather he died when she was very small. There's a note in her file that Mrs Broukalová had produced his death certificate thus excusing the school from consulting her father about any aspect of her education.'

'Do you still have it?'

'I don't, I'm afraid. We would have returned it once we'd seen it. And I don't honestly recall seeing it myself, but that would have been four or five years ago and I may well have forgotten.'

'Can you describe Mrs Broukalová to me?'

'Not particularly tall, very dark hair, not quite shoulder length, dark brown eyes. She must have worked somewhere nearby but I don't think we know where. She must have lavished a lot of money and attention on Viktorie, who was always immaculately turned out. The mother was clean and tidy, but obviously didn't spent similar amounts on herself.'

'Slightly built?'

'Not overweight, by any means. If anything she was probably a kilo or two under average weight for her height, I'd have said.'

'Could you describe her stepfather?'

The teacher frowned. 'He looked like a professional type. Collar and tie whenever I saw him — rather like you. So many men don't wear ties these days. Mid to late thirties, clean shaven, light brown hair cut quite neatly. He said very little to us, but left his partner to do most of the talking.'

'I don't suppose you know his name?'

'I've been trying hard to think of it, but I don't think I do. I think his first name may have been Daniel, but I wouldn't swear to that. Miss Fantlová was her class teacher. Why don't I take you to ask her?'

Navrátil agreed, and they walked along the corridor. The head teacher exchanged a few quiet words with Miss Fantlová and then took over the class while the younger woman stepped outside.

'I understand this is about little Viktorie,' she said.

Navrátil nodded. 'I'm afraid it is. Her body…'

He got no further. Miss Fantlová emitted a little shriek and slumped forward. It was only by dropping his notebook that he was able to grab her before she hit the concrete floor. In the absence of chairs he laid her gently on the ground in the recovery position and placed his folded jacket under her knees, having heard somewhere that this might help the blood flow to the brain. Tentatively he opened the classroom door and waited for the head teacher to notice him.

When she heard what had happened she took control.

'You're ten years old, not little children,' she announced. 'Please continue with your work quietly while I help Miss Fantlová.' She closed the door behind her. 'She can't stay here. Are we able to carry her?'

'I think so,' Navrátil decided, tucking his pen and notebook away. He had expected to carry her himself, because she was shorter and thinner than Kristýna Peiperová, and he had reason to believe that he could pick his girlfriend up. However, an unconscious and uncooperative woman is a very different load. On top of that, he was by no means certain where he could put his hands with due propriety. This conundrum was solved for him by the head teacher, who looped her arms through Miss Fantlová's armpits.

'If you'll take her legs we can get her to my office and put her in one of the armchairs.'

Navrátil grasped the ankles, but that wasn't helping much, so he decided the best bet was to grip her by clasping his hands behind her knees. As they lifted her Miss Fantlová's dress flopped upwards revealing that, however dowdy her outer layer, her choice in underwear veered towards the pink and lacy.

Navrátil grabbed the hem of her dress and gripped it between his thumbs to preserve her decency as she was manhandled to the office, propped in a chair and gently shaken by the head teacher. When this produced no response the first aid kit was produced, which proved to contain a small bottle of smelling salts. In no time at all Miss Fantlová was coughing and spluttering and gratefully accepting the offer of a glass of water.

'I feel so embarrassed,' she said.

This did not seem the time to apologise for having seen her panties, so Navrátil assured her that she had nothing to be embarrassed about, the head teacher returned to the classroom, and Navrátil pulled up a chair to resume his questioning. He sat down before he realised that it was a special little chair for the smaller children. Miss Fantlová broke into a gentle chuckle.

'I'm sorry, I shouldn't laugh,' she said.

'It's better than fainting,' Navrátil answered. 'I'm sorry I gave you a shock.'

'I guessed something must have happened when the head showed me the photo to confirm that we both thought it was Viktorie, but she took it away again before I could read the fax fully. How did it happen?'

'She suffocated somehow. Her body was found in the river.'

Miss Fantlová's eyes ran freely with tears which smudged her make-up and left a black trail across her cheeks. 'Not an accident, then?'

'If it was, someone still has to explain why they put her in the river. The head teacher has told me most of what I need to know, but you spent more time with Viktorie and her family. I'd be very pleased to have your comments.'

'Of course,' said Miss Fantlová, visibly trying to pull herself together. At that moment she looked rather like an eleven-year-old who had borrowed her big sister's clothes.

'Where do you want me to start?' she asked, looking for a tissue to dry her eyes in her pocket, and gratefully accepting Navrátil's handkerchief when she failed to find one.

'What was Viktorie like?'

'A polite girl, quiet, very keen to please.'

'Was she a loner?'

Miss Fantlová creased her brow in contemplation.

'You know, I'd never thought of it but until recently she wasn't. She'd play happily with the other children. But earlier this year something changed. Her school work suffered and she didn't want to go outside as much. She'd ask if there was anything she could do to help me in the classroom, so she'd help putting pens and paints out, or collecting the workbooks.'

'Did you have any idea what might have spurred that change?'

Miss Fantlová hesitated as if reluctant to say what she thought, but then decided that she ought to answer, and did it in a rather louder voice as if to emphasise that she was not holding anything back.

'I think her periods may have started. A couple of times I had to help her clean up.'

'I see,' said Navrátil, whose experience of menstrual cycles was limited. 'Would that explain the decline in schoolwork?'

'Not really. Obviously there might be a day or two when she didn't feel well and was uncomfortable or in pain. But it was more as if she found it psychologically difficult to deal with. I wondered if her mother hadn't told her what was happening to her, but when I mentioned it to Mrs Broukalová she assured me her daughter knew all she needed to know.'

Navrátil wanted to ask a question but was finding it difficult to phrase properly.

'Is it possible … it wasn't actually a period?'

'How do you mean?'

Navrátil broke eye contact for a second to make it easier for him to say.

'There is some evidence that she had been sexually abused.'

'Sweet Jesus! No!'

The tears began again, necessitating another outing for Navrátil's handkerchief.

'I'm afraid so.'

'That might explain the bleeding and the change in her performance,' Miss Fantlová commented. 'But I can't believe we didn't spot that. She didn't say anything, even to me.'

'Maybe she thought that was all part of growing up,' offered Navrátil. It sounded lame to him, but then he had never been a small girl. 'I'd be grateful if you didn't say anything about the abuse just yet.'

Miss Fantlová agreed. When her voice failed her, she simply nodded her head.

'What about Viktorie's mother?'

'A nice woman. She would do anything for Viktorie. They weren't well off, but Viktorie never looked neglected. She always had shoes that fitted properly, for example. I can't say that for all my class, sadly.'

'And her partner?'

'Much the same. Always polite, quite well presented. He looked like he had some kind of office job. It can't have been particularly well paid unless he spent it all on himself.'

'Do you remember his name?'

'Daniel. Daniel … no, I don't think I recall his surname.'

'Have you seen either of them since Viktorie stopped coming to school?'

'No, but then I didn't expect to. Mrs Broukalová called in to tell us she was taking Viktorie away and hinting at a break-up with her partner. She thanked us but there was no prior notice. She just picked the girl up, said this was the last time she would be there and explained that she couldn't give a forwarding address because she didn't know exactly where she was going. Viktorie got upset at the idea of leaving school but her mother told her it was sad but they had no choice.'

'That would explain why you wouldn't see Viktorie and her mother, but not her stepfather. You haven't seen him either?'

'No, but I never did except at school events.'

Navrátil closed his notebook and stood up.

'Thank you for your help. I'll go to their house now to see if he is there.'

Slonský was gripping the steering wheel between the two smallest fingers of each hand. The thumb, ring and middle fingers were otherwise engaged, those of his left hand grasping a *párek* while those of the right were holding a cup of coffee. It was at this moment that his phone rang.

It is possible, if you have had enough practice, to eat a *párek* with no hands, gripping the sausage between the teeth and pulling it forward as you chomp on the bun, so Slonský freed his left hand, then realised that he could not reach his phone. He deftly transferred the coffee to his free hand and pressed the answer button.

Navrátil's voice filled the van, to the point where Slonský yelled that he was going to pull over to take the call once he had adjusted the volume.

'Sorry about that, lad. You now have my undivided attention.'

'I'm at the girl's house, sir. The girl was registered at the school as Viktorie Broukalová. As I said, the mother told them she and her daughter were moving away. I'll fill you in on the detail when I see you. The point is that they gave me her address and I'm here now.'

'Well done. I'm glad you can find a house once someone gives you the address. Is there a point to this call?'

'I can see in through the downstairs windows. The house is in pretty good order downstairs, but one of the neighbours let me look from her upstairs window so I could see into the bedroom.'

'This neighbour knew you could see into the bedroom, did he?'

'She, sir. An old lady. She says she hasn't seen any sign of life in the house for a while. But it looks like the bedroom has been ransacked. I can see the wardrobe and some of the drawers are open. Can I get a search warrant?'

'Does anyone have a key?'

'Not that I've discovered, sir.'

'We have reason to believe that Viktorie was murdered there, don't we?'

'Do we?'

'Navrátil, it's as likely as anywhere else. Did the mother have a suitcase with her when she collected Viktorie at the school?'

'Nobody mentioned one.'

'Then if they were moving away the likeliest place to go was home to get some clothes. So that's the last place we have a definite link with the victim. That justifies breaking in to secure evidence. The man of the house isn't around either?'

'Not been seen, sir.'

'Do you know where he works?'

'Not yet, sir.'

'Right. Ring Mucha and get him to organise a search warrant just to be on the safe side. I also want a forensic technician there when you go in so that they can treat it as a crime scene. Mucha can ring Novák. Don't go in till the technician arrives. We'll have to send a couple of officers to guard the house until it's secure again. You're probably okay to smash a downstairs window to get in if you have to, but the technician may have a glass cutter with him.'

'Won't that take time, sir?'

'I've arrested people who could have been in through those windows while we were on this call, lad. See if you can borrow a ladder to have a better look upstairs while you're waiting.'

'Very good, sir.'

'Speak to you later — and well done.'

Slonský took a gulp of coffee and unfolded the list of names he had been given. There was no-one called Broukalová on it.

He was torn between turning back to supervise the search and carrying through his own enquiries, but reasoning that he had to allow Navrátil some independence at some time he started the engine again and drove on.

The women who were first and third on his list were nearest to the main road. Nothing about their homes suggested that a young girl was living there — other, that is, than the daughter of one of them, who was younger than Viktorie. The second name was registered as living in a block of flats but when Slonský called he was told she had moved away about three months earlier. However, the new resident had a forwarding address and Slonský found her there.

Lucie Jerneková was an angry woman. Slonský had no idea why, but she seemed to be upset with everyone about everything. She reluctantly let him into her flat, taking the opportunity to ask her neighbour what she was looking at as she did so, then stood with her arms folded looking combative.

'Is this about my old flat?'

'No. Should it be?'

'That bastard of a landlord keeps claiming I damaged his plumbing and caused a flood. The shower pipe came off the wall. Is that my fault? Jesus Maria! He won't let it drop.'

'I'm not remotely interested in that and I don't run around on behalf of landlords. I'm here because I'm told that you used to work at the kindergarten.'

'I did. They sacked me. Reckoned I had a bad attitude and it rubbed off on the kids.'

'When was this?'

'About two years ago.'

'But you were there when Viktorie Dlasková went missing?'

'Now, hang on. I was off duty that day. Ask anyone. Except that bitch of a Director. She'd probably stitch me up.'

'No, she said you weren't there. But the case has been reopened and the evidence points to someone who worked at the kindergarten being implicated, hence why I'm talking to everyone who worked there then. You haven't been singled out. Do you have any children?'

'I don't have a man, so how can I have children?'

'A reasonable question, but if you don't tell me you haven't got a man, how am I to know?'

She swept her fingers through her hair and flopped on a red vinyl sofa with a conspicuous tear in the seat.

'Sorry. It all gets on top of me sometimes.'

'Don't worry. It takes more than that to upset me. Is there a café near here?'

That Lucie was surprised at the question was evident from her face.

'There's a bar round the corner that does coffee if that helps.'

'If I go into a bar I'm not wasting my time buying coffee. Come on, you look like an hour out would do you some good.'

She picked up her jacket and followed this curious policeman in his antique overcoat and crumpled suit.

'Walking behind me isn't going to work too well, because I don't know where I'm going,' he called over his shoulder.

'Next left.'

'Ah yes. I can smell beer. Come on, step lively.'

He held the door open and they took seats by a pane of glass that would have been a window had it not been plastered with handwritten notices about items for sale.

'I'll have a beer,' Slonský announced.

'What size?' asked the owner.

'Man size. And give this lady whatever she wants to drink.'

Lucie asked for a hot chocolate with all the trimmings. Since Slonský had no idea what all the trimmings could be, he took a keen interest when the mug arrived.

'Is there some hot chocolate under there somewhere?' he asked.

'Whipped cream, marshmallows and chocolate sprinkles like the lady ordered,' said the owner, giving an inflection to "lady" that suggested he might have used another word. He plonked a glass of beer in front of Slonský.

Slonský picked it up, admired its colour and took a satisfying slurp.

'I could tell you how to sell a lot more beer,' he said.

'Oh, yes?' replied the owner, not without sarcasm.

'Yes,' said Slonský definitively. 'Fill the glasses up to the damn top.'

The owner marched away affronted, but Lucie was smirking.

'You told him,' she said. 'He's a bas—'

'I know,' Slonský interrupted. 'Is the chocolate good?'

'Haven't had one of these for ages. Very nice, thanks.'

'Let's assume, for the sake of clarity, that I'm convinced you didn't abduct young Viktorie. Who do you think might have done?'

Lucie considered for a moment. 'Why is this all coming up again now?'

'We've found her body, I'm afraid.'

'Poor little mite. I didn't work in that classroom very often but I knew her to look at. I wasn't there when it happened, but I could never work out how it could be done. But I suppose if it was one of us then it wouldn't be too hard. You could just take her hand and walk her out, but not to the gate. But you'd surely be seen.'

'Suppose it happened too quickly. Suppose the other helper in the room was busy. But don't worry yourself about how it was done. That's my job. I want your opinion on who had it in them to do this.'

'I'd like to think none of them could. But I suppose the Director would be on her own. Nobody would be watching what she was doing.'

'And is she evil enough to do this?'

Lucie shrugged. 'Probably not. But then you must have arrested plenty of people who weren't thought evil enough to do things.'

'You have a point there,' conceded Slonský. 'But where would she hide a child for seven years?'

'Seven years? You mean she's been alive all this time?'

'Until now.'

'Jesus Maria! Poor child. Why her?'

'I can't answer that. Not yet, anyway. Maybe she was the one nearest the door. Who knows?'

Lucie took another drink of her chocolate and absentmindedly wiped her mouth on the back of her hand. 'Why are you talking to me about this?'

'Because I'm working on the theory that Viktorie didn't cry out because she knew the person who took her. That means her family, which seems unlikely, or the people who looked after her day by day. We got a list of staff from the Director. Those who were on duty were cleared at the time, but they didn't talk to those who were off duty.'

'You're right there. This is the first time I've been asked about it.'

'Can you remember what you were doing on the day she was taken?'

'No. Only that I wasn't at work. I worked Mondays and Thursdays then.'

'And you didn't drop in when you were off duty?'

'Not on that day. Other times, yes. If you're passing and you need the toilet, why not? Or if it's someone's birthday and there's cake going. But I kept away. The problem was that if you went in you'd finish up being given things to do and not getting paid for it. The Director was a bitch for that.'

Slonský told himself that you didn't need to be much of a detective to realise that Lucie and the Director didn't get on.

'I've spoken to three of the four of you. The only one I still have to find is someone called...' He consulted his list. 'Tereza Jandová.'

'Good luck with that. She's dead.'

'Dead?'

'About three years ago. Drank herself to death. Pretty good alibi, I'd say.'

'It's not much of an alibi, actually. The fact that she died since doesn't stop her being the one who took Viktorie seven years ago.'

'No,' Lucie conceded, 'but she was in her fifties and not the sharpest knife in the drawer. She couldn't have come up with a plan like that. It was all she could do to get the children's drinks ready at lunchtime.'

'She worked in the kitchen?'

'She worked anywhere she was needed, but she spent very little time with the children. Besides, most of them were scared of her.'

'Why was that?'

'She had funny eyes. Something medical, I think. They were a bit goggly and you couldn't tell what she was looking at.'

Slonský made a note on his list and knocked back the remainder of his beer.

'What do you do now?'

'A bit of cleaning if I can get the work, but there aren't many jobs going around here.'

'Ever thought of looking for something in Prague?'

She laughed. 'It might as well be the moon. I don't have the money to go up there and stay somewhere while I look. I get by most days.'

Slonský put his hat back on. 'I'd better get going. Thanks for the help.'

'Thanks for the chocolate. You're an unusual type of cop.'

'So people tell me. You're an unusual type of witness.'

'Yeah, they tell me that too.'

Lucie rose to her feet and drank the last part of her chocolate.

'You don't have to leave just because I'm going,' Slonský said.

'Yes, I do. As soon as you're gone he'll throw me out anyway.'

'Why?'

Lucie shrugged again. 'It's his place. He makes the rules. Oh, and he thinks I'm a whore.'

'Are you?'

'No. I'd live better if I was.'

'If I think of anything else, is there a phone number I can reach you on?'

'No. You'll have to send me a postcard. Make it a picture one.'

Slonský walked to the van with a smile breaking through. An idea was forming in his mind. It was completely deranged, but then many of his best ideas were.

Chapter 8

Navrátil was surprised when a car pulled up alongside his and Dr Novák climbed out.

'I was only expecting a technician, Doctor,' he explained.

'They're right behind me. But if there is any chance that this is a murder scene I want to supervise the sample collection.'

The arrival of a small van produced two technicians, one of whom marched straight to the front door. After a brief inspection he decided the back door was a better option, and the party walked round the house.

Navrátil was just wondering which window they should break when he realised that the back door was open.

'I'm sure that was locked,' he said in some confusion.

'It was,' smiled the technician. 'It isn't now.'

'We'll let them go first,' said Novák. 'They know what they're doing. We'll wait here.'

'This isn't going to look good if Viktorie's stepfather returns,' Navrátil offered.

Novák opened the fridge. 'I don't think he's been here for a while. And if he comes back and eats any of this stuff I'll be back here once again.'

'Rancid, is it?'

'The milk is the best guide. That hasn't been disturbed for a week or more, I think.'

One of the technicians came downstairs.

'I think you'd better see the girl's bedroom, doctor.'

Novák followed at once, and was gone for a quarter of an hour or so before coming back down.

'You can come up, but don't go beyond the doorway, please,' he said to Navrátil.

The room was quite small. It was dominated by a single bed whose head was in the centre of the wall opposite. On the nearer side there was a chair and on the farther side a small nightstand. The window was to the left as Navrátil looked into the room, and a small wardrobe was positioned to the left of the window. Navrátil could not see it clearly with the door open.

Novák stood in his lint-free suit on the far side of the bed and used a laser pen to point to items of interest.

'The wardrobe is full of her clothes, so if the mother was planning to take her away they never got to finish the packing. Of course, they may have travelled light. Let me draw your attention to the bed. Although it has been made, someone has been lying on it, as shown by the indentations in the coverlet and the pillow.'

'That's a big dent in the pillow,' observed Navrátil.

'Yes, because she was pushed down into it, I think. There are traces of saliva and blood there. I think she suffocated when someone laid on top of her and shoved her head into the pillow. She tore her frenulum trying to turn her head.'

'Her what?'

'The frenulum. The piece of tissue that connects the top lip to the top of the gum. When she was struggling to breath she would try to gasp like a fish. With her lip pushed into the pillow that wouldn't be possible but she would tear her mouth trying to force her lips apart.'

'Would it be quick?' asked Navrátil.

'Not quick enough,' Novák replied. 'She must have suffered. Apart from anything else, I think a man was lying on top of her while she was face down, and I think we're going to find that those stains halfway down the bed are due to semen. We should be able to get a good DNA sample from them.'

Navrátil wanted to sit down but had to make do with rubbing his face vigorously.

'So let me get this right, doctor. You're saying she died here while she was being raped?'

'I don't know that there was penetration, but it's likely because there's some blood too.'

'And the person most likely to be raping a young girl in her own home is a family member.'

'A male family member, to be precise. And we only know of one. If we can't find the stepfather we need to find out who he is so that we can get DNA from a family member for comparison. Are you all right, Officer Navrátil?'

'Sorry, just a bit faint. It's my first experience of this sort of thing.'

Novák smiled in a kindly way. 'We all had a first time. Why don't you go downstairs and make some notes while I finish off in here?'

'Thank you — yes.'

Navrátil returned to the kitchen and had just started writing when the back door was flung open and a familiar figure strode in.

'This is no time for writing love letters, lad. Was that Novák's car I saw outside?'

'Yes, sir. He's upstairs.'

'Good. Why aren't you?'

'He suggested I write up what we've found so far while he finished off.'

'Even better. You can tell me what you've found as you write.'

'How did you know where to come, sir?'

'Mucha told me. Remember, you told him where to send Novák.'

'But Most is over a hundred kilometres away.'

'I know,' beamed Slonský. 'I'll have to tell old Dlouhý he was wrong. That van can do a hundred and forty, no problem. Well, a bit of juddering now and again, but there's no point in hanging around. You don't solve crime driving down the highway.'

Navrátil opened his notebook and began to read. 'It looks as if Viktorie died in her bedroom, sir. She was face down on the bed with a man on top of her and her face was stuck in the pillow. Dr Novák has taken some semen samples and will be able to identify the male involved.'

'So will everyone else once I lay hands on him because he'll be missing some of his key bits,' snarled Slonský. 'Anything else?'

'Her clothes seem to be here but perhaps the mother only packed a small bag.'

'We can check that. Come on.'

Slonský bounded up the stairs but instead of entering the small bedroom he opened the door to the adults' room. Walking to the wardrobe he opened the door.

'Full set of clothes, I reckon. Now, on the other hand, look at the chest of drawers, lad. Don't touch it until Novák's men have been in here, but what do you notice?'

'One drawer sticking out. It appears to be empty.'

'And the others?'

'I can't tell without touching them, sir.'

'Then put some gloves on and just peek in.'

'More or less full, sir.'

'Yes. And what are they not full of?'

'Sir?'

Slonský adopted his slow and loud speaking-to-an-idiot voice. 'What are you not finding?'

'There's no underwear, sir.'

'Exactly. When a woman is packing as fast as she can, she just tips her underwear drawer into a bag. She can manage with one or two tops and skirts or trousers, but women like plenty of underwear. If she had packed before she went to the school, she'd probably have been more selective about the underwear and taken more of her other clothes. I suspect that she packed after Viktorie was killed, lad. She fled the crime scene. So was that in horror at what she had found, or guilt at what she'd been part of?'

Navrátil and Slonský examined the drawers to see if Viktorie's stepfather's clothes were also missing, but that was not so clear-cut. Many were still there, but without knowing how many there had been before the events of that September day it was not possible to draw any firm conclusion, except, possibly, that the stepfather had not left in as much of a hurry as her mother.

'Does that mean that they didn't leave together, sir?'

'Maybe. But perhaps it just means he doesn't get as agitated as she does by killing children, Navrátil. Have you found a name for him yet?'

'There's some letters addressed to Daniel Nágl, sir. Recent dates.'

'Good work. When we get back see if you can trace a car and mobile phone for him. For that matter look for one for his wife while you're at it. I doubt she has a car but she may have a phone, and if she has I want to find it. Is there anything else we can do here?'

'You're in charge, sir.'

'Yes, Navrátil, but I'm giving you your big break. Remember, you're flying solo.'

'How can I fly solo if you're here?'

'Think of it as me being your instructor. I can take the controls if you're going to go down in flames, but you've got to fly sometime. So,' continued Slonský, 'I'm pushing you out of the nest.'

The mixed metaphor was not lost on Navrátil, but he was keen to show he could manage, so he stood for a moment tapping his pen on his teeth while he thought.

'You're meant to be an eaglet, not a woodpecker,' Slonský complained. 'Well?'

'Let's see if there's anything that tells us what Mr Nágl does for a living.'

'Excellent. Well, you don't need me for that so I'll head back to town.'

'If you're going first, sir, you could start the car and phone traces.'

Navrátil was convinced that he had overstepped the mark, judging by the look on Slonský's face, and braced himself for a flow of invective that never came. Instead, Slonský walked past and patted him on the shoulder as he went.

'Jolly good idea, lad. I'll get the desk sergeant onto it right away.'

Valentin must have had his hair cut. There was not that much of it, but what there was had been carefully arranged to conceal as much scalp as possible and bore traces of some fragrant oil.

'Have you been on one of those dating websites again?' posed Slonský.

'No,' replied Valentin. 'Why would you think that?'

'If you're not seeing a woman I'll sit here, but keep your distance. I don't want people thinking I've been turned by your tarted-up head.'

'It needed a cut,' Valentin protested. 'It was getting straggly.'

'It's been straggly since about 1983,' Slonský pointed out, 'but I don't remember you getting it properly cut before.'

'Then your observational powers are failing. For a start, you haven't noticed that my glass is empty.'

'So it is. While you're ordering a refill you can get one for me.'

Valentin bowed to the inevitable, the pain eased somewhat by the knowledge that in any lifetime reckoning he was well ahead so far as receiving goes, and beckoned a waiter to give their order.

'What have you been doing today?' Valentin asked.

'Driving a van up to the Most district.'

'Moonlighting? Police salary not enough for you?'

'No, it was the only vehicle Dlouhý would let me have.'

Valentin snorted. 'Are you surprised?' he said.

'Am I the only person around here who believes in letting bygones be bygones?' Slonský growled.

Valentin inspected him closely. 'You really mean that, don't you?'

'What?'

'You think that you're capable of forgetting a past slight. When did you last speak to Marián Krátký?'

'Around 1962, I think.'

'And the reason for your silence?'

'You know the reason.'

'Humour me.'

'He snapped one of my ski bindings.'

'Yes. When we were still at school. He keeps a bar not two hundred metres from here and it's the one place in Prague I'm certain never to find you.'

'The beer's like virgin's pee.'

'Undoubtedly true, but he does a decent sausage, I'm told.'

Slonský looked confused, as if someone had just proved to him that the world was flat. 'I can't be bought by a sausage. When he's ready to apologise, I'll think again.'

'He apologised in 1962.'

'He didn't mean it.'

'You don't know that.'

'I'm a policeman. It's my job to work out if people are telling the truth.'

'You weren't a policeman then.'

'No, but I was thinking of becoming one, so it's just as well I was demonstrating I had solid instincts for that kind of thing.'

Their beers arrived, so each man put aside their discussion for a moment to savour the first mouthful under the foamy head.

'That's nice. I needed that,' said Slonský.

'The first of the day is always the best,' Valentin opined.

'It's my second,' Slonský told him. 'I had one with a witness.'

'Isn't drinking with witnesses a slightly unusual approach for a policeman? I know you normally treat the Police Manual with contempt but this is a bit over the top even for you.'

'The woman hadn't two crowns in her purse and she needed to get out of her depressing flat. I took her somewhere she would relax and be less aggressive. And it worked. She saved me a fruitless trip by telling me the fourth woman on my list was dead.'

'If she was telling the truth.'

'Why would she lie?'

'According to you, everyone does.'

'They do. But they don't all lie all the time. Anyway, we've got a name for the victim, the mother and the mother's partner. Now we need to see if we can trace either of the adults back to Ústí.'

'Permit me to observe, as an interested bystander, that if you can't your case is shot.'

'You think I don't know that? Anyway, Sergeant Salzer is whiling away the night shift trying to track Mrs Broukalová's addresses, phone numbers and relationships.'

'Do you have all that on file then?'

'And more. I just can't get the hang of the computer stuff, but everybody else seems to be able to find out all sorts.'

'This place gets more and more like a police state,' Valentin grumbled.

'Compared with when I started in the police, it's a beacon of liberty,' Slonský corrected him.

'Yes, I suppose so.'

'The only difference is that Sergeant Salzer can do it all from his desk whereas before we had eighty-four clerks running up and down a kilometre of filing cabinets. I couldn't get the hang of that either.'

Chapter 9

Navrátil was always punctual in the morning and was used to being first to arrive, so it took him aback a little to find Slonský sitting at his desk surrounded by sheets of paper on which he had written with a large red marker pen.

'Good morning, sir. Has Sergeant Salzer found anything of interest?'

'Good morning, Navrátil. Yes, and no. He's discovered that Mrs Broukalová is a practised liar. She has an identity card and we can track it back for about six years, but where she was before that is not at all clear.'

'So Broukalová isn't her real name.'

'We can't say that. Either it isn't, but she got papers in that name to conceal what she was about, or it is and she previously used a different one.'

'And Nágl?'

'Prague resident going back a long way. He seems to be about thirty-eight and he's been hereabouts for at least the last twenty of those years. He owns a black Volkswagen Golf, about two years old. I've got the traffic police looking out for it but no sightings so far. I also sent a car to tour the neighbourhood where they lived to see if it's parked anywhere nearby, though why he would do that when he has a perfectly good driveway is hard to imagine.'

'Nágl seems to be some sort of draughtsman, judging by the books on his shelves.'

'That doesn't help us much in terms of finding his employers, but his tax records should.'

'I'll take a look, sir.'

Navrátil sat at his desk and worked in silence for a few minutes before deciding there was something he needed to say. 'I haven't had a chance to tell you that someone called Krob dropped his paperwork back. I put it in your in-tray.'

'Which one is my in-tray?'

'The top one.'

'Ah. I normally think of that as my tray for putting sandwiches in. Let's have a look — there it is. Thanks.'

'Which vacancy is he applying for, sir?'

'Navrátil, I know where this is going, and you can relax. My plan is that Krob should work under one of the lieutenants. He's not replacing anyone you know.'

'I suppose Kristýna and I have been fortunate in working together so far. We can't expect that to continue.'

'No, that was possible because I was around to make sure that the two of you didn't spend all your days parked up in a lay-by somewhere. But part of the point of letting you lead on parts of this case is so that I don't have to do that and I can spend more time with the new folks like Krob.'

'So will we be getting two new lieutenants to replace you and Doležal and a new officer to replace Rada, sir?'

'Budget cuts, lad! They'll only let us have two of the three for now. That's another reason why I'll have to split you and Peiperová up when she comes back, or there'll be a lieutenant with no little helper.'

Navrátil did not like what he was hearing, but he knew that it was inevitable. At least they would both be in the same team.

'Is there any news on Colonel Urban's promotion, sir?'

'You mean his lack of promotion, Navrátil. I don't know. And presumably Mucha doesn't know, or he'd have told me. And if Mucha doesn't know, nobody knows.'

The tax office provided an address for Nágl's employers so Navrátil was dispatched to see if he was there while Slonský continued his trawl though the paperwork trying to piece together Mrs Broukalová's life. The essential next step in this process was to visit the canteen to collect a coffee and some source of carbohydrates.

As usual, Dumpy Anna was behind the counter. Slonský had no romantic interest in her, but he enjoyed a chat with her and she mothered him occasionally.

'Ah, it's old Skin-and-Bones! What are you not going to have today?' she asked.

'Thank you for noticing that my rigorous exercise programme is bearing fruit,' replied Slonský.

The rigorous exercise programme in question had been forced on him by an impending police medical, for which he had managed to lose seven kilograms. Realising that at his age a medical was never going to be too far away he had continued to put in a bit of time in the gym when he could, because the alternative of continuing to go without beer, coffee, sausages and pastries was just too grim to contemplate. Not only was it unhealthy in his view to deny himself these pleasures, it had also, by common consent, made him even more grouchy and antisocial than had previously been the case, and it was his firm opinion that his brain did not function as well without beer to keep the cogs oiled. He had told anyone who would listen that his difficulty in solving the case in which poor Doležal had been beaten up was largely due to that period of enforced abstinence. Well, near-abstinence; that is, reducing to less than two litres a day.

Anna handed him a coffee and took the money for the pastry he had selected.

'Anna,' said Slonský on an impulse, 'do I remember that you've been married twice?'

'You do. They both died on me.'

'So you'll have had to get new national identity cards in your new name a couple of times?'

'Yes. I never remembered to do it right away, of course. And you don't have to change your name when you get married, do you?'

'No, but if you do, what do you have to do?'

'It's a bit stricter now. I think you have to take your marriage certificate and something that proves your address. Back when I did it they knew where you lived anyway.'

'But did they actually check anything?'

'You mean like going round to the flat to see if you were there? Not that I know of. They've got computers now so I suppose they can check things through that, but in my day it was all paper.'

'Did you keep your last husband's name after he died?'

'No point in changing, was there? It's not like I was going to be third time lucky.'

Slonský smiled benignly. 'There's no harm in hoping, is there?'

'Why would I want to get married again? At my age it just means double the ironing.'

Slonský skipped happily up the stairs now that an idea was forming. He knew that many of his ideas came to nothing, but the important thing was to have plenty of them. He never felt as bad as when he had run out of plausible ideas.

At the top of the stairs he was surprised to find his old boss, Captain Lukas, loitering in the corridor.

'This is a pleasant surprise, sir,' he remarked.

'Don't call me sir, Josef. I'm retired now, remember? I'm just plain old Mr Lukas now.'

'You'll always be Captain Lukas to me, sir. Come in and sit down. Coffee?'

'No, thanks. It's a kind offer but I don't hold my liquid so well these days. Besides, I remember what the canteen coffee is like.'

'Very wise, sir.'

'Don't let me keep you from work. I was just ... in the district and thought I would pop in. See how my old colleagues are doing.'

One of the things about the police headquarters was that it was not on the way to anywhere sensible. Knowing where Lukas lived, it was hard to see why he would be "in the district" unless dropping in was the main purpose of his outing. Lukas confirmed this obliquely, feeling that some additional explanation might be warranted.

'My wife and daughters are lovely, of course, and very attentive, but a fellow needs a little bit of male company now and again, Josef.'

Lukas was not a red-blooded alpha male, devoted to beer and hockey, so Slonský interpreted this as a need for a modicum of silence from time to time.

'I quite understand, sir. We'll always be pleased to see you here.'

'That's very kind. How are things?'

'On a scale of one for totally grim to ten for archangels singing, I'd say about one point five.'

'Oh dear.'

'Oh dear indeed. The bean counters won't let me fill all the vacancies but I've got permission for two so long as one is a woman. I've filled one but he can't start for a few more days.'

'I imagine that Navrátil is a great help, though.'

'He's a good lad. He's taking the lead on a current case and making a reasonable fist of it.'

'How about Peiperová?'

'Ah. She is miserable. I don't think she likes working for Colonel Urban.'

'I always thought Urban was a first-class officer.'

'He is. It's as a human being he's lacking at present.'

'He hasn't got the Director of Police job yet, I hear?'

'That's why he's roaming the corridors like a bear with piles. We all thought it was done and dusted, then suddenly the old one says he's staying on for another three months.'

'Really? Any idea why?'

'The rumour is that someone in high places wants the job to go to Colonel Dostál, whose secondment finishes then.'

'Dostál? My word! That would ruffle a few feathers.'

'That's an understatement. It's a bit like electing Lucifer as Pope.'

'And that's a bit of an overstatement. Dostál is a competent officer. He's just not very much of a team player.'

'You mean it's all about the greater glory of Dostál?'

'I wouldn't, perhaps, go quite that far myself. But others would.'

'More to the point, he's younger than Urban, so if he gets the job Urban never will. And you can imagine what that would do for his demeanour. And, in turn, what that means for Peiperová, who is counting the days until her year ends.'

Lukas took a sudden and keen interest in the stitching of his gloves. 'One hesitates to relate unsubstantiated gossip…' he began.

Slonský immediately pricked his ears up. He had never known Lukas to do this before.

'...but you might want to look at the details of the bank siege that brought Dostál to prominence.'

'What am I looking for?'

'I don't remember exactly. But I know that there were questions about the conduct of the operation. The Office of Internal Inspection looked into it, but Dostál was cleared. There were people who felt that the investigation had, perhaps, not been as vigorous as might have been warranted.'

'Really?'

'I'm not in a position to comment, of course, but I can't help wondering whether the fact that Dostál subsequently married the daughter of the then head of OII might have raised eyebrows.'

For someone who has no interest in gossip you certainly seem to know plenty, thought Slonský, at the same time wondering why Mucha had not told him this. He had long believed that nothing happened that Mucha did not know about, but his reputation as the all-seeing oracle was now on the line.

'I'll do that, sir. Thank you,' said Slonský.

Lukas left through the main door with a cheery wave to Slonský and Sergeant Mucha. As soon as he had gone Slonský moved in to the attack.

'You never told me Dostál married the daughter of Whatsisname.'

'If I knew who Whatsisname was meant to be I could answer that, but I don't recall that you asked me who Mrs Dostál was.'

'The daughter of the old head of OII.'

'Zednìček? He wouldn't have children, he'd have spawn.'

'That's as may be, but Dostál married one.'

'Actually, he married the *only* one. The apple of the old man's eye. Still, look on the bright side. They haven't had any children yet so with luck Zedniček's genes will die out.'

'Is she over there with Dostál?'

Mucha leant forward and lowered his voice. 'Rumour has it that Dostál was furthering international relations until she moved to be with him.'

'Was he indeed?'

'In a stationery storeroom with a Spanish woman.'

'Yes, but I doubt we'll get him sacked for that. If senior officers who shagged women on the premises were turfed out that posh corridor behind me would be looking pretty empty.'

'It would open up opportunities for the likes of you and me. I've never had a woman at work.'

'Me neither. But we'd both be displaced by Navrátil, who hasn't had a woman anywhere.'

'That's true.'

'Anyway, Captain Lukas has opened up a possible line of enquiry by telling me that Dostál was the subject of an OII investigation that was regarded by some as a cover-up.'

'Presumably because said Dostál was going out with the daughter of the head of OII.'

'Or he married her in gratitude for being exonerated. What's she like?'

Mucha thought for a moment. 'The phrase "traditionally built" comes to mind.'

'Well, if there was such an investigation Major Rajka may be able to tell us more, though he didn't volunteer it when we first talked about Dostál.'

'It'll be that need to know thing. You didn't need to know.'

'I always need to know, old pal. Always.'

'Ask him again, then.'

'I shall. But I need to check my facts first.'

Mucha emitted a whistle of surprise. 'That's a bit of a departure from normal practice for you, isn't it?'

'Desperate times need desperate measures, mate.'

The office at which Nágl worked, according to the tax authorities, turned out to be a curious unit on the upper floor of a block on a small industrial estate, accessible by one of two flights of steel stairs at the ends of the block. Navrátil climbed the nearer stairs and pulled open the door to find that there was no reception area, the stairs opening directly on to an open plan office in which there were six desks, four of which were being used at that moment.

Navrátil displayed his badge and addressed the room in general.

'I'm looking for a Daniel Nágl.'

'Join the club,' said the oldest man present.

'He works here then?' asked Navrátil.

'He does. But if he hasn't got a good explanation when he shows up it'll be "he did".'

'You are…?'

'Peterka, Bohumil.'

The man made to reach into his jacket for his identity card but Navrátil gestured not to bother.

'When did you last see him?'

Peterka looked round the room for inspiration. Eventually a man in the far left corner replied, 'He went missing in the middle of the month, didn't he? Didn't come to Václav's birthday do, and that was on the eighteenth.'

'Of September?'

'That's right.'

'Do you have a phone number for him?'

Peterka checked a list on the wall and wrote it on a piece of paper.

'I've tried ringing it. He just lets it ring and doesn't answer.'

'Battery will be dead by now, I shouldn't wonder,' argued one of the others.

'Thanks,' said Navrátil. 'We'll get our technical people onto it. What is he like?'

'Physically? Average height, very proper, always wears a tie to work. Meticulous in what he does. You can't fault his work,' Peterka admitted.

'What is his work?'

'We design electronic switches and control panels. Nágl is particularly good on designing control centres for office lighting. You know, the kind of thing where lights go off by themselves if there is nobody in the room.'

'Forgive my ignorance. Is it well paid work?'

'Not particularly. They bill our time at a high price but we don't get it. But it's better than working in a supermarket.'

'He runs a car, I understand. It isn't parked here, I suppose?'

'If it was it would be gone by now,' Peterka laughed. 'I wouldn't leave my car overnight in this district. But I don't remember him regularly coming by car. Usually he caught a bus into work. What's all this about?'

Navrátil pondered how much he could say and decided to stick to what was already public knowledge. 'I'm afraid his partner's daughter was found dead the other day. We're trying to trace him to ensure that he knows.'

'Is that the girl in the river?' asked the man at the back. 'Is he a suspect?'

'We don't yet have any evidence tying him to the crime,' said Navrátil.

'Yet,' emphasised Peterka.

'We don't have any evidence tying him to the crime at all,' Navrátil tried. 'Unless any of you have any?'

No evidence was put forward, though Peterka felt free to offer a comment.

'Strange how you can spend ten hours a day with someone and never really know them, eh?'

Slonský was puzzled. He was so deep in thought that he took a bite out of a vegetarian roll before he realised that there was no meat in it.

'You could have poisoned me!' he complained to Dumpy Anna.

'You picked it,' she pointed out.

'How was I to know?'

'The label "Salad Roll" might have been a clue to some people.'

'What else have you got?'

Anna smiled. 'How about I slip out the back and slide a slice of ham in this one? No charge.'

'You are a princess amongst women,' replied Slonský. 'Those two husbands of yours don't know what they've given up.'

'I don't think they chose to die,' she replied, quite reasonably. 'When your time comes the Grim Reaper isn't going to hold off just because you fancy a sandwich.'

Slonský preferred not to ruminate on his own mortality. He fully intended to live for ever, if only to annoy the police pensions department.

Resuming his seat, ham salad roll in hand, coffee before him, he took out his pen and made a list of the questions that he was struggling to answer.

1. He had been sure that one of the off duty workers had been responsible for the abduction, but they all had alibis or were vouched for in some other way.

2. In any event, none of them was called Broukalová, which was obviously an assumed name. But how had the woman managed to persuade a civil servant to issue an identity card to her in that name, given that they were notorious sceptics at the best of times?

3. And whoever she was, where was she?

4. Assuming that her partner had killed Viktorie (which was not proven but seemed the most likely explanation), had Broukalová fled with him, or from him?

5. And where was Daniel Nágl, not to mention his car and mobile phone?

6. On the other matter, what had Lukas been hinting at (given that he couldn't remember the exact details even if he'd tried)?

7. Why hadn't Rajka shared this with him? There was that tiresome need to know stuff, but they were mates. A mate shares stuff with his mates. Except Klinger from the Fraud Squad, but then he had no mates.

8. Where was he going to find another officer to fill the remaining approved vacancy? They could advertise, of course, but then he might get someone completely unsuitable. Slonský firmly believed that choosing a work partner was as important — and as difficult — as choosing a life partner, Mind you, he had screwed that up royally. Which reminded him…

9. What was he going to do for Věra's birthday? She was bound to remember his in November. He recalled that Věra's birthday was the first of October; or perhaps it was the fifth? Anyway, if he took her out for dinner when he was free, it wouldn't matter if he didn't get the date exactly right, so long as he told her it was for her birthday.

10. What bizarre impulse drove people of sound mind to eat salad?

Valentin was inclined to be cooperative, especially after Slonský bought him a beer and a schnapps without entering even the mildest protest.

'I remember that siege,' he said. 'A few years ago now, though.'

'I don't know, but it must be at least five because he's been a colonel that long, and you wouldn't get a colonel putting themselves in harm's way at an armed bank robbery. They'd be sat in the car outside feeding useless suggestions through one of those funny earpieces the special teams wear along with their body armour.'

'Why do they always wear short sleeved shirts?' asked Valentin.

'It's to make them look tough,' Slonský decided. 'They're willing to risk both being shot and getting cold elbows. It shows how hard they are. It's like the Russian soldiers wearing those weird foot nappies instead of socks.'

'Poor so-and-so's. Imagine doing sentry duty in St Petersburg in those things. A couple of hours of standing still and you'd be leaving your toes behind.'

'You were a non-combatant, weren't you?'

'I didn't have the feet for it. But I did my national service in the army. Just not in boots, that's all.'

'Yes,' mused Slonský, 'I never saw the sense in that. Surely a flat-footed soldier is just as able to get himself shot as any other man, and that's what the army private is for, after all. You could even say that it's interference with nature.'

'In what way?'

'Suppose the Cold War had ended badly and the Socialist bloc and the evil Westerners had finished up slogging it out on the plains of Hungary? And we'd done as we said we would, and fought until the last soldier was dead.'

'Ye-es,' said Valentin, unsure where this was leading.

'Well, the only people left to keep the human race going would be a bunch of flat-foots excused frontline service. In no time all the little babies born here would have flat feet now that the curvy-foot gene had been extinguished.'

'I see where you're coming from,' Valentin agreed, 'but I'm pretty sure if things had been going that badly those of us who were medically less than A1 would have been sent up the front to make the supreme sacrifice.'

Slonský took a long pull of his beer. 'I suppose so. Anyway, I was rather hoping you would hunt through your newspaper's files to give me a bit of background on the events so that I don't look a complete know-nothing when I go to see Major Rajka.'

'Can I come?'

'Of course not. I can't drag a reporter in to an off the record discussion about how two senior policemen can stitch up a top colleague. It wouldn't be professional.'

Valentin fumbled for his handkerchief so he could deal with the beer which seemed to have made its way down his nose when he laughed. 'I had something more cunning in mind.'

'Oh, yes? Let's hear it.'

'Well, suppose my paper were to feature an article on what a fine character Colonel Urban was and how he would make an excellent Chief of Police one day? Can't do any harm, can it?'

'It's a bit transparent, isn't it? All of a sudden one of our newspapers starts a campaign to get Urban the top job. If I read it I'd immediately assume you were up to something and you'd bought him off.'

'Ah, a very likely conclusion if it was all on its own. But suppose it was part of a series of profiles designed to give the great Czech public confidence in the rising stars of the police service? We could start with Major Rajka.'

'So you're suggesting we put out highly slanted stories about senior officers that show them in a good light?'

'Basically, that's about it.'

'I can't see the police public relations team going along with it.'

'Why not?'

'Because we pay them a lot to write lies for us and here you are offering to do it for nothing. They'll feel they've been undercut.'

'They'll still get paid. They just won't have to do any work.'

'Oh, they'll go for that! Once it's expressed in that light I can see they'll fall over themselves for it.'

'I'll pitch it to my editor tomorrow. You know the sort of thing — show the human face of law enforcement. Give me three or four other names so Urban is nicely hidden in the mix, then if he approves the plan I'll approach the police PR mob.'

'Right, well — there's Rajka, Urban…' A long pause followed.

'There must be others,' Valentin prompted.

'You said they had to be human,' said Slonský. 'Narrows the field a bit.'

Navrátil had done it.

He had never thought he would be able to, when it came to it. It was such a big step, a real rite of passage in his life. It was an irreversible step, made possible only by his deep passion for Kristýna Peiperová.

He had told his mother he was engaged.

To his surprise, there were no temper tantrums, sobs or histrionics. No pottery was thrown.

'All the more important that I should spend some time with my future daughter-in-law, don't you think?' said his mother.

'You're not going to put her through the mill to check she's suitable, I hope,' he replied.

'Certainly not, my dear boy. If you've chosen her she's bound to be a good choice. You've always been such a serious young man. You don't do things frivolously or on a whim.'

Navrátil was now lying on his old bed, arms behind his head, staring at the ceiling. He had a little flat in town, but there was something comforting about returning to the room in which he had grown up. He might have lived there still, were it not for the difficulties of getting to work by seven in the morning on public transport. It could be done — just — but if they worked late he could not guarantee a bus home, and it was a long way to walk.

Anyway, life was good, he decided, feeling rather like St George must have felt when he slew the dragon and sauntered into town with its head. He felt good about himself, and when he rang Kristýna and told her she had been delighted and had promised him a reward. He had no idea what the reward was and just hoped it wasn't going to be the sort that he would have to mention at Confession next week.

Chapter 10

The morning brought further good news. Nágl's car had been found in a car park near the main railway station in Prague.

'Why abandon his car if he wanted to get away?' asked Navrátil.

'A number of possibilities, lad,' Slonský replied. 'He thought we'd be looking for it. He could make a more efficient getaway by train. He and his wife could flee by train. Or his wife was scarpering by train and it was easier to follow her by jumping on the train than trying to drive, especially if he didn't know where she was going to get off.'

'If he was chasing his wife and they were on the same train it's hard to imagine he didn't find her,' Navrátil suggested, 'but we haven't heard of a body by the tracks.'

'He doesn't have to kill her. He just catches up and tells her if she wants to stay alive she goes with him and keeps her mouth shut.'

'I suppose. She'd have to tag along and just hope an opportunity to escape presented itself later.'

'Let's hope we don't find any more bodies, lad. Now, two things we need to do with that car. First, we need to get the forensic team over there to give it a thorough going over, and while they're doing that you can check out the CCTV at the entrance to see when he got there.'

'I thought I was supposed to be in charge of this part of the enquiry, sir?'

'Oops. Quite right, so you are. So what are you going to do, Navrátil?'

'I thought I'd get the forensic team over there to give it a thorough going over, and while they're doing that I can check out the CCTV at the entrance to see when he got there, sir.'

'Excellent idea, lad. With initiative like that you'll be high up in the police force in no time.'

Valentin had an aversion to entering Slonský's place of work, this being the result of an unlooked-for visit under the previous regime. Slonský had tried to convince him that the chances that he would once more be thrown down a flight of concrete steps and kicked in the ribs a few times were extremely small, no matter how aggravating he was, but Valentin preferred not to take the chance. They had therefore agreed to meet for a mid-morning snifter at a nearby bar. To Slonský's surprise Valentin asked for a coffee, which shamed Slonský into doing likewise, despite the fact that 11 o'clock is very nearly lunchtime and a lunchtime sausage can be very dry without a little something of a hoppy nature to help it on its way.

'What have you got there?' asked Slonský.

Valentin handed over a folder containing a number of photocopies.

'Everything I could find about the bank siege. Some good stuff in there, even though I didn't write it. And the editor liked the idea of profiling senior police officers. He thought it wouldn't do us any harm to earn a few merit points from the forces of law and order. Got any more names?'

'I thought perhaps Major Klinger?'

'You said human.'

'He is. More or less. And just think — he's almost singlehandedly defending the value of people's savings against the evils of fraud and corruption. Besides, you're a creative writer. Write something creative about him.'

'You mean lie.'

'No, just write something creative. Something that makes him sound cuddly, like your favourite uncle.'

'You overstate my powers. But since Urban is the real prize here, I'll give it a go. Who else?'

'I thought maybe the head of PR?'

'Fine. Name?'

'I've no idea. You'll have to look it up.'

'Okay. I can do that. A fifth one would be good, then we can run one a day from Monday to Friday for a week.'

'Malý.'

'Malý?'

'Yes, Malý. He's a police dog.'

Valentin put his pad down so that he could use both hands to make a point.

'Slonský, I can't interview a dog.'

'He's a very clever dog.'

'No doubt. But I'm not printing a quote that goes "Woof woof, woof woof woof!"'

'People love dogs. It'll be very popular.'

'That's as may be. But I can't profile a dog.'

'Not Malý then. We have around eight hundred others.'

'Not a dog.'

'How about the Head of Cynology?'

'Cynology? What's that?'

'Dog training. Interview him about all the wonderful things dogs do.'

Valentin sighed. 'Okay. What's his name?'

'I've no idea. You'll have to look it up.'

When Slonský returned to the office he was intercepted by Mucha.

'Navrátil says when you get back could you please meet him in the Situation Control Room?'

'The what?'

'The Situation Control Room. The room where we control situations.'

'I didn't know we had one of those. We can't be using it very much.'

'The room two floors up with a television on the wall.'

'Oh, that! Is that what we call it these days?'

'Why, what do you call it?'

'The room where we watch big football matches together.'

Slonský laboriously climbed two flights of stairs and pushed open the door of the room. Navrátil was sitting on the table using a remote control to manage a video recording that he was watching on the big screen.

'Have you borrowed a movie, lad?'

'CCTV of the car park. I wanted you to watch it with me to see if you draw the same conclusions that I did.'

'This, I imagine, is the moment when Daniel Nágl's car arrives at the car park.'

'That's right. But the first thing to notice is the date and time.'

'Sunday 16th September, 14:34. So if she planned to run off on Friday, why didn't she get on with it?' Slonský asked.

'I think I've got an answer to that. That's the black Golf now, coming off Wilsonová into the slip road for the car park. Let me freeze it as it gets to the barrier.'

'Right. What am I looking at?'

'We can't really see the driver too well because the sun visor is down. But note they've only got one hand on the steering wheel.'

'The left hand.'

'Then they have to take the ticket from the machine on their left, so they wind down the window and use the left hand.'

'Okay.'

'So they now have no hands on the wheel.'

'Agreed.'

'Drive through, then we switch to this camera at the far end. There are quite a few spaces on Sunday afternoon but the driver chooses a place well away from other parked cars. The Golf comes to a stop, and the driver gets out, picks a bag out of the back seat, again using only the left hand, and locks the car.'

'It looks awkward, doesn't it? Something wrong with their right arm?'

'I think so. And we might get a reason for that when they walk into the station…'

'It's a woman! That must be Mrs Broukalová.'

'Wearing dark glasses but that looks to me like a swelling on her cheek. I think she probably has a black eye she's hiding, and she has to hold the door with her left hand, cumbersome as that is. I think Nágl has beaten her.'

'Well, somebody certainly has.'

'And she parked well away from other cars because she doesn't have a driving licence. So far as I know, she can't drive, but it's an automatic and if she takes it carefully and only has to work the wheel and the pedals, it's not impossible that this woman who allegedly can't drive could use a car to get away.'

'And if she's using the car, he can't, so he will have problems following. So why only drive to the station?'

'She doesn't want to push her luck. She certainly doesn't want to get out onto the motorway. But driving in from Komořany is not too terrible. It's about eleven kilometres, and it doesn't matter if it takes her thirty minutes. He can't follow. She just drives up Modřanská then she either crosses to the left bank and comes back across the river via Jiráskův bridge, which is the shortest route, or she keeps going and makes a right turn onto Podolská. It's a little longer but for a novice driver it's more straightforward.'

'Good work, lad. Are there any images that show her face?'

'I haven't found one, sir. That's what I've been doing.'

'Have the forensic boys removed the Golf?'

'They've examined it on site, but the Car Park operators want to know who is going to pay the twelve thousand crowns due for the parking? I told them to speak to you, sir.'

Slonský was doggedly ploughing his way through the photocopies that Valentin had found, and decided that he now had enough to go and see Major Rajka. A telephone call ascertained that Rajka was free so Slonský gathered the papers back into the folder and made his way to the plush corridor that housed senior officers.

Rajka's office was not in that corridor. This was his choice. He thought being housed with senior officers might tend to give the impression to people that they could influence his enquiries, not to mention sneak in and tamper with the evidence, so to get to Rajka's team you had to go along the corridor, down a flight of stairs at the end and along to the farthest point of the wing. There was a security door where you had to wait for someone to let you in, but if Rajka's secretary was in her office it was left open.

Rajka was sitting at his desk when Slonský entered, but sprang to his feet with alacrity and offered his hand. Slonský was very impressed that Rajka was able to stand without the use of his arms, his desk or emitting a low grunt of effort.

'You intrigue me. Sit down. Green tea?'

Slonský peered into Rajka's mug. 'What is it? Cabbage?'

'Actual tea. It's just green. Full of antioxidants.'

'Are you full of oxidants, then?'

'We all are,' smiled Rajka.

On the basis that if drinking this stuff contributed in any way to the impressive musculature underlying Rajka's shirt, Slonský would be a fool to miss out, he accepted a cup and tried hard to look as if he was enjoying it.

'I assume that folder is the reason for your visit.'

'It might be. When we were discussing Colonel Dostál you didn't tell me that he had been the subject of an Office of Internal Inspection enquiry.'

'That's because I didn't know.'

Rajka turned to his computer and tapped a succession of keys with the practised ease of a concert pianist. 'There's nothing about it in our index,' he frowned.

'Captain Lukas remembers being told it was happening. But more to the point, this folder consists of press cuttings relating to the bank siege that made his name, and one of them mentions that OII will be investigating a complaint of unnecessary violence by the police attending the siege.'

Rajka walked to the door to summon his secretary.

'Do you have a date there, Slonský?'

'Eight years ago. The siege was in June 1999.'

Rajka instructed his secretary to go to the evidence store and look for anything relating to an inquiry into a man called Dostál in the latter part of 1999.

'We'll see if we can get to the bottom of this. Summarise what's in here for me.'

'It was Friday, 18th June. A team of three bank robbers targeted a bank in the old town. They walked inside like normal customers, and two of them joined the queues for the tellers. The third one pretended to be reading some leaflets. Suddenly the two men produced guns and the third one slipped through a door into the area behind the counter. It's possible that they waited until someone came out so they could get in without having to force the lock.

'They ordered the staff to fill their holdalls with cash and the one who was inside made sure they did it. He told them to leave the small stuff, just fill it with large denomination banknotes, and get a move on. It seems likely that he knew there was a silent alarm button but they didn't know where so they planned to be only a minute or two and to leave before the police arrived. Which they did, or at least one of them did.'

Rajka raised a quizzical eyebrow at the suggestion that only one had tried to leave, but said nothing.

'The problem was that Prague City Police are not much good at preventing bank robberies but they're red hot on illegal parking in the old town, so the getaway driver had been moved on by a couple of City cops. He planned to go around the block and come back, but by then the alarm had been raised and they'd heard on the radio what was happening, so when robber number one pokes his head out he sees two police running towards him with their guns drawn. So he retreats inside and slams and bolts the door.'

'And I assume the next step was to open negotiations with the robbers while all the time filling the district with troops?'

'Pretty much. Dostál and his squad were able to get into the building using extending ladders provided by the fire service.

The robbers had barricaded the ground floor but could not cover the whole building. What happened next is anybody's guess. There was a lot of sound and fury, and the two men in the main customer area were shot by Dostál's men. The third one tried to hide in the back office but was pointed out by staff. After a bit more drama he too was dead and Dostál and his men were the heroes of the day. Dostál was promoted to major and everyone was happy. Except, presumably, the robbers, but you can't have everything.'

Slonský sipped his green tea and made an involuntary face.

'It's an acquired taste,' Rajka explained.

'Evidently, and I haven't acquired it. Anyway, there it would have rested except that one of the members of the public in the bank at the time must have been feeling very public-spirited and brave, because she wrote to the newspaper saying that she didn't think they should be making heroes of Dostál's men given that at least one of the robbers was unarmed and had surrendered when he was shot. The newspaper knew better than to print the letter, but they forwarded a copy to OII and kept the original. Some days later OII demanded the original, so we wouldn't know the letter existed except that the newspaper made another copy.'

'And was there an inquiry?'

'The demand says that the letter is needed as part of the evidence for the inquiry and so that they could contact the sender. I called her just before I came here. She says that nobody ever interviewed her. And the newspaper editor of the time wrote a memo in which he said that he asked after a while — to be precise, on Monday 11th October — whether the inquiry had reached any conclusions and was told that all involved had been exonerated and that the witness had been mistaken.'

Rajka's secretary returned with a small document box which she handed to her boss.

'This is all there is, by the looks of it,' said Rajka. He spread out the documents, paying particular attention to some photographs taken at the scene.

'That's odd,' said Slonský.

'What is?'

'This is plainly a still from a videotape, but I'd have expected the videotape itself to be retained as evidence.'

'So would I. And do you notice anything about these three photos of dead robbers with their guns beside them?'

'You mean apart from the fact that two of the guns look suspiciously identical and that no serial numbers are quoted?'

'No, that'll do. I smell a rat. It's just possible that the robbers obtained two identical guns in identical condition, but otherwise I'd suspect that a gun was moved after being photographed by one body to place it near the third, particularly since someone alleges that the third robber was unarmed. Are you busy?'

'I'm trying to solve an abduction and murder, but I've given Navrátil his head. He won't miss me for an hour or two.'

'Excellent. Let's go and see if anyone who was there in 1999 is still working at that bank, and then we might drop by the woman's house and take a proper statement. The enquiry into Colonel Dostál's behaviour has just been reopened.'

Rajka drove a vehicle that was definitely not police issue. Sleek, white and very foreign, it contained a number of enhancements that suggested to Slonský that the extras may have cost as much as the car. He was particularly impressed by the voice activated entertainment system, not that he wanted to use it. It was just that he had never come across anything before that did what you wanted as soon as you mentioned it. Except, now he thought about it, Navrátil.

Rajka's car had at least six gears but not, it seemed, a brake. Either that, or Rajka was trying to avoid wearing it out with overuse.

'Don't you get a police issue car?' asked Slonský.

'I could,' said Rajka, 'but it's important that people don't immediately recognise the car as a police vehicle.'

Well, they'd never suspect this was one, thought Slonský. The chances are the Chief of the whole Czech police force doesn't drive one of these.

'But you've got a siren and lights,' Slonský pointed out.

'Yes, but concealed lights, not stuck on the roof like a normal police car. If I want to drive down the highway I can do so without attracting attention to myself.'

That struck Slonský as inherently unlikely. It reminded him of a prostitute he had once known who used to claim that she was "blending in" when she entered expensive hotels wearing an ocelot coat and no underwear.

Rajka turned right without any obvious signal and parked in exactly the same place as the getaway driver had eight years ago.

'Aren't you worried about being ticketed?' asked Slonský.

'No, because I'd tear it up and in any event there's a sticker in the front window that tells those who need to know that it's an unmarked police car.'

I never knew that, thought Slonský, who wondered what the point of doing that was, since it seemed to defeat the object of an unmarked police car if you then marked it in some way.

Rajka presented his credentials at the counter and asked to speak to the senior manager on duty.

'He has someone with him,' replied the assistant tentatively.

'I'm sure he has. He'll be a busy man. So am I. I can give him five minutes to wrap things up.'

Slonský turned over in his mind whether there was any semantic difference between the Rajka approach — "I can give him five minutes" — and his own — "Five minutes, then I kick the door in" — and decided they were broadly equivalent.

The assistant rushed away to consult the manager and soon returned to invite them to wait in the corridor outside the office.

'He'll only be a minute or two,' she explained.

Slonský and Rajka sat on the indicated chairs.

'Do you bank here?' asked Slonský.

'No,' said Rajka. 'I don't go to banks that have a history of being robbed. What about you?'

'No, I use the one nearest the office. Banks don't fall over themselves to get my business.'

The manager emerged, ushering a woman in front of him who was still trying to put her coat on as he shook her hand.

'Thank you so much. We must talk again soon,' he said, before turning to Rajka and Slonský and inviting them to enter and take a seat. He was one of those people who readily displays his anxieties, as evidenced by his sweaty hands and his rictus smile. 'Is there a problem, gentlemen?'

'Not at all,' said Rajka. 'We are reopening an old case on a confidential basis and need to review the evidence relating to a robbery you had here eight years ago. Were you here then?'

'No, not at all!' the relieved manager replied. 'That would be my predecessor.'

'Do you have an address for him?'

'Not really. He's dead.'

'So are there any staff here now, or with whom we could make contact, who may be able to answer our questions?'

Rajka asked, slowing his speech to ensure that he made himself very clear.

'Ah, yes. Our chief teller, Mrs Klimentová, was here then. I've heard her talking about it. Should I fetch her?'

'That would be helpful,' Rajka agreed. 'And perhaps there is a spare room we could use?'

'Certainly. If there isn't you can use mine.'

'We'll try to avoid that,' said Rajka, 'to reduce the inconvenience to you.'

'Most thoughtful,' the manager said before rushing off to find Mrs Klimentová.

The chief teller proved to be a woman of around fifty with hair that Slonský for one found intriguing. First, it appeared to have been made from tightly coiled steel wire that had then been lacquered into a style that could outlast eternity. You could have thrown an owl at it and watched it bounce off. It also had a dashing blue streak. With the exception of an occasion in the sixties when the young Slonský had asked his barber for a Tony Curtis cut (and received the usual short back and sides) it had not crossed his mind that hairstyles could depart from nature so radically. Nowadays when his barber asked what he wanted, Slonský usually answered "a discount".

They were offered an interview room adjoining the manager's office, and settled themselves with the two policemen on the window side and Mrs Klimentová opposite them.

'I am Major Rajka and this is Captain Slonský,' Rajka began. 'I understand you were here on the day that the bank was robbed eight years ago. Is that correct?'

'Yes. It was a ghastly day. I shall never forget it,' Mrs Klimentová responded.

'That should make you a good witness, then,' Rajka smiled. 'Perhaps you could tell us, in your own words, where you were and what you saw.'

'I wasn't on the counter at that time, but in the back reconciling the cash from the morning shift. There was a large desk immediately behind the counter that we used for the purpose because it had privacy screens at one end that stopped the coins rolling off. So I was standing there counting the cash received and ensuring it was correctly bagged.

'That was when Julia asked me if I could help her. She was carrying a bundle of printouts from the fax machine. At that time if you wanted to get out of the back into the bank lobby you had to go through a door at the end of the counter. It had two locks and you had to turn the knobs simultaneously to open it. We have an electronic system now. Anyway, Julia couldn't carry her printout and open both locks, so I went to open the door for her. No sooner had we pulled the door back than a man ran in and pushed Julia over.'

'I hope she wasn't hurt,' Rajka commented.

'Shocked more than hurt, I think. There was a lot of shouting as two accomplices in front of the counter produced guns and demanded that we fill their holdalls. I couldn't see any way of preventing them robbing us but I was determined that they were going to get as little as possible, so I started filling the holdall with coin bags and blank paying-in slips, but the one in the back, who must have been their leader, shouted that they only wanted banknotes, ideally in large denominations.'

'Did he have a gun?' Rajka asked casually.

'I didn't see one. He was using both hands to fill the bags so if he had one he wasn't holding it. Anyway, if I couldn't hamper him as I had planned the next option was to slow him down, because I knew that Matěj on the counter would have pressed the silent alarm. It wasn't very well designed, because the bank was worried that we'd knock it accidentally, so it was under a small cover. You had to flip it up with your hand and hit it with the other one. The other problem was that it was very obvious what you were doing. Fortunately Matěj was quite a big lad and while he stood with his hands up one of the girls slipped behind him to trigger the alarm.'

'And how quickly did the police come?'

'Very quickly. One of the armed men opened the door slightly and shouted that someone wasn't there. That seemed to panic them, and the leader told him to shut the door and barricade it, because a couple of City Police had turned up outside. I don't know exactly when the assault team arrived.'

'Is there a back door they could have used?'

'There is, but it wouldn't help them a lot. For safety reasons you can open it from the inside by pressing on a bar and a button simultaneously, so if there's a fire we can escape, but only into a back courtyard. We then have to wait for someone to unlock the outer gate. The leader grabbed one of the girls and made her lead him to the door but he soon returned and said there was no way out in that direction.'

'So what did he do then?'

'He told each of the robbers to grab someone. He grabbed Julia and the robbers each seized a customer. By this time someone outside had telephoned the bank and they were beginning negotiations. The robbers asked for a car and safe passage out of the country. I don't think they had any idea where they could go but that's what they asked for.'

'What makes you say that?'

'The robbers started arguing about where they could go where the police couldn't extradite them. One of them suggested Ukraine, and another thought Moldova might work.'

'I doubt they knew where either of those was,' interrupted Slonský.

Rajka arched an eyebrow but decided not to pursue that discussion.

'And then?' he asked.

'We could hear people in boots running around upstairs. I don't know how long they'd been there. The leader looked out of a window and saw a fireman's ladder being used to lift armed police in at one of the upper levels. Because this is an old building there are restrictions on alterations we can make, you see. The upper floors can't be secured, so we have a cage separating the lower two floors from the upper ones. People may get into the building, but they still have to get into the caged area.'

'And how did the police do that?'

'It was during working hours, so one of the two doors was open. I think the police just blew the other one off its hinges somehow.'

That's exactly what Dostál would do, thought Slonský, but he said nothing.

'Then they came running down the stairs. The leader told the other two to shoot, but they clearly didn't want to. They held their guns to their hostage's heads but an open lobby area and police spreading into a wide semi-circle meant that sooner or later they'd be shot. There was a stand-off for a moment, then they pushed the hostages away and dropped their guns, but it was too late. The police had fired at the same time.'

'This is very important. Are you sure that the police fired at the same time as the men dropped their guns?'

'It was all so fast. It's really difficult to decide.'

'Put it another way,' said Slonský. 'When they pushed the hostages away, was there any reason for the police to think that they, or anyone in the room, was under direct threat from their guns?'

'I don't think so. Their arms weren't raised to a firing stance.'

'And the leader?' asked Rajka.

'He tried to mingle with the staff at the back with a view to slipping out. He edged round to the staircase they'd come in at and was just making for the stairs when they shot him.'

'But you don't think he had a gun?'

'I never saw one, and he wasn't holding one when he fell to the floor.'

Something had occurred to Slonský. 'Just a minute. You said he was shot at the foot of the staircase. That's to the back left of the room, if I remember correctly?'

'That's right.'

'Yet I have a photograph here that shows his body lying behind the large table you talked about.' He riffled through the folder to find it. He had not planned to show it to Mrs Klimentová but she held out her hand for it.

'No, that's not right at all. He died by the stairs. And he didn't have that gun.'

Rajka sat back quite satisfied. 'I don't want to hold you up now. We'll need a proper statement but I can construct a draft and come back tomorrow. You can amend it in any way you think fit, so please don't let me put words in your mouth.'

Mrs Klimentová indicated that she understood by nodding gently.

'Now,' Rajka asked, 'are there any colleagues here who were working then?'

Navrátil had a definite gift for extracting information from large datasets. He was never happier than when he was surrounded by sheets of paper and trying to meld them together into some sort of coherent whole.

At that particular moment he was browsing through a selection of train timetables when a frighteningly cheerful Slonský walked in and threw his hat in the general direction of the hook behind the door.

'I've had a good day, lad. How has yours been?'

'Disappointing, sir. None of the ticket clerks on duty that Sunday recall serving a woman with dark glasses and a bruised face, but they admitted that they don't always scrutinise the customer's face. And, of course, she may have bought her ticket on the train from the conductor.'

'No credit card slip?'

'For a single journey nearly everyone uses cash. So my next thought was — where could she go? She'd just missed a train to Most and there wasn't another one for over two hours, so if she has someone there to go to, she'd have to hang around the station.'

'That sounds unlikely. If you're running away you want to get out of the area. You can always triangulate to your original destination later.'

'That's what I thought, sir. So, assuming it takes her about five minutes after she parks the car to get into the station, choose her train and get to it, there's a train to Pardubice at two minutes to three, and a train to Brno at 14:50 too. She'd probably just miss the train to Plzeň.'

'Either of those might do.'

'Unfortunately the Brno train then goes to Vienna. But the Pardubice one left from platform 3 and the Brno train from platform 6, which is that much further away. I'm not sure she could have got to the train before it left.'

'It would be tight, even allowing for the fact that a Czech train doesn't always leave on time.'

'There's another reason for thinking she may have taken the Pardubice train. She withdrew some money from an ATM on Saturday but there's not much in that account. A ticket to Vienna would have eaten into it and she needs to have something left to live on. Even so, she has to find someone who will let her live with them cheaply.'

'And the likeliest place will be friends or family. If we're right and she originates from somewhere near the kindergarten, then that's the place she's likely to go, but it's also where her partner will go looking for her.'

'Try this then, sir. She goes to a third place. Let's say it's Pardubice for the moment. Her partner isn't likely to be able to follow that trail. From there she phones someone in Most explaining her problem and checking whether Nágl has shown up there yet. If he has, she stays put. If he hasn't, she completes her journey. Even if he went there on the Sunday, he can't stay indefinitely. Sooner or later the coast will be clear.'

'That's probably our best guess for the moment. Has he used his credit cards or bank account?'

'I'm still waiting for that information, sir.'

'There are just too many variables to try tracking her. I doubt she'd go south because then she'd have to come back through Prague. But until she shows up somewhere there's not much we can do. Any mobile phone information?'

'She has one but it's been switched off since she caught the train. I'm also keeping a lookout for Nágl's but no sign of that either since that weekend.'

'If they were fleeing together that would make sense, but why would he switch his phone off while he's chasing her? It's not as if she can track him.'

'Maybe he's more worried about us, sir. By the same token, why has she turned hers off when he can't track her? And the safest place for her to be is in one of our cells.'

'You haven't tasted the lunches we give prisoners, Navrátil. On top of that, she's probably a bit wary of us too given that if our suppositions are right she's looking at a lengthy jail sentence for abducting Viktorie in the first place.'

'So what do we do now, sir?'

Slonský flopped in his chair and folded his arms slowly.

'Navrátil, my long experience of police work has taught me that there are occasions when the most important thing to do is nothing.'

'Nothing?'

'Nothing. Rien du tout. Nada.'

'Isn't that a dereliction of our duty, sir?'

'It would be if we had something useful to do. But there is no merit in mindless activity, lad. It just wastes valuable energy. Let's go and think this through over a coffee and a pastry or two. Good work, by the way.'

'Thank you, sir.'

'No, I mean it. You know, when I first saw you, I thought I'd been saddled with a complete deadweight. I am happy to admit that I was wrong.'

Navrátil smiled.

'Or, at least,' added Slonský, 'not entirely right.'

Chapter 11

Major Rajka rubbed his chin thoughtfully.

'The big problem here,' he said, 'is that however good Mrs Klimentová's statement is, it's just her word against Dostál's.'

'Her colleagues support her,' Slonský pointed out.

'No, they don't contradict her, which is not quite the same thing. Too many of them didn't see enough to be useful.'

'We don't need to prove it. We just need enough to get an enquiry rolling, then Dr Pilik won't dare appoint him.'

'You don't need to prove it for your purposes, but as Head of OII I need to know there's a good chance we'll prove our case. I have my department's reputation to consider.'

To Slonský's way of thinking the reputation of OII was streets ahead of most other police departments, at least with him. Unlike, say, Organised Crime, some of whose members had been found to be doing the organising of quite a bit of crime, or the Fraud Squad, who had that unfortunate incident with Kobr on their record. And as for Vice, a more shady bunch of rampant trouser-droppers had yet to cross his path.

It was not a great concern to him if the enquiry petered out in December, so long as it lasted long enough to ruin Dostál's chance of getting the post Urban wanted, thus making Urban happy and, by extension, Urban's PA, Peiperová. However, he could see that if the investigation came to nothing and Dostál had been denied the top job as a result of some character assassination Rajka's position vis-à-vis his new boss could be difficult. And he could be fairly certain that Dostál's second action upon taking over would be to send a retirement letter to one Slonský, J.

‘So how do we beef up the evidence?’

Rajka pressed his temples with his fingers as if it might help to stimulate thought.

‘We need some corroborating evidence. It’s a shame that videotape went missing.’

‘It didn’t go missing. It was removed.’

‘Yes, I know, but we can’t prove that.’

‘What about the woman who wrote to the newspaper?’

‘Obviously we have to visit her. Have we got an address?’

Slonský patted his pockets. ‘Yes,’ he announced firmly. ‘Somewhere.’

After a bit more rummaging he unfolded a grubby piece of paper. It proved to be a receipt for two sandwiches and a half-litre of beer. Even deeper in his pocket than that he found the address he wanted and handed it over.

Rajka bounded from his chair.

‘Off we go, then. Shall I drive?’

But he had left the room before Slonský could answer.

Not all of Prague is picture postcard beautiful, and the area where Božena Moserová lived was fairly decayed. Chunks of render were missing from the walls of some of the buildings and too many of the shops had steel shutters for Slonský’s liking. Rajka had to concentrate on the road so Slonský was left to look for the apartment block unaided.

‘Ninety-eight, ninety-two, next block, I think.’

He was just about to announce that they had arrived when he was thrown forward in his seat by Rajka’s enthusiastic use of the brake.

‘An empty legal parking space. You don’t see those too often,’ Rajka remarked.

As they climbed out of the car a boy of about eleven eyed them suspiciously as he juggled his football.

Rajka beckoned him towards them.

'We're going in there. We'll be on the third floor. If you make sure nobody touches this car I'll give you ten crowns when we come back.'

'Twenty,' said the boy.

Rajka opened his jacket to show his badge. This move ensured that the boy also got a glimpse of his shoulder holster.

'No, ten'll do,' the boy corrected himself.

They began to climb the stairs. While Rajka skipped upwards with the grace and ease of a chamois Slonský looked more like an arthritic bear, but in time they were both on the landing outside Mrs Moserová's apartment.

Mrs Moserová was in much better condition than her apartment block, but then she seemed to have had much more remedial work done over the years. Her nails were beautifully tended and she wore a cameo brooch on her white blouse. She invited the officers in and offered them coffee, which Slonský accepted. Rajka asked for a glass of water.

'Must be money in the family,' whispered Slonský as he pointed at the tasteful *objets d'art* that fringed the sitting room.

'Given the district I'm surprised they're still here,' murmured Rajka.

Mrs Moserová returned with a tray bearing their drinks, including a coffee for herself, and a plate of vanilla crescents.

'I have a woman who helps me now I'm older,' she explained. 'She loves baking. Do help yourselves, please.'

Slonský tasted the coffee and took a bite from the biscuit. If he had not already been married he might have proposed to Mrs Moserová on the spot. The coffee was excellent, and the biscuits were beyond any of the type that he had ever bought in a bakery.

'You have a very nice flat here,' Rajka began.

'Thank you,' the old lady smiled. 'I owe many of the objects to my late husband's taste. He was a professor at the university where he taught the history of art. And of course he knew many artists. That accounts for the collection here. I doubt we could have bought so many on the open market, but they were very kind to him.'

'We're here about a letter you wrote to a newspaper some years ago after you were caught up in a bank siege. Do you remember?'

'Young man, I don't see how I could ever forget it. Have you come round to tell me I'm a stupid old woman who didn't see what she thought?'

'Not at all,' said Rajka. 'Why — has someone done that?'

'A policeman came shortly afterwards and told me my complaint had been investigated and found to be unfounded, and I wasn't to repeat such scurrilous allegations again. I was rather upset to be called a liar like that, but my husband persuaded me that I had done my duty by drawing attention to it and we must trust that the authorities would have investigated it thoroughly.'

'Unfortunately,' Rajka replied, 'we now have reason to believe that your evidence was ... not properly assessed.'

Hidden in an old drawer and ignored for eight years was how Slonský might have phrased it, but he let the matter drop.

'I wonder if you'd mind telling us what you saw once again,' Rajka asked, 'if it isn't too distressing for you.'

'It's not distressing at all,' said Mrs Moserová.

'It must have been quite an ordeal,' Slonský chipped in.

'I've had worse,' sniffed Mrs Moserová. 'As a young woman in the fifties I was arrested several times. In those days you weren't even guaranteed a trial.'

Not for the first time Slonský found himself admiring a seemingly frail old lady who proved to be made of granite.

'I was in the bank to pay in a money order my sister had sent us,' Mrs Moserová continued. 'It wasn't a lot but her feelings would have been hurt if we hadn't banked it. It was quite a long walk from the bus and there was a queue so I sat on one of the chairs just inside the door to collect myself. Three men came in.'

'Did they arrive together?' Rajka interrupted.

'Two were talking as they came in, and they joined the line. The third one started picking up leaflets or forms of some kind.'

'I see. Please, do continue.'

'I'm afraid I wasn't really concentrating when it all started. Suddenly the two men produced guns and the third one had somehow managed to get behind the counter and was collecting all the money in a bag. We were all told to keep our hands up, so of course we did. After just a little while — not much more than a minute I'd have said — one of the men went to the door and looked out. They must have been expecting to meet someone because the man came back and said "He's not there."'

'Those exact words?'

'I believe so. Then the man behind the counter, who seemed to be the leader of the group, said something rather vulgar and told his colleague to bolt the door. I've often wondered why they didn't just run away but I think the bags were rather heavy with so much money in them, particularly because the bank staff had added coins as well as notes. Then we heard someone banging on the door and shouting "Police! Open up!" at which the leader told them all to grab the nearest person to use as a shield. They all grabbed young women and then they gathered at the end of the counter to discuss their next steps. I couldn't hear what they were saying.'

Slonský was very impressed with Mrs Moserová. She spoke clearly and didn't pretend to know anything just to complete her story. This was quite novel in Prague. When he was a new policeman Slonský had discovered that at most traffic accidents people were prepared to give statements clearly attributing blame even if they could not have seen the incident in question, based to a large extent on the principle that a man who had a car was a bigwig and therefore not to be trusted. He had a special fondness for the old boys who insisted that the Deputy Secretary of the Communist Party in Prague had driven into the back of a young man's vehicle and continued to insist on the point even after the honest young fellow had admitted selecting reverse gear by mistake. This, they explained, was clear proof that he had sustained a head injury due to the Secretary's inept driving.

Mrs Moserová took a sip of coffee before continuing.

'I don't know how long the police took to get into the bank, but they came down the back stairs and there was a loud noise as they came through the door at the foot of the stairs. There was a horrible smell so I suppose they must have used some sort of explosive. Then the policemen spread out in a large arc which must have made it difficult for the robbers to see all of them at once. The two in the bank foyer realised that they could not escape, so they pushed their hostages away but as soon as they did so they were shot.'

'Did you see who shot them?' Rajka wanted to know.

'At that stage I could only see three of the police clearly because they were so spread out. The only one I saw shoot was the one in the middle. But there were at least two I couldn't see.'

'What about the third man?'

'Well, he didn't have a gun, so he tried to escape up the stairs, but the wreckage from the door was in his way, and one of the police shot him. Now, I know that can only have been the one in the middle. That's what I thought was so upsetting, do you see? One doesn't expect to see bloodshed on a little trip to the bank, but to see an unarmed man shot seemed completely abhorrent to me, and I said so in my letter.'

Rajka turned to Slonský. 'Any questions, Captain?'

'No, sir. Mrs Moserová's evidence is admirably straightforward.'

They thanked her for her co-operation and her hospitality, and strolled back to the car.

'If only we knew who the middle one was,' Rajka said.

'Surely the commander of the mission.'

'We need a bit more than that, Slonský. If only we still had that videotape that went missing.'

The boy was waiting by the car with his hand outstretched. Rajka fished in his pocket and handed the lad twenty crowns.

'You're right,' said Rajka. 'It was worth twenty.'

It was late afternoon by now and Rajka suggested they return to the office so he could write up the draft statements.

'Where do we go next?' posed Slonský.

'I don't know,' said Rajka. 'We've got enough to start an enquiry but not enough to conclude it successfully.'

'On the basis of three heads being better than two, why don't we go to see Colonel Urban?'

Urban heard them out without comment, but when they had finished he slapped his desk hard with the palm of his hand.

'I knew it! It's that idiot Zedniček's fault. If he'd conducted a proper enquiry we wouldn't be having this trouble now. Of course, the fact that one of the men was subsequently found not to have a gun is not proof that Dostál didn't genuinely believe he had when he shot him. If he was the one who did the shooting, that is.'

'If he has nothing to feel guilty about, why falsify the evidence?' Slonský answered. 'The body didn't move itself or go and fetch a gun.'

'Why didn't the other police say anything? Do we know who they were?'

Rajka made a note. 'I don't know how we'll find out who they are, given that the case file has been so thoroughly edited. But I'll see if we can find a staff list of the time,' he said.

Urban stood up and walked round his desk to stand next to them.

'I really appreciate the effort you're putting in on my behalf.'

Rajka would have protested that this was his job, but decided that this was not the time to split hairs.

'Slonský, you're working flat out anyway. Haven't you got an abduction and murder to solve?' Urban asked.

'I'm letting Navrátil lead on that one, sir.'

'Navrátil? He has the makings of a good officer, doesn't he? But I seem to remember you were whingeing about a shortage of people before all this.'

'Krob joins us next week. And I've got to recruit a woman from somewhere.'

'What's Lieutenant Dvorník doing?'

In all the fuss of the last few days Slonský had completely forgotten about Dvorník and his assistant Hauzer. Neither of them was lazy, but they obviously thought that if he showed no interest in them it was not their place to come to him to explain how they were filling in their time.

'I'm just about to get a report from him, sir,' Slonský improvised.

'Why don't I let you have Peiperová back until this is sorted?'

'That will leave you without a Personal Assistant, sir,' Slonský protested.

'I put up with that nincompoop Kuchař for a year. That was as good as doing without.'

Kuchař was a young officer who scored surprisingly high marks at the police academy in the light of his subsequent performance in the force, but it appeared that you could make up for a lack of diligence, organisation and intelligence by having a senior politician for a father, as a result of which he was now part of the Czech contingent at Europol.

'In that case, sir…' Slonský began.

'Needless to say, the quid pro quo is that you get results, Slonský.'

There's always a catch, Slonský thought. But it would be worth it to have Peiperová in the team again. She was sharp, fearless, supremely organised, and she made much better coffee than Navrátil. Not that coffee making fell within her normal duties, he hurriedly added mentally, in case she could read his thoughts.

Peiperová herself was sitting opposite Navrátil as he tidied his desk at the end of the day.

'It's good that you're being given some responsibility,' she said. 'I'm just a skivvy at the moment.'

'But you're being introduced to some very important people,' Navrátil pointed out.

'I am,' conceded Peiperová, 'but you may have noticed that very important people quite often seem to end up as very important prisoners.'

'That's true,' Navrátil agreed. 'You need real influence to be truly corrupt.'

'That's probably why you and I are so honest.'

Navrátil said nothing for a moment or two. When he finally found his voice, he averted his gaze so as not to convey his feelings fully.

'I miss you,' he said. 'It's not the same.'

'You see me almost every day.'

'Yes, but not to work with. The Captain is a good man but he's stretched at the minute. He's not as much fun as he used to be. I think he misses you too.'

'He wouldn't say so, would he?'

'Not to me. Or to you. Or to anyone else, I suppose. He's trying to carry on as if nothing has happened but you can't get over the fact that he now has a department to run, and on top of that he's dreading the thought that Colonel Dostál may become Chief of Police and your boss won't get the job.'

'There's nothing he can do about that, Jan. What will be will be.'

Navrátil smiled. 'Are you going to tell him that, or will I?'

'Probably best if neither of us says a word. Anyway, he has enough on his plate with this abduction and murder. At least we know why the mother didn't report the murdered child missing, if she thought it might lead to us discovering she wasn't her daughter in the first place.'

'It seems she'd got into an abusive relationship. In the last picture I can find of her you can see she'd taken a beating.'

'What makes men think they can do that?' snapped Peiperová.

'We don't all do that,' Navrátil replied. 'I'd never lay a finger on you.'

'I was rather hoping you might once we were married.'

'I mean I'd never lay a finger on you in anger.'

'We don't know what we'd do in anger, do we? But I think I'm safer with you than anyone else I know.'

Navrátil smiled again.

'Besides,' Peiperová added, 'if you hurt me I'd complain to Captain Slonský and he'd give you the kicking of a lifetime.'

'That's true. He hates domestic violence.'

'Where is he, by the way?'

'I've no idea. I haven't seen him since yesterday afternoon. He said he was going to see Major Rajka this morning.'

'Maybe they've found something.'

'Let's hope. I reckon if Captain Slonský can pin something on Dostál that gets Urban that job you'll be back here in no time, probably with your lieutenant's star on your shoulder.'

'We wear plain clothes. Insignia aren't that important.'

'I'd get mine sewn on my shirt just to make the point.'

Peiperová laughed. 'Have you finished there? Let's go and get something to eat and maybe we can find a movie.'

'Almost. Are you all packed for the weekend?'

'It doesn't take me long to pack for a weekend. I'm looking forward to it.'

'I'm not. My mother is too nosey for her own good sometimes.'

'She's lovely. And we'll get along perfectly well. After all, we already have something in common.'

'What's that?'

Peiperová stood up and draped her arms round Navrátil's neck.

'Your mum thinks you're smashing. And so do I.'

Dvorník was still at his desk when Slonský marched into the room.

'Still here?'

'There's a lot on. I know you're busy so I didn't like to worry you about it.'

Slonský pulled up a chair. 'If I haven't spoken to you it's because I trust you just to get on with things. After all, now that I've been moved up you're the senior lieutenant.'

'That's because I'm the only lieutenant,' Dvorník corrected him. 'Any news of another one?'

'Still pushing Human Resources to let me have one.'

'We need two. One to replace you, and one to replace poor old Doležal.'

'I know. It's not for want of trying, believe me. How's Hauzer doing?'

'He's okay. Keeps himself to himself. Some days he barely says a word.'

'Can you keep him occupied?'

'Oh, yes! We've got a grievous bodily harm and a hit and run on the go. And I'm still liaising with Organised Crime about that gang thing.'

'Don't let them saddle you with all the work. Our interest is only in the woundings. They can sort out the gangs themselves.'

Slonský noticed a new picture of Dvorník's family on the corner of the desk. Since new Dvorníks arrived at depressingly frequent intervals he quietly counted the children.

'Still eight?' he asked.

'That's right,' said Dvorník. 'I don't think we'll have any more.'

'That's what you said after number seven.'

'I mean it this time. It wasn't too bad when they were small but the oldest is fifteen now and the house feels a bit crowded.'

Dvorník and his wife had each been married before, and each had brought three children to the new relationship. Slonský had enough trouble remembering the first names of people he knew well. How anyone remembered the names of eight children was beyond him. Perhaps Dvorník made them wear shirts with their names on the front. Maybe they had individual numbers like a hockey team.

'I'll leave you to get on,' said Slonský. 'I just want you to know that even when we get new lieutenants, if we ever do, you'll still be the senior one.'

Dvorník was touched. 'Thanks. I appreciate your faith in me.'

Slonský had some reservations about Dvorník. His willingness to resort to firearms was a bit of an issue, but at least he put in the hours on the range perfecting his technique. Slonský himself had to be prodded to do his mandatory firearms training; in fact, come to think of it, now that Captain Lukas was not around to do the prodding, he thought he should check when it had to be completed. He flicked through his training logbook when he returned to his office.

Two weeks ago.

Chapter 12

Slonský tipped his glass as far as it would go to catch the very last drains of his beer. Valentin had another one waiting for him, but it would be a shame to waste any when the devoted brewers of Plzeň had put so much effort into making it.

'Better?' asked Valentin.

'Oh yes,' said Slonský. 'The little grey cells are beginning to buzz. I can feel them all lining up for maximum efficiency. I reckon another one of those and the old brain will be purring along like a well-tuned engine.'

'You hang on here. I need to go and sort out a problem with my hydraulics.'

'It's your age. Have one for me while you're at it.'

As Valentin waddled off Slonský took his first sip through the foamy head of a new beer and sighed with deep satisfaction. It rarely disappointed, unlike most other things in life. Valentin didn't. He'd been the same since they started school on the same day over fifty years ago. They had their first drink together when they were eleven, a glug from a bottle of homemade schnapps Valentin's father had distilled.

Captain Lukas was always reliable too. I never thought I'd miss him, thought Slonský, at least not until the last few months when it became clear he was going. It was a bit like a bereavement — there were so many things he wished he'd said to Lukas before it was too late. Things like "How do you get all the staff you're supposed to have?", "Why do you wear uniform when you don't have to?" and "Can I have another couple of pairs of police issue shoes?"

Then there was Navrátil. Slonský had never wanted a partner, and fortunately he was such a cussed and difficult character to work with that most potential partners didn't want him either, but then came the day when Captain Lukas had been assigned Navrátil for further training and the only person who didn't already have a regular assistant was Slonský. When he declined, Lukas brought up the matter of his closeness to retirement age and hinted heavily that Slonský's continued service after the age of fifty-nine might be contingent on his training Navrátil.

And so this slightly-built, fresh-faced youngster had turned up, eager to learn, willing to work hard, and scrupulously honest. He went to Mass every weekend even though Slonský had offered to write him a note for the priest saying he had a cold or he'd left his kit at home. Slonský had joined the police wanting to stamp out crime and make the lives of ordinary people better, and it hurt to think that he was going to retire without having made much of a dent in the crime statistics. But he could see that same fire in Navrátil. If there was any justice, Navrátil was going to be at the top of the tree one day.

Unless Peiperová beat him to it. She had joined the police straight from school, whereas Navrátil had taken a law degree and then joined under a graduate entry scheme. She had been in uniform, walked the beat, thrown drunks into cells or taken them home. She was competent, organised, meticulous and had interpersonal skills of which Slonský could only dream. Not to mention such magical powers as remembering people's names, birthdays and spouses' names. She could interrogate people, especially women, and make it seem like a chat over a coffee.

Mind, she was ferociously ambitious. Navrátil was too polite. He'd stand back and open the door for her, and next thing he knew she'd be Director of the Police Presidium or whatever they called the top job these days. And these two were an item. God knows what any child they produced would be like — if Navrátil ever overcame his scruples and decided that sex after marriage was permitted.

Of course, they didn't have Slonský's occasional flashes of beer-fuelled brilliance, the moments when he broke through the barriers and experienced enlightenment. He never knew how those eureka times came about. He just mulled over a problem and suddenly it seemed to crack open. He was aware that many of the solutions were a little strange, but they worked more often than not, and he needed one now as he tried to think how to screw Dostál over.

And then it came to him. An answer of such luminous brilliance that even he was stunned momentarily. It might not work, but if it did it was possibly the most cunning idea he had had for nearly a fortnight.

Slonský did not share the entirety of his idea with Major Rajka, because he feared that if he did Rajka would stop him carrying it through. However, once he sprang his trap he thought Rajka would go along with it.

'Visit Zedniček? Why?' asked Rajka.

'Because the whole mess is of his making. If he'd done his job properly we wouldn't be having to do this now. If he protected Dostál then he'll make touch to tell Dostál it's all been reopened, and Dostál, knowing he's guilty as hell, will try to throw a spanner in our works. I bet he'll suddenly come back for a few days' leave instead of hitting the French vineyards as usual. He'll try to find out what you've discovered. Of course, there's always the possibility that Zedniček let

Dostál off the hook because he's crap at his job, but you'll be able to work that out from his answers.'

Rajka sat back and chewed his lip while he thought. 'It's worth a try,' he said. 'Have you got his address?'

Slonský produced a piece of paper from his inside jacket pocket. Rajka unfolded it, fully expecting it to be a laundry bill or a receipt for some pastries, but it was an immaculately written address.

'Hang on — that's not your handwriting,' he said.

'I got Peiperová to find it for me.'

Rajka was driving through the northern area of Prague with his usual disregard for the traffic laws when Slonský gave him advance notice that they would need to pull over after about five hundred metres. When they did, Slonský alighted and went into a seedy looking second hand store. He was gone just a couple of minutes and emerged with something in a brown paper bag. Rajka could not see what it was, but out of the corner of his eye he could see Slonský pulling bits of paper off it and dropping them back in the bag.

Zednîček lived in a very smart area with a hedge around his house and a double garage.

'Two cars?' said Slonský. 'There's posh. And look at that garage. I've known families living in smaller spaces than that.'

The retired officer was not pleased to discover who was at his door, but being an ex-colonel now he could hardly refuse to co-operate. He invited them to sit, did not offer any refreshment, and looked about as sour as a man could look in the absence of a mouthful of lemon.

Rajka explained that in the light of new evidence the enquiry into what had happened at the bank siege had been reopened.

'New evidence? What new evidence?' Zednîček asked.

'I'm not at liberty to say just yet,' Rajka said smoothly. 'But it has caused us to revisit the file relating to your original enquiry. I'm afraid it's surprisingly thin.'

Zedniček did not attempt to deny this, but moved straight in with an explanation.

'You can't clutter up the place with useless materials. Once an enquiry is completed and your superiors are satisfied that there's nothing more to do, papers are shredded or returned. You keep the investigating officer's report, of course. I think you'll find that all that needed to be said is in there.'

'Well, since we don't know what else was said, it's hard to be certain on that point. I'm interested to know on what basis you decided that Mrs Moserová's account was incorrect and that the bank robbers were all armed, for example.'

'If they hadn't been armed, the assault team wouldn't have shot them, would they?' Zedniček had the effrontery to point out as if dealing with a particularly stupid child.

'And what about the forensic evidence? Were the bullets that shot the robbers ever tied to a particular gun or guns?'

'You can't expect me to remember that after this length of time. But I suppose if they had it would be in my report.'

'It would, but it isn't. And I can't trace a request to the ballistics team to examine the guns or bullets.'

'You will remember,' said Zedniček icily, 'that it was not the function of OII to conduct the initial investigation of the deaths. That fell to the homicide division. I only became involved some time later, when the allegation of impropriety on the part of the assault team was made.'

'Indeed,' said Rajka. 'But you would have reviewed the homicide team's work and if you were unsatisfied you could have made appropriate orders to rectify any shortcomings.'

'It was one old woman's fantasy. There was absolutely no evidence to back it up. Nobody else made that allegation.'

'Actually, others have,' said Rajka.

'And there's no concrete evidence to help us,' protested Zedniček.

It was at this point that Slonský opened his brown bag and placed a rectangular black object on the table top, carefully keeping his hand on it so it could not be snatched away.

'A videotape?' stammered Zedniček. 'Where did that come from?'

Rajka was just as surprised as Zedniček but hid it well.

'I'm not at liberty to say,' he answered.

Zedniček's mouth appeared to have dried up on him. He licked his lips a few times as he tried to assess where this revelation left him. Would he admit that he had conducted an inadequate enquiry designed to clear the police and brazen out whatever the tape showed, or would he decide to come clean? Rajka decided to give him a little nudge.

'You'll know that conspiracy to pervert the course of justice is a very serious offence,' he said.

'Am I accused of that?' Zedniček replied.

'No, not yet,' said Rajka.

Zedniček shifted awkwardly in his seat. A couple of times he looked as if he was about to say something, then he thought better of it and kept his mouth shut. Slonský was experienced enough to follow the advice he regularly gave Navrátil, namely, to keep quiet and let the suspect fill the silence. The fact that it was advice that he very rarely followed himself did not make it any less sage.

Finally Zedniček leaned forward and pointed at the tape.

'It is, I'm sure, entirely possible that if that tape had been available to me at the time I might have reached different conclusions. Who can say?'

'You didn't have it?' asked Slonský.

'I understood it had gone missing,' Zedniček replied.

You have to admire his brass neck, thought Slonský, resisting the considerable temptation to lean over and give Zedniček a slap for lying to a policeman.

Rajka was in a more forgiving mood.

'No doubt there was evidence pointing in each direction,' he began.

Zedniček seemed to relax a little. He could seem a tiny glimmer of light indicating a way out of the tunnel he had put himself in.

'Certainly,' he agreed. 'But to discipline an officer you have to have evidence showing a strong probability of guilt, if not beyond reasonable doubt.'

'So what evidence was there against the commander of the squad?'

That's clever, thought Slonský, not using the name as if you weren't fully aware it was this villain's son-in-law.

'There was the letter, of course. But nothing much else. On questioning, the other witnesses agreed that things happened so quickly that they couldn't swear to what happened in what order.'

'That's all in the questioning, though, isn't it?' Slonský chipped in. 'Ask a question one way and they say "yes"; ask it another way and they say "perhaps not".'

Zedniček bristled at the suggestion. 'We did not start with any pre-determined conclusion.'

'So the fact that the officer was soon to become your son-in-law did not influence your enquiry at all?' Slonský growled.

'That wasn't the case at the time,' Zedniček fired back.

Rajka glared at Slonský to make clear that he was asking the questions.

'So,' Rajka said smoothly, 'there was no reason, in your view, for you to recuse yourself from the investigation?'

'Certainly not. I don't mind saying that when my daughter declared her intention of marrying Dostál I was quick to point out that this put me in a very invidious position. Of course, I couldn't prevent the match, nor would I, but I did ask them to wait a while.'

'How long is "a while"?' Slonský interrupted.

'At least three months,' said Zedniček.

Slonský did some quick sums. Since the wedding took place around eight months after the siege, it must have been set up pretty soon thereafter if there was time to delay it three months. It seemed unlikely to him that there had not been some relationship between them at the time. On the other hand, Dostál may have been scheming enough to quickly cuddle up to the colonel's daughter when trouble came calling.

Rajka was waiting for Zedniček to say something, and Zedniček was equally certain that he had said enough and anything further would be too much information. Finally Rajka ostentatiously made a note and resumed his questioning.

'Is it fair to say, then, that you accept that your conclusions could only be regarded as provisional and that it was always possible that new evidence could invalidate them?'

Slonský was impressed. Rajka wasn't actually saying that there was any new evidence, and his question was phrased so that only an obstinate fool would say no; and since Zedniček was not a fool, he obliged with the answer Rajka wanted to record.

'Of course.'

'I realise,' Rajka smoothly continued, 'that your family connection with Colonel Dostál cannot be ignored, but you will understand that I have to ask you not to discuss this matter with him. He will be informed officially that the enquiry has been reopened.'

'Naturally,' Zedniček agreed. 'It goes without saying. We must guard against collusion.'

Was the word "we" intended to indicate that Zedniček could see which side his bread was buttered and had decided to switch sides? If so, Dostál was now floating in the sea and his father-in-law had chosen to put the lifebelts back in storage. Slonský had never had a daughter, and therefore no son-in-law either, but he had an idea this wasn't how family relationships were meant to work.

Rajka wrote the answer down, put his pen and notebook away, and stood up, so Slonský did the same.

'Thank you for your co-operation. If we need to speak to you again I'll contact you to arrange a convenient time.'

This notion of agreeing a time for an interrogation was completely alien to Slonský, who had long been accustomed to asking questions whenever he wanted and taking the maximum time that the law allowed to do it.

He followed Rajka out to the car, carefully tucking the videotape in his coat pocket first.

'Just out of interest,' Rajka murmured as they walked, 'what's on the tape?'

'A performance of *Swan Lake*,' Slonský admitted. 'Not my sort of thing, really, but it was all they had.'

'You were taking a chance. Suppose he'd had a video player?'

'If he had I wouldn't have mentioned the tape.'

'Good choice.'

Peiperová was celebrating her first day of freedom by reading all the papers Navrátil could find about the disappearance and death of Viktorie Dlasková. She viewed the video footage from the car park, rewound it and watched it twice more. Navrátil knew better than to speak while this was happening.

'It's awful,' she declared at last. 'Nágl raped and murdered the child, and at some point he gave her mother a good beating into the bargain. Those look like new injuries. You can almost see the pain she's in.'

'I agree. And you can't blame her for getting away by any method she can. I don't think anyone wants to charge her with driving without a licence or insurance in the circumstances.'

'Do you think Nágl knows where she was going?'

'All we can discover suggests that he didn't meet her until after she'd left the Most area, so perhaps he only knows what she's told him, but who knows what that could be? The saving grace is that she should know what he knows. If she told him where her friends and family are he'll know that's where she's likely to go. She's got a head start and I suppose she abandoned the car because the train would be quicker.'

'The main thing for her was to deprive him of the use of it.'

'That's right. And she's not a practised driver. She might know the road if she caught the bus into the city centre now and again, but once you head out to the north she wouldn't know what she might find.'

Peiperová looked up at Navrátil and shook her head.

'No, there's something wrong here.'

'Something wrong? How do you mean?'

'When Captain Slonský and I went to the kindergarten, he concluded that the abductor must have had a car waiting at the back. It's the only way that she could escape quickly. But if she can't drive, and she doesn't have a car, how is that possible?

We've been assuming that Broukalová kidnapped Viktorie, took her away and brought her up. But the argument you're putting forward is that she could drive seven years ago, but she can't drive today. How does that work?'

Navrátil pinched the bridge of his nose. How had he missed that? 'So she isn't the abductor?'

'We can't say that. But we have to revisit the sequence of events because even if we found her we wouldn't get a conviction with that argument.'

'Nágl can drive. Could he have snatched Viktorie?'

'There's no evidence that she knew him. Wouldn't she have yelled out?'

'Well, perhaps Broukalová took her, but Nágl was waiting in the car.'

'Then we've got to show that Nágl was in that part of the country then, but nothing we've found so far suggests he had a home there.'

'He could have been visiting.'

'But can we show he even knew Broukalová then?'

Navrátil sighed. 'We'll just have to question him on that when we find him.'

Slonský listened with increasing dismay as Navrátil and Peiperová expounded their thoughts on the hypothesis he had so lovingly cobbled together, and realised, not for the first time, that Peiperová was right. As things stood the theory just didn't work.

'What do we do now, sir?' Navrátil asked.

'It's your case, lad,' Slonský answered.

'But if I get stuck I'm supposed to come to you for guidance, which is what I'm doing now.'

This pair are altogether too bright for their own good, thought Slonský. 'We'll do what we usually do when things get tough. I need a sugar rush. Let's get some coffee and pastries.'

As they descended to the canteen they met Sergeant Mucha coming up the stairs.

'How kind of you to save me a long walk,' he chuckled. 'The trace you asked for has borne some fruit.'

Slonský held out his hand, but Mucha reached past him and handed the pages to Navrátil.

'It's Nágl's credit card. It was used in Kolín on the day after Mrs Broukalová caught the train.'

'Kolín?' said Slonský. 'Isn't that on the line to Brno?'

'It's the fourth stop on the way,' Mucha agreed. 'Kutná Hora is the next one, where the wife's sister lives, when she's not infesting us.'

'And Kolín has a direct line to Ústí,' Slonský added.

Navrátil ran down to the main desk and began flicking through a large book kept under the counter. 'The amount charged to the card is the cost of a ticket from Kolín to Ústí,' he said. 'Nágl's hot on her trail, isn't he?'

'Damn!' said Slonský. 'We'll have to alert the police up there. It's probably not a bad idea for us to drive up and see what we can find. There's not a moment to lose.'

Navrátil and Peiperová ran back up the stairs to fetch their coats.

'Where are you going?' called Slonský.

'We're getting our things,' answered Navrátil. 'You said there's not a moment to lose.'

'There's not a moment to lose after coffee, I meant. First things first. It could be a long day. I don't want us fainting from hunger.'

Mucha coughed eloquently.

'Yes, humble servant?' Slonský said.

'Far be it from me to poke my untrained and distinctively non-detective nose into things, but you might want to look at the second page.'

Navrátil belatedly did so. 'He's taken a load of cash out of his account.'

'When?' demanded Slonský.

'Last Monday.'

'Where?'

Navrátil swallowed hard. 'He was in Most.'

Chapter 13

Peiperová was thrown the keys.

'You drive,' said Slonský. 'I'll sit up the front. Navrátil can go in the baby seat because he's the shortest.'

'It's just as well I don't have a complex about my height,' Navrátil remarked ruefully.

'He's not that small,' Peiperová jumped to his defence. 'Anyway, they don't make diamonds as big as bricks.'

Slonský looked out of the side window so they couldn't see him smiling. It felt good to be back as a team of three again. He was confident that they would get somewhere now. Without Peiperová he had felt as if one arm was tied behind his back.

'It's a shame this car doesn't have a siren,' he said. 'Navrátil, wind down the window and make wah-wah noises.'

'I don't think that'll fool anyone, sir,' Navrátil replied. He too felt a curious sense of relaxation. He had never lost his positivity but it had been tested a bit over the last three months or so.

There was no denying that Peiperová was a much better driver than Rajka. On the other hand, she didn't have the better part of three and a half litres of engine to play with. On top of that, she was scrupulously attentive to traffic lights and give way signs and kept meticulously to her own side of the road.

'Thank you for getting me back, sir,' she said.

'Hold your horses. It's only temporary. Colonel Urban realised we were really stretched at the moment. Greater love hath no man than this, that he lay down his PA for his friends.'

'I don't think that's exactly what the bible says,' Navrátil observed.

'Well, I bow to your insider knowledge on that,' Slonský told him, 'but it's how I feel. Of course, while we're on the abduction we can't be looking into the Dostál matter, which is what Colonel Urban really wants me to push ahead with, but I think Major Rajka can manage that himself now I've given him a nudge in the right direction. Hang on, lass, that bakery has a special offer on cream cakes. Pull over.'

'I'll pull in up there on the right, sir.'

'Suit yourself. It only means you'll have an extra sixty metres to walk to the bakery.'

Slonský produced a banknote suitable for the task in hand, and Peiperová trotted back down the road, returning in a few minutes with a large bag.

'You'd better not eat while you're driving,' Slonský told her. 'We'll save some for you.'

Peiperová dipped her hand into the bag and fished out a cake. 'I'm a woman. I can multitask,' she said, and took a large bite.

Navrátil decided they ought to talk a bit of shop on the way.

'Where do you think Nágl could be staying, sir? We don't know of any friends so he'd have to pay cash, but even the money he took out on Monday wouldn't go far if he's in a hotel or guest house.'

'Look on the bright side, lad. If he's still in Most, that must mean he hasn't found Broukalová yet. And unless he's managed to get a new car, which I doubt, he's doing his searching by public transport and on foot, which will slow him down.'

'So where do we start, sir?'

'Let's see if the cash machine where he withdrew his money is covered by any cameras,' Slonský decided. 'Then we'll play it by ear. We may have to stay over, so I hope you've brought your nightwear.'

'I can manage,' Navrátil said.

They both looked quizzically at Peiperová.

'I'm saying nothing,' she said. 'And it's none of your business anyhow.'

Slonský was unsurprised to find that there were no useful cameras anywhere near the ATM, so he deployed his troops to minimise the time that they would have to spend there.

'You two go to the kindergarten and see if the name Broukalová means anything to the Director. If that Katja woman isn't there, drop in on her house. You've got the address, haven't you?'

Peiperová agreed that she had. 'Katja Švandová, wasn't it, sir?'

Slonský agreed, although if the truth were told he could not remember her surname exactly. It ended -ová, but then most women's names did.

'I'm going to visit Lucie Jerneková. She left before the events but if Broukalová used to work there perhaps she would have known her.'

'Where will we meet, sir?' asked Peiperová, ever practical.

'At Ms Jerneková's house.'

'I don't know where that is, sir.'

'No, but you will when you've dropped me off there, won't you?'

Slonský produced Lucie's address and gave Peiperová some cursory directions. He somehow managed to find the bar they had gone to and worked out how to get to the flat from there, suggesting to Peiperová and Navrátil that the bar would be a good place to meet up when they were done.

He banged on the door which was flung open by Lucie, who was about to launch into some street Czech when she realised who it was.

'Oh, it's you,' she said.

'Undoubtedly true,' said Slonský. 'I'm certainly me. Have you got a minute?'

Lucie shrugged and stepped aside to allow him to go in.

'Sit on the sofa. I can perch on the wobbly chair,' she said.

'Thanks. I won't be long. First, have you ever been arrested?'

'No!' said Lucie indignantly.

'That's good. It makes life easier.'

'Why? Can't criminals be witnesses now?'

'Not a problem so far as I know. I wasn't asking for that reason.'

'So what were you asking for?'

'I wondered if you'd ever thought of joining the police.'

Lucie goggled at him. She was obviously in the company of someone with a loose grip on reality.

'Why would I do that?' she said at length.

'Steady work. You can get accommodation, at least when you start. You seem like an observant, honest type. And it would be reasonable money, so long as you only want to eat properly every other day.'

'That's what I do now,' she said.

'Then you've got nothing to lose. I'd put in a word for you.'

'Sorry — is this some sort of weird job interview?'

Peiperová and Navrátil had been perplexed to discover that the Director had been suspended. Whether it was true or not, the staff seemed to think that Slonský had been responsible for this. As a result, a couple were nakedly hostile while others offered them coffee and the more comfortable chairs.

'It seems that Viktorie Dlasková had been living with a woman called Broukalová. We wondered if any of you knew anyone of that name,' Navrátil asked.

There was a general shaking of heads.

'We've got a poor quality photograph of her,' Peiperová added, showing it to each of them in turn.

'Goodness, she's taken a thumping, hasn't she?' remarked one of the teachers.

'We think she may be trying to escape from an abusive relationship, and the indications are that she has come back here.'

The handyman asked to see the picture again. 'I think if you saw anyone with a shiner like that you'd remember it,' he said. 'I'll keep my eyes open when I'm out and about, but I'm sure I haven't seen her.'

'Do you think she might come here?' asked a nervous young teacher.

'I doubt it,' said Navrátil. 'I think she'll stay clear of the kindergarten, but it's not that big a town. She must be staying with friends or family but we can't find anyone of that name in any records we have.'

'Not everyone keeps their ID information up to date, I suppose,' the young teacher replied.

The two detectives walked back to the car.

'I was sure someone would know the name,' said Navrátil.

'Obviously not,' Peiperová answered. 'We're no further forward. I hope Captain Slonský is having better luck.'

Slonský had been busy expounding his master plan to Lucie Jerneková.

'You want me to do my basic training, then come to work for you?'

'That's the long and short of it.'

'You don't know me.'

'I didn't know Navrátil when he came to work for me, and that's worked out pretty well. At least I've spoken to you. I didn't know him from Adam when he turned up for his first day.'

'I might fail the course.'

'Yes, you might,' Slonský conceded, 'but I don't think so. I've seen a lot of police in my time, so I think I'm qualified to judge. And when you look at some of the no-hopers we currently employ, I'd say you'd have a glittering career ahead of you. Anyway, think it over. The vacancy won't be there for long.'

'But I wouldn't be working for you straight away, and you need help now, you said.'

'This is where I've been unusually cunning, even by my standards. I don't have the money yet to pay you, but while you're in basic training, I don't have to. But I've been promised the money so long as I take on a woman.'

'I qualify on that basis,' Lucie said.

'I'd worked that out for myself. I'm not a detective for nothing.'

'Is that what you drove all this way for?'

'What? Ah, no, I'm glad you reminded me. Does the name Broukalová mean anything to you? We think someone who calls herself Broukalová may have abducted Viktorie.'

Lucie appeared to be in deep thought.

'The answer can only be yes or no,' Slonský prompted her.

'It's yes, sort of,' she replied. 'I don't know a Broukalová, but I'm pretty sure that one of the staff had a dad called Broukal. So presumably Broukalová was her maiden name. I just can't remember who it was.'

Slonský slapped his leg in annoyance. That's how she had managed to get an ID card in the name of Broukalová. She must have turned up with her old card and some kind of sob story about having lost the one in-between. If the clerk had done their job properly they would have looked for proof that one had ever been issued, but if you're surrendering an old one that has your picture on most of them wouldn't worry.

'Would a hot chocolate help you think?'

'No,' replied Lucie. 'But a beer might.'

When Navrátil and Peiperová walked into the bar they were surprised to see Slonský laughing with a young woman. He was in a very good mood, which boded well for the investigation.

'Meet Lucie Jerneková,' he said. 'She has come up with a name for us. We're looking for Magdalena Novotná, née Broukalová.'

'So is Mr Novotný masquerading as Nágl?' asked Navrátil.

'I doubt it. It seems that he was off the scene when she left. They'd broken up and she was going to make a new life somewhere else. No doubt we can begin to flesh that out now that we've got a target name. In the meantime, order yourselves a drink if you want. Put it on my tab.'

He is in a good mood, thought Navrátil. Either that, or he's had a bang on the head.

'Shouldn't we have stayed on to pursue enquiries locally?' asked Peiperová as they drove back. Navrátil was having a turn at the wheel so she was sitting in the back.

'We can probably do more at our desks than we can here. Or, more accurately, you and Navrátil can. I can never get the hang of those computers. She's stayed safe so far and once we find her old address we can ask the local police to drop by and see if she's there. Although I'd probably rather we did it ourselves.'

Navrátil had an ethical question to ask. 'Sir, isn't it poor practice to take witnesses for a drink?'

'Yes, absolutely shocking. But she was dehydrated. Consider it as first aid. And she wasn't being consulted as a witness. By that time it was a job interview. Navrátil, I think if you're going to swerve across lanes like that you're expected to signal.'

'Sorry, sir. You took me by surprise a bit.'

'And don't think I didn't spot that. I'll explain it to you. We need a bit of gender balance, lad.'

'Gender balance, sir?'

'Navrátil, if you're going to do that thing where you repeat the last couple of words of each of my sentences I may attack you while the balance of my mind is disturbed. Yes, gender balance. There are five of us in the team. Four are men, unless Hauzer is a better actor than I give him credit for. Only one is female.' He dropped to a stage whisper. 'Don't turn round but she's in the back.'

'Yes, sir.'

'When Krob joins us that will be five to one, and the deal I have with HR is that I'll fill the next vacancy with a woman. And we obviously don't want to advertise it widely or we could be saddled with somebody completely unsuitable. Now, I have been keeping my eyes peeled in the canteen, and no obvious candidate has come to my notice. Ms Jerneková, on the other hand, is astute, aggressive, streetwise and generally nobody's fool. She reminds me of my younger self, if you disregard some small cosmetic differences. I can make something of her. Or, more truthfully, you can, Peiperová.'

'Me, sir?'

'Well, if Navrátil is helping Krob to settle in, we can't have you at a loose end, so you can have Jerneková to help you. If she signs up, which I think she will because the cleaning job isn't doing too well at the minute.'

'But you have to have a certain minimum experience before you can be a detective, sir,' Peiperová protested.

'Yes, but not before you can join the crime department. We just won't call her a detective. We've actually got the same problem with Krob, who is joining from the City Police. Technically, City Police are civilians, so it wouldn't count towards his service. Fortunately a nice man in HR explained that this is how we get round it. And if that works for Krob it'll work for Jerneková.'

'She'll still have to do her basic training, sir,' Navrátil pointed out.

'So she will, but she'll finish it just as Peiperová's year is up. Couldn't be better.'

Peiperová and Navrátil knew that in the long run they would not be able to work together, but since Slonský appeared to ignore every other employment rule they had been hoping he might have turned a blind eye to that one too and allowed them to carry on working in tandem despite their romantic attachment.

'You surely can't have expected to work together as a couple once I'm not there to exercise chaperoning duties?' Slonský asked.

'No, sir,' they chorused.

'Good, because I won't last forever and the white powder I put in Navrátil's coffee to curb his urges is expensive.'

Navrátil decided that this was a good moment to change the subject.

'Do you think we'll find her, sir?'

'It's more likely than not. It's very difficult not to come to the notice of authority these days. As soon as she buys a phone or sees a doctor she'll be traceable. It's just a case of us keeping alert. Of course, we don't all have to be alert at the same time, so you two keep your eyes peeled while I inspect the back of my eyelids.'

He leaned back in his seat and tipped his hat over his face.

Chapter 14

The following morning started very well. Slonský was just collecting his first coffee of the day when Rajka strode into the canteen and shepherded him to a nearby table.

'I thought you'd like to see this,' he said, and handed Slonský a letter from the Ministry of the Interior.

'Let's see. "I am directed by the Minister to thank you for your courtesy in keeping him informed of the context of a current investigation. I am further directed to clarify that the officer in question is not currently being considered for any senior position within the police service." So what does that mean?'

'It means that Dr Pilik wants nothing to do with Dostál and his application for the Chief of Police job has been cut into small squares and hung on a nail in the gents' toilet.'

'How appropriate a metaphor.'

'It doesn't mean Colonel Urban is guaranteed to get it though.'

'We've done all we can. And, frankly, if not him, then who?'

'Who indeed?'

'Can I show it to him?'

'Certainly not. It's a confidential letter to me.'

'So if it's confidential why are you showing it to me?'

'Because I know that you'll tell him all about it, and then I won't have to.'

'I might not tell him just yet in case he asks for the return of Peiperová. I'll have to think of somewhere to send her before I say anything. Somewhere that doesn't allow mobile phones.'

'Do you want anything looking up in the police archives?'

'That would be ideal, but I don't think I do.'

'He doesn't need to know that.'

'Good point. Thanks for bringing me this good news. Now let's see what sequence of musical chairs is going to change a lot of top jobs.'

Rajka returned to his office, leaving Slonský with his coffee and a ham and cheese croissant he had forgotten having ordered, from which he had just taken a bite when Navrátil and Peiperová rushed in.

'Sir, Peiperová has just thought of something,' said Navrátil.

'Was it so exciting that she couldn't tell me herself?'

'Officer Navrátil is being over-dramatic, sir. All I did was ask a question he can't answer.'

'Goodness, we can all do that. His knowledge of Czech films of the fifties is pretty minimal and he's fairly dodgy on anything to do with football.'

'Not that sort of question, sir. I was explaining to Officer Peiperová where we had got to with the bank siege case when she asked me something I think is important.'

'Go on, then, lass. Astound me.'

'Navrátil was telling me that the getaway driver was moved on by the city police, so he wasn't there when the robbers tried to leave.'

'Yes, that's right.'

'How do we know that?'

Slonský was so surprised that he dropped his croissant. 'How indeed? The robbers can't have told us, because they were all dead before they got the chance to share their plans. But Valentin's newspaper cuttings said it, so somebody knew it, and I never thought to ask how. Well done, lass.'

He carefully reassembled his croissant.

'Shouldn't we go and follow this up?' asked Navrátil.

'No point,' said Slonský with his mouth full of breakfast, obliging him to repeat it when he had swallowed.

'Why not, sir?'

'Because the person best able to tell us will still be in his pit until around eleven. He keeps journalists' hours. But if we shuffle around the bars about then we're sure to find him somewhere, and then you can ask your question again, my girl.'

At ten to eleven Peiperová put her coat on.

'Going out?' said Slonský.

'We're going to the bar in the cellar you sometimes go to.'

'Are we? Is it someone's birthday I've forgotten?'

'Not today. But it's your wife's next week.'

'So it is. Peiperová, may I hold your hand a moment?'

'Sir?'

'I was going to get my wife a pair of gloves but I don't know the size. Once I know if her hand is bigger or smaller than yours you can tell me what size I should get.'

Peiperová held her hand out in the manner of a baroness permitting a commoner to kiss it.

'About the same length but a bit wider, I'd say.'

'Size seven, sir.'

'Thank you.'

'I could get them for you if you want, sir.'

'No, thanks for the offer, but I can't send people out to do my shopping for me. It wouldn't be right.'

Obviously Slonský's definition of shopping did not include the hundreds of coffees and pastries that Peiperová had been sent to fetch over the past seventeen months or so.

'I rang Mr Valentin's newspaper and left a message for him, sir. I said you'd be in the cellar around the corner about eleven o'clock.'

'Very enterprising of you. I suppose we'd better go, then. He hates being stood up. Is Love's Young Dream coming?'

'Navrátil is waiting for a death notice, sir.'

'So long as it's not mine.'

'He's trying to find out when Magdalena Broukalová's parents died. The registry was going to ring him back but that was an hour ago and they still haven't done it.'

'Peiperová, you'll both have to learn a cardinal rule of dealing with Czech civil servants. Always ask their name, and always write it down. Then if there are any deficiencies in the service they know that you'll be able to direct your boot to the right bottom. Watch and learn, lass.'

Slonský picked up his desk telephone and dialled a number.

'Captain Slonský speaking. And you are…?'

There was a pause.

'Indeed you can help me, Mr Škára. A while ago someone from your department came to look at my office with a view to knocking down a wall but I've heard no more about it… Mr Mráz, is that him? … If you would get him to call I'd be very grateful. Goodbye.'

He put the phone down.

'Now, you see, Peiperová, Škára now knows that I know his name and if I'm not happy I'll make his life miserable. But he also knows that Mráz is the real culprit, so he'll get on his back, and I won't have to.'

The phone rang.

'Who? Oh, Mr Mráz, how good of you to call.'

Valentin felt the natural order of the world had been overturned. He was used to being the one sitting with a drink when Slonský arrived, but he could see his detective friend was already in place, along with Officer Peiperová. Even more alarming, Slonský was drinking a coffee.

'Have they run out of beer?' asked Valentin.

'No, despite your best efforts they can struggle on for at least another few hours.'

Valentin glanced at his watch. 'I suppose it's a bit early for beer. I'll just have a coffee.'

The waiter nodded and was about to walk away when Valentin added, 'With a small schnapps.'

'So what's the reason for your demand for a piece of my time?' the journalist asked.

'Those cuttings you gave me were very useful, but they raise an intriguing question that this talented young lady needs answering.'

Slonský produced one of the articles and pointed to the paragraph in question.

'It says here,' he began, 'that the getaway driver was moved on by the City Police when he tried to park outside. But how did your reporter know that, because the robbers didn't survive long enough to give him an interview? And so far as we know the driver pushed off and we don't know who he was.'

Valentin read the report again. 'Written by Honza Hanzl, I see. I don't know the answer to your question, but you're in luck, because Honza Hanzl still works for us and he's only a few metres away.'

'He does?'

'Yes. He's now the news editor. If you promise to leave my drink unadulterated I'll step over and persuade him to join us.' He leaned forward to whisper into Slonský's ear. 'A word of warning. He drinks like a fish.'

Hanzl was an overweight man with a waddle for a walk and a wardrobe that must have been acquired when he was two sizes smaller because neither the jacket nor the waistcoat below it could be fastened. His trousers, though adequate in size, were held up with a pair of braces that were showing signs of fatigue.

Invited to sit by Slonský, he accepted a coffee and schnapps combo and listened attentively as Slonský set out the question that was bamboozling them.

'Ah, that's easy,' said Hanzl. 'The police told me.'

'The police? You mean the real police or the City lot?'

'It was a joint effort. One of the witnesses had overheard one of the robbers telling the others that their driver wasn't there. When the City Police heard this they checked their notebooks and discovered that the same car's registration plate had been noted by two of their officers as being illegally parked outside the bank, so they drove round to the place where the car was registered. By that time the driver knew what had happened to his mates so he was very happy to surrender to the City Police because he felt safer in their custody. He was charged with conspiracy to commit theft and got three years, I think. I can't remember his name exactly — Petrovský, Pernovský, something like that — but I can check when I get back. I covered his trial.'

'Was there anything said about the robbery that didn't get into your first report?' asked Slonský.

'When I say I covered his trial, I didn't actually go there. I just bought the usher a drink at the end of the day and got the info I needed.'

'You see,' said Valentin. 'There's not much difference between journalism and police work after all.'

On their return to the office Slonský stopped at the main desk to share this new development with Sergeant Mucha.

'Very enterprising of him,' said Mucha. 'Saves a lot of time, in much the same way as we save valuable police hours finding out what the villains have been doing by reading the newspapers.'

'So does the name Petrovský or Pernovský mean anything to you, O Oracle?'

'Strangely enough, it does. Vladimír Petrovský is a regular client of ours. He has a little sideline in tarting up old cars that have been written off by insurance companies.'

'Is it lucrative?'

'I doubt it. He keeps getting caught. Somebody was arrested only a month or so back for causing a breach of the peace when he turned up at Petrovský's workshop with the front end of a car that had fallen off as he drove through town. Petrovský offered to bolt it back on but the customer told him of an alternative place where he could stick it and volunteered to do it for him.'

'So does that magic box of tricks at your side have any useful information relating to Petrovský's part in a bank robbery eight years ago?'

'I tell you what. Why don't I check?'

'That would be good.'

'For you — no charge.'

'Even better.'

'I'll let you know.'

Slonský made for the stairs but was stopped in his track by a mighty roar.

'Captain Slonský!'

I can't pretend I didn't hear that, he thought, and turned to see who was calling. Colonel Urban was striding across the hallway towards him.

'I thought I should let you know I've just taken a call from the Ministry of the Interior. I've got the job, starting on the first of November.'

Slonský shook Urban's hand enthusiastically.

'I'm really pleased, sir.'

'I won't forget this, Slonský. You and Rajka stood up for me and I'm not a man to turn his back on his friends.'

'I never thought you were, sir,' Slonský replied, crossing his fingers behind his back.

'Best say nothing about this until it's in the public domain,' Urban said quietly.

Since the earlier part of the conversation had been conducted in the entrance hall of a large and busy police building at full volume this seemed to Slonský to be shutting the stable door after an entire team of horses had bolted, but he smiled and agreed.

Urban slapped him manfully on the shoulder. 'Good work. Well done. Thanks. Won't forget this.'

'Neither will I, sir.'

As Urban turned away something occurred to him. 'Hardly worth Peiperová coming back just for a month. If she can drop by from time to time to help me get things tidy for whoever succeeds me, that's enough.'

Now that was cause for celebration indeed.

There are events for which it is fair to say that no matter how much a man has conceptualized them, imagined them, anticipated them, when they come to pass he finds himself utterly unprepared for the reality. Such a moment befell

Slonský when he reached his office and told Peiperová what he had just heard.

Peiperová was so pleased that she executed a couple of small jumps on the spot, thus building momentum for the move in which she launched herself into first Slonský, then Navrátil, culminating in a hug which could have been terminal in someone with a heart condition. Fortunately Navrátil had been vaccinated against this by repeated doses of the same thing and was able to withstand the onslaught.

'I understand your excitement,' Slonský told her, 'but we have work to do. Let's piece together all we can of the lives of Novotná-Broukalová and Nágl.'

'We've made some progress, sir,' reported Navrátil. 'It seems that Mr Broukal died in 1999 and his wife followed three years ago. So far as I can discover Magdalena is their only child. She's now forty-eight years old and married Jan Novotný twenty-seven years ago.'

'Any children?'

'Not that I can trace thus far. And they don't seem to have divorced until 2003. The court transcript indicates that he was granted a decree because she could not be traced to be served the papers. With three years' separation and no counter-petition on her part alleging hardship if the divorce were granted it would have been automatic.'

'So they separated around the time that Viktorie was taken?'

'If Novotný's deposition can be trusted, he had walked out about a month before because she was behaving unreasonably.'

'Anything else?'

'Not yet, sir. I can't find when she left the north or when she arrived in Prague. The first sign we have of her here is a little over two years ago when she registered her new ID card. That was May 2005.'

Slonský made some notes on a pad and pinned the page on the notice board.

'So they separate in January 2000, Viktorie is snatched in February and by 2003 they've been apart long enough for him to get a divorce. Then she reappears in Prague in May 2005. That's five years we've got to account for. Anything on Nágl?'

'He seems to have lived in the southern part of the city since he became an adult. He moved to the present house in the second half of 2005. By the way, forensics have sent their report on his car. I put it on your desk.'

Slonský retrieved it and read through the summary. Something caught his attention and he turned to one of the interior pages which he read in detail.

'If he doesn't have a car, he's got to use public transport. And if he's given up his job to go looking for her it tells us that it's very important to him to silence her. This can't be his word against hers. She must have some sort of hard evidence.'

'Maybe he just can't face losing control of her,' Peiperová interjected. 'Some men do that. He wants to punish her for deserting him.'

'He's punished her once. Why didn't he finish the job off then instead of doing half a job and then having to chase round the country looking for her?'

Navrátil bristled at the suggestion. 'You're surely not advocating that he should have killed her in the first place, sir?'

'No, of course not, lad. I'm surprised you should even think of construing it that way. I'm looking at it from his point of view. He clearly maltreated her over that weekend, and she ran away. That must have panicked him, otherwise he could just have let her go.'

'Exactly my point, sir,' said Peiperová. 'He thought she was under his thumb and he could treat her however he wanted with no consequences. She plucked up the courage to leave and we can't protect her because she won't ask us for help.'

'But we can't ignore the fact that she is likely to have kidnapped a child. It's the prospect of punishment for that crime that stops her coming to us. For any other woman we'd tell her just to get in touch, but that won't work with her. The only answer is for us to find her before Nágl does. And we don't know how much he knows about her past.'

'Presumably he knew about the abduction, sir,' Navrátil said. 'That's why she couldn't say anything about Viktorie being abused. If she filed a report he would accuse her of having abducted the child and they'd both go inside for a long time.'

'That's the obvious conclusion, but whatever went before, the issue for us is finding the pair of them. The child's real parents deserve no less than an explanation of what happened to their daughter. Peiperová, I want you to go back to Broukalová's parents' district and go door to door. Find out anything you can that might help us to piece together those missing five years. Navrátil, your job is to find out all you can about Nágl. Does he have any family he might be keeping in touch with? Is anyone supplying him to cash to enable him to keep this search going? We didn't get much out of his work colleagues but perhaps they know something helpful, so try again.'

'And what will you be doing, sir?' Navrátil asked.

'Thinking,' said Slonský. 'Thinking very hard.'

Peterka seemed to regard Navrátil's return to the office as a clear pointer that Nágl was suspected of something.

'I can't comment on that. I'm trying to find anyone who was close to him.'

'You don't get close to men like Nágl. I worked with him. I wouldn't have spent a weekend with him.'

'He didn't have any special mates?'

'He was famous for having no mates at all. He devoted his time to his wife and child. He showed us plenty of photos of them, especially the girl. But now it turns out she wasn't actually his.'

'His stepdaughter, I believe.'

'So I hear.'

'Did he ever bring her here?'

'Not to the office, but we have an annual summer picnic. She came to that a couple of times.'

'What did you make of her?'

'Pretty girl, nicely dressed, very well-behaved. She was very shy. I might almost say timid. Didn't play much with our children. In fact, she didn't play at all. It was as if she was frightened that she'd be told off if she got dirty. She was like a little adult.'

'Did you ever hear him mention parents, brothers, sisters?'

'His parents were still alive last year but I don't know where they are. They can't be far away because he said he sometimes visited for lunch on Saturdays. I don't know anything about other family.'

Navrátil was building a picture of the man but he felt he was getting nothing that would help him to understand what Nágl was capable of doing. He decided he needed to push a little harder.

'I have to emphasise that we're looking for Mr Nágl to question him. There is suspicion that he may have abused his stepdaughter and maltreated his wife.'

Peterka's reaction was telling. There wasn't one.

'You're not commenting,' Navrátil said.

'Nothing much to say. Am I surprised? No. He was an insignificant man leading an insignificant life. If he had an opportunity to bully someone he'd take it just because they'd be the only people who had to pay any attention to him.'

Navrátil snapped his notebook shut. 'Thanks for your help,' he said.

'No problem. I hope you catch him. And when you do, I hope you'll make sure the country isn't put to the expense of a trial.'

Peiperová had been making more headway. After drinking more coffee than was good for her she had pieced together a coherent history from people who had known the Broukal family. She decided to call Slonský to update him before she drove back.

'It seems that Magdalena was a model daughter. Her father was a respected mining engineer. He thought the world of her, she idolised him. There was never any suggestion of impropriety, just a very close father-daughter relationship. She was a daddy's girl. She wasn't so close to her mother but while her father was alive that wasn't an issue. She held her tongue for his sake.'

'Any siblings?'

'No. The neighbours said she was a late baby.'

'How do they mean, late?'

'Her mother had been trying for a long time when she finally got pregnant. That's worth noting because we'll come back to it later. Magdalena married around 1982 when she was about twenty-two. She and her husband were very happy for quite some time by all accounts, but she wanted a baby and despite lots of medical help it wasn't happening for her. She seems to have inherited her mother's low fertility.

'Anyway, she finally got pregnant when she was in her late thirties and carried the baby for about six months, but then she lost it. She became very depressed. The local doctor said he couldn't discuss it in detail without a court order but he could at least confirm that. Obviously the neighbours couldn't tell me anything about what went on in their household but it seems the whole thing broke them apart. She gave up her job with the kindergarten because being with children was making her feel worse.'

'And the Director didn't think to tell us that?'

'It was about six months before Viktorie went missing. Maybe she didn't connect the two.'

'You've got a child that goes missing and a woman who badly wants a baby and she doesn't connect them?'

'Lots of women badly want a baby, sir, but very few go round stealing them.'

'Fair point. So presumably at some stage she left the district to start a new life?'

'Yes, sir. Nobody quite knows when, though. Her father died in 1999, just after she discovered she was pregnant. At some point during her depression she had an enormous row with her mother. The women I spoke to were at pains to stress that they only had the mother's side of the story, but it seems they never spoke again, and because she cut off contact with her mother they don't know any more about what happened to her. However, her doctor says he never saw her again after December 1999. Unless she abruptly stopped her medication she would have needed to see another doctor within about three months, so he assumes she moved away then, but he was never asked to send on her records.'

'And that's right on the time that Viktorie was taken.'

'Couldn't fit better, sir. She took Viktorie when she was leaving town.'

Slonský tossed the new information around in his mind. This resulted in a silence that Peiperová finally broke.

'Are you still there, sir?'

'Yes, still here. The question now is how she lived when she came to Prague. Let's say she decides to leave and she grabs the girl. Is she really going to come to a new city where she knows nobody, doesn't have anywhere to stay or a job? What would she do?'

'I know what I'd do, sir. I'd head for a women's refuge.'

'Good thinking, Peiperová. When you get back here find out all you can about the options she had. If they're too many for you to visit we'll share them out between us. She may have used either the Novotná or Broukalová name, so we'll have to check for both.'

'Will do, sir. Is it all right if I do that in the morning?'

'You work hard enough. I don't expect you to give all your evenings up. Anyway, I can't expect you to work when I'm having the evening off next week. I'm taking my wife out to dinner.'

'That's nice, sir. I hope you both enjoy it.'

'So do I. It's been a long time. I'm out of practice.'

Chapter 15

The following morning began with a considerable surprise. Officer Krob reported for duty.

'I wasn't expecting you until the first,' Slonský told him.

'I know, sir, but I had to use my leave up so I actually finished a few days early. I thought it might be helpful if I came in today so I could get up to speed before I start in earnest on Monday.'

This sort of enthusiasm surpassed even Navrátil's. Admittedly Navrátil couldn't turn up early because he didn't know until his first day to whom he had been assigned, this being the inevitable outcome of Slonský's attempts to get out of mentoring him, but Slonský was impressed with Krob.

'This is Officer Navrátil. Pay no attention to that open and trusting expression. He is a considerable asset to this department. I expect great things of him, if he listens carefully to all the pearls of wisdom I dispense. He'll take care of you. In a minute he'll give you a tour of the building, organise your passes and your badge, and take you to the very hub of policing in the Czech Republic.'

'What's that, then, sir?' Navrátil enquired.

'The canteen, lad. It's where we take on board the necessary calories that keep our brains ticking over. A good detective needs three things, Krob. He needs a good pair of shoes, a bottom that can withstand prolonged periods of sitting down and a mind to gather and process all that comes in.'

'Yes, sir.'

The door swung open behind them to display Mucha standing with a large cardboard box in his arms. He indicated Slonský's desk with a nod of his head.

'Can you make some space? This thing is heavy.'

Slonský cleared an area by simply dumping the papers on the floor behind the desk.

'What have you got there?'

'Something that I think will make you very happy,' said Mucha.

'Is it Navrátil's mother's recipe for cinnamon buns?'

'Better than that.'

'Now I know you're lying,' said Slonský. 'There is nothing on earth better than Navrátil's mother's cinnamon buns.'

Mucha removed the lid of the box with a flourish and plunged his arm inside.

'This,' he said, 'is the evidence box for The State v Petrovský. We hadn't got round to throwing it out. And this is a copy of a video tape I think you've been looking for.'

Slonský goggled. 'How did you find it?'

'The ruthless application of logic, coupled with an appreciation of how the Czech bureaucrat's mind works. Petrovský was charged with conspiracy to commit a robbery, remember? To prove that, the prosecutors would have to prove that there had actually been a robbery. And since they were asking for a six-year sentence they had to show it was an aggravated robbery, meaning that violence or threats were used. The easy way to do that would have been to show the video. But the original video was needed for the OII enquiry into Dostál's handling of the siege. I know that enquiry was a complete fraud but the prosecutors didn't know that, so they made a certified copy of the tape in case they couldn't have the original when the trial was on. At some stage someone —

probably Zedniček — threw out the original tape but he didn't know that there was a copy.'

'He does now,' said Slonský. 'I showed him one the other day.'

'Where did you get that?' asked a perplexed Mucha.

'In a second hand shop. It was actually a tape of *Swan Lake*.'

'And he didn't notice the difference between a vicious armed bank siege and a bunch of woman in tutus tiptoeing around a stage pretending to be pond birds?'

'I didn't actually run the tape. I just waved it at him. Anyway, now we've got it, we'd better have a look at it. Just one question — why bring the whole evidence box?'

'Because I didn't want to sign out the videotape alone in case anyone is watching what we're doing. I haven't been a policeman for nearly forty years without learning that sometimes it's better if other police don't know your business.'

'You're wrong there,' said Slonský. 'It's always better if other police don't know your business.'

The whole party trooped to the Situation Control Room where Navrátil, who had already shown his mastery of the equipment, was tasked with putting the videotape in the player and turning the right television on.

The tape did not show the whole of the bank's ground floor. It concentrated on the public area and the counter. The picture covered the part of the room behind the counter, but the private area extended in an L-shape down the left of the picture and there was a strip there hard against the wall that could not be clearly seen.

The relevant part of the tape showed the assault team entering the room and fanning out into an arc. Five could be seen at various points, but at the key moment there were three in a horizontal line across the screen. Slonský designated these 3, 4 and 5. 1 and 2 were on the left edge and were not always visible.

The two armed robbers each held a customer in front of them. At one point they each pushed the hostage away and were shot. The tape had to be run slowly to verify the sequence of events.

'It's a shame the tape is silent, sir,' said Navrátil, 'but the fact that the two robbers both push the hostages away at the same time suggests a countdown.'

Mucha pointed to policemen 4 and 5. 'Those two have clear lines of fire, but of course they can't know which one each will shoot at so they could be hit before they got a second shot in. But even people as thick as most bank robbers would realise that with a semi-circle of armed police around you, the game is up. It's just a case of bargaining for their lives at this stage.'

'Let's not jump to conclusions,' said Slonský. 'That's not our job. Peiperová, would you give Major Rajka a call and invite him to join us if he's free? And if he isn't free, suggest he makes himself free to come and see this.'

Rajka needed no second invitation when he heard what they were watching and soon joined them as they replayed the video.

'We can't be sure whether policeman 1 or policeman 2 pulled the trigger,' said Slonský.

'No, but for my purpose that doesn't really matter,' Rajka answered. 'Dostál was the commander and he had an obligation to give a truthful account to any OII enquiry, which he plainly failed to do. As to the matter of unlawful homicide, I'd be passing that back to you, so you're the one who'd have to make that call.'

'Based on the way they fall, I think I could make a case for it being number 2 who shoots. The more difficult bit is proving that he knew the men were no threat. And of course the shooting of the third man isn't on here.'

Lieutenant Dvorník appeared in the doorway.

'I heard you might be in here,' he began. 'Is this that bank robbery you've been looking into?'

'That's right.'

Navrátil started the tape for the third time. Suddenly Dvorník became very animated.

'Whoa! Go back!'

'To where?' Navrátil asked him.

'Just before they let the hostages go. There! This is all wrong. Look at those two at the back. They begin to lower their guns. They know there's no threat. In fact the one on the right looks like he's applying the safety catch on his weapon.'

Slonský took no convincing. Dvorník knew more about firearms than he ever would.

'Good enough for me. Did you want me for something?'

'Yes — there's some woman called Jerneková on the phone for you. She says it's important.'

Slonský ran to Dvorník's office and picked up the phone. Jerneková had rung off.

'I've got the number she rang from on the pad,' said Dvorník. 'Why not call her back?'

Slonský dialled the number and was delighted when Jerneková picked up.

'Sorry — I didn't have any more money,' she explained.

'I'll pay you back. What's this about?'

'Well, two things. First, if you were serious about the police thing, I'm up for it.'

'That's good to hear. I'll send you the papers.'

'But the bigger thing is I remembered something about Magdalena. She doesn't have any family left, but she was very close to Petra Novotná.'

'Should that name mean something to me?'

'Her husband's sister. If she had nowhere else to go, she might have got in touch with Petra.'

'I thought she'd divorced the brother?'

'The brother divorced her. But he loved the woman she was. It was the woman she'd become that he couldn't live with. It doesn't mean Petra would feel the same way.'

'I'll look into it, thanks.'

Slonský returned to the Situation Control Room. Rajka had left but the others were still watching the tape.

'Any more ideas?' he asked.

'Only that I should take this to the technicians and get a digital copy made in case this disappears again,' Navrátil answered.

'That would be good,' Slonský agreed. 'When you've done that, I want you to give Peiperová a hand. She's tracking down any Prague hostels or refuges for women to see if we can discover where Broukalová was staying when she came here. I want you to find out if there are any refuges or hostels near Most where she could be staying now.'

Krob wasted no time. 'Can I help?'

'Krob, you certainly can. I have no idea how but Navrátil will tell you. Go with him.'

Navrátil felt there was a potential impediment to Krob's involvement in the enquiry. 'Sir, he hasn't got a desk.'

'He can use mine for now. I'll use Lukas's old desk until such time as the buildings mob get that wall knocked down. Just don't let him change the PIN number on the answerphone. It's taken me years to learn that.'

The junior officers dispersed and Slonský was left with Mucha.

'You did well,' said Slonský. 'I'm afraid I forget to say that to you sometimes.'

'That's true.'

'Sometimes I take you for granted.'

'That's true too.'

'If you ever feel like joining the detective team, just let me know.'

'I will.'

'There's just one catch. You'll have to have a sex change. Don't blame me, it's police policy now, apparently.'

'I doubt the wife would notice,' sniffed Mucha, and returned to his post at the front desk.

Later that afternoon Slonský returned to his office to find two men in overalls making chalk marks on his wall.

'Are you here officially or just a graffiti team who have forgotten to buy spray paint?' he asked.

'We've got orders to knock a wall through.'

'Right through? The length of the wall?'

'Almost. It's a big job so we'll need you to move out for a couple of days. They'll have to get a custom-made steel beam fabricated to take the weight. We've got to put in some props, take out the space for the beam, lodge that in place then rip out the wall underneath. Start Friday night, finish Sunday night. Once we've got the beam, of course. Here's the estimate for the work.'

Slonský looked at the proposed hit to his budget. 'How much would a cat flap be?' he asked.

'I dread to think what our phone bill will be this month,' Slonský pondered.

'That's not your problem,' Mucha replied. 'Unless they've started docking the departmental expenses out of our wages and not told me.'

Slonský took another bite of pastry. 'Peiperová and Navrátil must have a knowledge of women's refuges second to none. I think they've rung most of them. Speak of the devils…'

The two young officers, with Krob trailing behind, were entering the canteen. They collected cups of coffee and responded to Slonský's invitation to sit with him.

'I thought this might be a private conversation,' Navrátil explained.

'I have no secrets from you, lad. Or, more accurately, I have plenty of secrets but I wouldn't tell Mucha about them. He knows enough already.'

'That's my pension plan you're talking about,' Mucha expostulated. 'My little black book of secrets about my fellow officers. I'm relying on that to keep me in sandwiches for my first day of retirement.'

'What are you going to do when you retire, old friend?'

'What have you heard?' Mucha asked suspiciously.

'Nothing! I mean, when the time comes, which I hope will be a long way off yet.'

'I don't know. Sit around the house getting in my wife's way, I expect. Occasional forays to meet up with old mates. Digging a big hole in a patch of wasteland large enough to take the wife's sister if I ever find I can't take any more and run amok.'

'You need a hobby.'

'Says the hobby guru. When have we got time for hobbies?'

'Good point. But with this new hand-picked team of bright young things beneath me I am confident that I'll soon have nothing to do most of the time because they'll mop it all up. I'll just sit in Captain Lukas' old office signing expense claims and processing requests for leave.'

'You'll hate that.'

'Only if I grant them. If I don't allow success to spoil me and carry on being my old self I anticipate a lot of job satisfaction out of saying no. For a start, I'm thinking of making everyone work all day on 21st June next year.'

Navrátil and Peiperová exchanged glances. That was the well-publicized date planned for their wedding. They decided not to rise to the bait.

'Are you getting married in uniform?' Krob asked.

It didn't take them long to tell you all about it, Slonský thought.

'I don't know,' Navrátil replied. 'I hadn't thought about it.'

'Only if you do, I suppose Officer Peiperová would have to as well.'

Peiperová gulped her coffee. 'And miss out on the one chance in my life to wear the big white dress? No, thank you.'

'You could always have the police insignia sewn on its shoulders,' Slonský proposed, 'if you want to find a middle way.'

'A traditional white wedding, that's what we said, isn't it, Jan?'

Navrátil nodded emphatically. 'That's right. We want a wedding just like other Czech brides and grooms have.'

'You mean with the bride three months gone?' Slonský asked.

Peiperová was about to snap at him until she realised that he was smirking.

'Sorry,' he said. 'Couldn't resist. I'm sure it'll be lovely. I'll make sure you get the whole day off.' He finished off his pastry, emptied his cup and pushed them away. 'I guess we ought to talk shop at some point. How have you got on?'

Peiperová was first to speak. 'I've got a list of places from social services. I had no idea there were so many. I've rung about eight but it'll take me all day, I think.'

'Not quite so difficult up north,' Navrátil added. 'Social services didn't have much of a list. I rang the local priest to ask where he would send anyone who asked him for help. He was understandably reluctant to give me addresses because I suppose he couldn't be sure I wasn't a husband chasing after a runaway wife, but he gave me phone numbers. Between us Krob and I have rung all those without finding anything out. We've got a couple of hostels we've got to ring back once they've spoken to whoever was on duty at the relevant time in case they turned her away.'

'Do they often turn women away?' asked Slonský.

'Only when they're full. They give them introductions to another place but some don't ever present themselves there, it seems.'

'Okay. Keep pegging away at it. Has Krob got his new badge?'

'They wouldn't give it to me until Monday, but it's all ready. And I've been measured for my uniform and they tell me that will be waiting for me on Monday too,' Krob replied.

'Excellent. By long-established tradition the newest member of the team gets to organise the staff Christmas party, just so you know.'

'That's a long-established tradition that dates back to last year,' Peiperová helpfully added.

Slonský was deep in thought.

'Something puzzling you, sir?' asked Peiperová.

'It's the timing of the whole thing. Let's walk through it. Maybe you folks can spot something I've missed. Broukalová goes to school on Friday 14th September to tell them she and Viktorie are moving away and not to expect her on Monday. In fact, for whatever reason she doesn't actually go until Sunday 16th, and Viktorie doesn't go with her, so let's assume Viktorie has been killed on Friday or Saturday. So why, having decided to leave, does Broukalová not immediately go? If she'd left that afternoon she'd have been away before Nágl came home. She'd be safe and Viktorie would still be alive. So what kept her?'

'Presumably she had to wait for something,' Navrátil suggested.

'Pay day,' Krob interjected.

Slonský's eyes lit up. 'Money would make sense. She doesn't have the money to get away.'

'We're all paid direct into our banks once a month but she's probably paid weekly because if I understand correctly she worked in a local shop. And if it closes on Sunday then Saturday would be the last working day and therefore pay day.'

'Good thinking, Krob. When we're done here see if you can find out where she worked and when she was last paid.'

'When she enrolled Viktorie at the school she showed them a death certificate that allegedly belonged to the father,' Peiperová pointed out.

'Since we know she was using the name Broukalová I expect she used her father's. It would have the right name and enough women marry men a generation older for it not to be a complete surprise. She may even have altered the date of birth,' Slonský responded.

'And he'd died the year before Viktorie was taken,' Navrátil added. 'That bit fits.'

'Right, so we may be able to explain why she doesn't leave on the Friday. But where was she on the Saturday night? You see, we know of a number of events, but we can't assign them to a sequence. There are four that we have to get into order. Viktorie is killed, Magdalena is beaten up, Viktorie's body is disposed of and Magdalena runs away. The last one has to be Nágl chasing after her, and since I can't imagine that he broke off the chase to go back and put Viktorie in the river, and since we know Magdalena left on Sunday afternoon and he followed, it seems that Viktorie's body must have been put in the river before then.'

'Would he risk it in daylight, sir?' Navrátil wanted to know.

'It's much more likely he'd go when it was dark. That leaves us Friday or Saturday night for the disposal of the body. So Nágl would get in from work at six or seven on Friday, somehow discover they were planning to leave, there's an argument, Magdalena gets hurt…'

Krob interrupted. 'If she did, wouldn't they notice at work when she went to collect her pay?'

'Good point. Check that. We should have done it before, but I'm afraid I let the Dostál thing distract me. Mucha here can show you how to get employment records, so unless she was paid illegally cash in hand we should be able to find out where she worked.'

'Isn't it more likely that Magdalena would try to make Friday night entirely normal,' said Navrátil, 'if she knew that she couldn't leave till Saturday? Then she collects her pay, and if she didn't take Viktorie with her when she did so — and we can check that — she'd have left her alone with Nágl. And she must have known that was a risk because she knew Nágl had molested the child before.'

'She doesn't have a good option though, does she?' Slonský argued. 'If she's going to keep things as normal as possible she can't take Viktorie if she wouldn't normally take her. She can't pack her bags without giving the game away. She's obviously hoping that Nágl will go out over the weekend and she and Viktorie can get away. If all else fails they can go on Monday morning when he has gone to work. But until then, it has to be normal. Except that somehow he seems to have worked out what was happening.'

There was a short silence while they processed the information they had just shared.

'Viktorie told him,' said Peiperová.

'What? Why?' asked Navrátil.

'Not deliberately, of course. But she let it slip somehow. Perhaps she said she wasn't going to school on Monday. Maybe he asked her if she was good at keeping secrets and she told him one she was keeping. Or it could be that she thought he was coming too. They're a family in her eyes, so they would go together. All she'd need to do is ask where they're going and he'd tease the rest out of her.'

It seemed plausible.

'So when Magdalena comes back he lays into her. Viktorie starts to scream, he pushes her face into the pillow to keep her quiet…' Slonský continued the sequence. 'Then after dark he goes to dispose of the body, Magdalena hurriedly packs and gets out of the house. But where can she go? Why does she wait until Sunday to leave town?'

'Maybe the beating is so severe she can't go any earlier,' Peiperová suggested.

'Or perhaps he takes her with him while he disposes of Viktorie's body to make sure she doesn't leave,' added Navrátil. 'Then he thinks she's too badly hurt to travel on

Sunday, relaxes his guard and she steals the car and drives off, leaving him to trail behind.'

'He used his bank card on the Monday in Kolín,' Peiperová read from her notebook, 'then he uses it again in Most on Monday 24th.'

'And our best guess at present is that Magdalena is surviving thanks to the charity of Petra Novotná. We need to find an address for her,' said Slonský.

'I'll see what I can find,' Mucha replied.

Slonský looked at his watch. 'Let's meet up again in two hours for lunch and see what we've got.' He looked up at the menu board on the wall. 'On second thoughts, let's meet somewhere else for lunch.'

A murder enquiry can be a frustrating thing. Some days the police work ferociously hard tracking every possible piece of evidence, and at the end of it all the investigation seems to have gone backwards. On other occasions they find that witnesses introduce other witnesses, facts fall nicely into place and — if they're really lucky — someone confesses and saves them a lot of trouble.

Over the next two hours the team felt that they were really making some headway. Mucha found the name of Magdalena's employer. Navrátil was doubtful that they would be able to make contact since it was St Wenceslas' Day and therefore a public holiday (albeit that the non-believers referred to it as Czech Statehood Day) but when they telephoned the number they had the owner of the small local shop picked up.

Krob explained the reason for their call and the owner agreed that Magdalena Broukalová had worked there. She only worked from nine o'clock to two o'clock four days a week but she was a hard worker and flexible about her schedule. The owner had been disappointed when Magdalena had said that she would have to leave and explained that her relationship had broken down; so much so that the owner had suggested that she could keep her job if she could find somewhere else to live in Prague. However, Magdalena said she couldn't settle knowing that she might bump into her ex-partner.

'I don't like to gossip,' said the store owner, 'but I think she was hinting that she feared violence.'

'Did you ever see her bruised or harmed in any way?'

'No, never,' said the owner. 'That's one reason why I was surprised at her hint.'

'Not even on the last day? We gather she worked on Friday and came in on Saturday to collect her wages.'

'No, she seemed fit and well. She could have had the wages on Friday but she said she had better follow the usual routine so her partner would not become suspicious. I could quite understand that. She also had to pick up her work papers, of course, with her employment record so that she could get another job elsewhere. I gathered those together into a folder for her but she took them out and folded them so that they would fit in her bag.'

'Was her daughter with her?'

'No, she never brought her daughter to work. Occasionally in the summer holidays she would leave her with one of the other workers and they would meet here to hand their children over, because on her days off she would look after someone else's child in return, but otherwise we never saw her.'

'And just to confirm she hasn't been in touch since she left?'

'No, not at all. May I ask what this is about?'

'I'm sorry to have to tell you that her daughter died an unexpected death a few days later and Ms Broukalová hasn't been seen since. We'd like to confirm her safety if we can.'

When Krob put the phone down Navrátil complimented him on the call. 'That was a nice construction. "An unexpected death" sounds much better than "murdered by her stepfather".'

'We're assuming it was her stepfather,' said Krob. 'Do we know that?'

Navrátil was stopped in his tracks. They had built such a compelling picture of the events of that weekend that they had not stopped to consider an alternative. Could Magdalena have suffocated Viktorie? Was that why Nágl had beaten her?

Slonský listened to Navrátil's questions with increasing unease. 'Those things are possible, but there are two ways to conduct an investigation. You can either keep all the possibilities running at the same time, in which event you risk ending up with chaos, or you pick the likeliest one or two and go with them until they're disproved, when you have to retrace your steps and think again. Why would Magdalena suffocate Viktorie?'

'So she could start a new life, I suppose.'

'And why would she do it when she had already risked so much to snatch her in the first place?'

'Well, she could hardly return her to her mother, sir.'

'And I could understand that Nágl might have thumped her if he caught her red-handed, but after the event why chase her across the Czech Republic when he could just call us and get us to do it for him? He's given up his job and he's using his savings trying to find her. Why would he do that if she's the guilty one? It makes no sense to me.'

Mucha had found an address for Petra Novotná but he had not been able to trace a telephone number. It was a cause of continuing disappointment to Czech officials that some people seemed to be able to live their lives without possessing a telephone or even a computer. Novotná was described as self-employed, so he assumed that she used a business phone registered in a business name. It ought not to be difficult to find — after all, self-employed people want others to be able to find them — but it was going to take him a little while longer.

Peiperová was still ploughing through the list of refuges and hostels in Prague. Slonský had no idea that there were so many. He had sorted out enough cases of domestic violence over the years to be under no illusions about their frequency, but as a man who would never think of hitting a woman and would have been deeply ashamed of himself if he had he could not understand why so many men demeaned themselves in this way. In the interests of balance Peiperová had felt obliged to note that violence in relationships did not always flow in the same direction, but agreed that it was a considerable task and expressed her thanks to Krob for helping her work through the list after his phone call to the shop owner.

Navrátil had completed his ring-round, but without finding anyone who would admit to having received a woman of about fifty with a bruised face last Sunday or Monday. 'If she isn't staying with Novotná I don't know where she is,' said Slonský. 'It's hard to imagine that she has the money for a hotel or guest house.'

'She might for a few days, but she'd quickly run out,' said Peiperová. 'I'm better paid than she was and I doubt I could stay in one for more than a fortnight, and then only if I bought food and prepared it myself somehow.'

Slonský drained his glass. 'I have to go to see Colonel Urban now. Keep up the good work and give one another a hand. We'll get to the bottom of this somehow.' I just can't see how unless we strike very lucky, he thought to himself.

Chapter 16

Colonel Urban was in a very good mood. He remained in a very good mood even when he saw what Slonský was expecting him to sign off.

'You might like to know,' he began, 'that Dr Pilik has today written to Interpol terminating Colonel Dostál's secondment and requiring his return to Prague to face serious criminal charges. I haven't seen the letter, of course, but that's what the Minister's office has told me.'

'I've had some experience of the Minister, sir. Dr Pilik is very good at sticking the knife in once he's been shown where he has gone wrong.'

'As you climb the greasy pole, Slonský, you come to realise that he's not alone amongst politicians when it comes to that.'

'I imagine not, sir.'

Urban read the first couple of documents and signed them without any fuss. The third one produced a deep furrowing of his brow.

'This Jerneková woman — why do you want her?'

'I could go through the normal processes, sir, and spend weeks reading applications and interviewing only to be saddled with somebody unsuitable. I just took the view that if I went out and found the right person it would save a lot of time that I could devote to doing my actual job of fighting crime.'

'And you think she can do it?'

'She's a bit rough and ready but she's streetwise, she observes well and she's honest. She's also a woman, which is seemingly the most important characteristic of all in the eyes of the Human Resources department, since they made that the top requirement on their list.'

'She'll still have to do her basic training.'

'I know, sir. She doesn't qualify for the Police Academy, not having completed higher schooling, so she'd have to go to a Police School, but after six months she can apply for a placement with my team, which we will of course grant. She'd be a uniformed officer in the crime department for another year, then she can apply for detective training, which we would again grant. So eighteen months from now I'll have the officer I want, and that's worth waiting for. But it needs your signature to say that she'll be given a placement with us. And if you have any pull to get her into the police school that would be good too.'

'Getting her into the school won't be too hard, Slonský. We're not meeting the target for recruits as it is. It's just a little irregular to recruit someone by promising that they'll get postings and promotions before they start.'

'I'm just being innovative, sir. The current Director of Police always says that's what he wants us to be.'

'I don't think he had that sort of innovative in mind, Slonský.'

Urban read it through one more time and signed it.

'There! If it all goes belly up, on your head be it.'

'I'm entirely confident, sir.'

'Now, this building quote. Why do you need a wall knocked down?'

'Because my old office and my new office have a wall between them. I can't see my staff to supervise them. It would foster team spirit to be together. Besides, Krob would find it much more convenient because as things stand the old office will hold three and a half and the new one could hold one and a half, and he's the unlucky beggar who won't have a proper desk in either.'

'But you also have an office that used to house Dvorník, Hauzer, Doležal and Rada, and now that the latter pair have been posted to Pardubice two people are occupying a room designed for four. You could simply swap them over.'

'Ah, but with all due respect, sir, Lieutenant Dvorník doesn't need the level of personal supervision that the younger officers need, and if I swapped them over I'd be even further from Navrátil and Peiperová than I am now. And the derogation that allows them to work together despite their relationship was based upon the supposition that I would be physically close enough to intervene if they showed signs of unprofessional canoodling.'

'And have they?'

'Certainly not. Navrátil has strong opinions about that sort of thing. But as his nuptials approach, the pressure on his scruples to anticipate the lawful joys of matrimony will surely increase.'

'Slonský, I've heard some tosh in my time, but that's pretty high up the list of bunkum I've experienced. How about if I move the officers out of the room on the other side of yours and give you three in a row plus Dvorník's room just along the corridor?'

Slonský had not considered that possibility but it sounded good. He could have Navrátil and Krob on one side and Peiperová and Jerneková on the other and still have space to squeeze a desk of his own in each if he wanted, so he extended his hand to shake Colonel Urban's and watched as his superior tore up the fourth piece of paper.

Navrátil was keen to bring matters to a head.

'Why don't we go to Petra Novotná's house and just see if there's any sign that Magdalena Broukalová is there? If she is we have enough evidence to bring her in for questioning on the abduction charge, and she might come voluntarily anyway if it means Nágl can't get at her.'

'But what if she isn't there? Or, more exactly, what if she is there, but not at the time when you call? We'll have given away that we know what she did.'

'That's true, but she has very limited options for survival. She's not earning and she has very little in the way of savings.'

'Ah,' sighed Slonský, 'that's why rich people make more successful criminals. Having money gives you options that poor people don't have.'

'My point exactly. She has no real options. She can't get out of the country easily…'

'Hang on. We don't know for sure that she didn't get out before we knew who she was.'

'She couldn't afford the ticket to Vienna, sir.'

'Has it occurred to you, lad, that if you already have child abduction to your name not buying a ticket on a train may not be too much of a moral challenge? Thousands of Czechs do it every year.'

'You think she may have boarded the train without a ticket?'

'Don't look so astonished. I'm not saying she did. I'm saying she might have done.'

'Okay, but the only lead we have is that she may have sought help from Petra Novotná. I think we should at least pay an unannounced visit. We may be wasting our time, but we might not be.'

Slonský considered this for a moment. 'If you think you should go, that's fine. I said you needed to take the lead sometimes, and if you think that's a good use of your time I won't argue. But you can't go alone. We need two officers there. And since you're aiming to arrest a woman, you ought to take a female officer.' He looked round the room. 'If only we had a female officer spare…' he said.

Peiperová raised her hand. 'I could go.'

'You're ringing round hostels.'

'I can do that,' Krob said. 'I'm doing some anyway — I can just carry on with the rest of the list.'

'That's settled then,' Slonský announced. 'Go and book yourself a car and pay Petra Novotná a visit. If you time it right you should arrive after she finishes work, unless she's a nightclub hostess, I suppose.'

'I don't think it's the sort of place that has nightclubs, sir,' said Peiperová.

'And don't expect overtime payments,' Slonský added.

'I've never had one before,' said Navrátil. 'I didn't know they existed.'

'They don't. That's why you shouldn't expect one.'

'Which of us is going to drive?' asked Navrátil.

'You're in charge apparently,' said Peiperová. 'You decide.'

'I feel uncomfortable about giving you orders.'

'So you should. And I feel uncomfortable about taking them from you, but it's the police way. Someone's in charge, and this time it happens to be you. In the future things may be reversed.'

Navrátil decided that no answer that he could give would be convincing, and — more to the point — any kind of answer would be unwise, so he unlocked the car and climbed into the driver's seat.

'How about I drive going and you drive back?'

'But if we find her and arrest her I'll have to sit with her in the back, which will make driving difficult.'

'Okay. You drive going and I'll drive back.'

'Good decision, Officer Navrátil.'

Navrátil could feel the tension in the air, and didn't like it one bit. Suddenly Peiperová burst out laughing.

'If you could see the look on your face!' she said.

'You're not annoyed with me?'

'Of course not.'

'You looked annoyed,' he said suspiciously.

Peiperová took the keys and smiled. 'If I'm annoyed with you, you'll know about it.'

Navrátil did not doubt that for a minute.

They changed places and Peiperová pulled out into the traffic.

'What have you got planned for us this weekend?' Peiperová asked.

'I thought when we get back tonight, or tomorrow morning if we're back very late, we'll go over to my mother's place and you can spend some time with her.'

'Does she go to bed early? I wouldn't want to arrive after she's retired for the night.'

'She sits reading most evenings, unless it's very cold, when she may go to bed to keep warm. Then tomorrow I thought we'd all go into the woods for a picnic, if the weather is good. It'll do her good to get some fresh air.'

'And who's going to make this picnic?'

'She will. She won't let me. You may be permitted to assist, if you're favoured.'

'That will be nice. I intend to impress her, you know.'

'You won't have to try. She'll be won over.'

'You think? This is quite nerve-wracking, you know, meeting your future mother-in-law.'

'You didn't say that when I met your mother.'

'But she's my mother! She wouldn't wrack anyone's nerves.'

'Yes, but you know that. I didn't.'

'Anyway, brave knight won over the dragon. You were a big hit. Mother and father approve.'

'I assumed that or you wouldn't be marrying me next June.'

'Actually, they think I've done rather well for myself.'

'That's very kind of them.'

'That's mainly because my cousins didn't. My mother looks at the men her nieces married and shuddered to think I might do the same. They were swayed by big muscles, you see.'

'I'm glad I don't have any then.'

Peiperová busied herself removing imaginary fluff from her trousers. 'One thing we ought to get clear. My mother thinks that a woman's main function in life is to get pregnant as quickly as possible after she marries. I've already told her I am not going to be your personal baby factory.'

'Heaven forbid.'

'I have a career too, you know.'

'I know.'

'I just wanted to be sure your mother didn't have the same idea, because it might lead to some friction.'

'She's never said so. Of course, she'd like grandchildren some day. And I assume you have no objection to children as such?'

'Not ours, no. I'm not dewy-eyed over other people's.'

It crossed Navrátil's mind that there were a number of topics related to their forthcoming marriage and life together that they had not discussed, and probably should have done, but a police car was not the place. Peiperová had no such inhibitions.

'Just in case there's any doubt, I don't want a baby any time soon.'

'No. Right.'

'And I'm relying on you to make sure I don't have one.'

'How do you m— oh, right. Yes. That'll be my job.'

'Just getting it out in the open.'

'I understand.'

'And I'm not taking your name. At least, not professionally. I don't mind being Mrs Navrátilová when we're off duty, but I'll still be Peiperová at work. I don't want anyone thinking that I'm riding on your coat-tails.'

'You may advance faster than me,' Navrátil pointed out.

'Even so. Just managing expectations.'

'That's fine by me. Anything else you want to make clear now?'

'Yes. Your tennis is going to have to improve. I can't get better if you can't return my serves.'

'I do my best, but after your arm goes up the next thing I know is the ball smacking into the wall behind me. You could always practise with someone else.'

'Where's the fun in that?' Peiperová asked.

Slonský was enjoying an evening (or, perhaps, late afternoon) of solitude. He had a beer in front of him, and a plate of sausage and onions was on its way, so life was good. He needed to think, and since Valentin was busy at the radio station where he had just been reinstated as one of the late night chat show hosts, Slonský anticipated no interruptions. He had promised that at ten o'clock he would listen to the programme so that he could give informed feedback on

Valentin's pithy social commentary, unburdened as it was by either research or excessive reliance on facts, and just hoped he could stay awake through the whole programme, something he had never achieved during Valentin's earlier stint. This was less of a handicap than might have been thought, partly because Valentin kept repeating himself ('As I said earlier…') and partly because Slonský already knew his views on almost any subject that might be raised so if asked he could probably busk a critique.

He turned over the sequence of events that weekend when Viktorie died. Within his head, he walked through various possibilities, but almost all of them came up against a problem. Sometimes it was that the sequence made no sense. Why did Nágl choose that weekend to kill the child? Was it fear because he had discovered they were leaving him? Did Magdalena decide to leave because she foresaw this happening some day? But if he killed the girl, why didn't he kill Magdalena too? Why did he let her escape? Did he think he had such a hold over her that she would be pliable in future? And how had he managed to track her to Kolín and then back to her original home? They'd been together some years so he supposed that something must have been said at some time. He thought of his wife Věra; they'd only been together for two or three years nearly forty years ago but he'd known where her family home had been, which school she had attended, where her first job was.

Magdalena had hurriedly packed a bag. Her partner seemed to have chased after her without pausing to do so. It must have been a shock to him when she drove off in their car and left him having to use public transport. Slonský considered whether Nágl might have been able to persuade a friend to lend him a car or give him a lift, but concluded that Nágl didn't seem to have any real friends. He would have used public transport, but that would not necessarily have left him far behind her. The Prague traffic system gave priority to public transport in some places so it was often faster than driving. That's why Slonský rarely drove. If he took a car it was usually so he would have some way of conveying a prisoner.

There was then the question of what Broukalová was going to do next. She could not hide forever, especially with no money coming in. Even if Petra Novotná was the best friend a woman ever had, she would not want to house and feed her indefinitely. They had only to wait, and one day Magdalena Broukalová would take a job or rent a flat and her details would come up on an ID trace. It just seemed cruel to him for Mr Dlask and Mrs Dlasková to have to wait that bit longer to get justice.

Major Rajka could have done with a stiff drink himself, but as a teetotaller he was denied that pleasure. He had just spent an hour closeted with the Minister of the Interior, Dr Pilik, as the latter raged about the response he had received from Colonel Dostál.

Pilik had written to Interpol withdrawing Dostál's credentials. Interpol had, of course, immediately complied and had informed Dostál that he must return to his home country, but Dostál was not that stupid, and had last been seen enquiring about a flight to Taiwan, which did not appear to have an extradition treaty with the Czech Republic. What really irritated Pilik was that when he had enquired of his officials how they should begin the extradition process he had been told that he needed to contact Interpol where, it transpired, Dostál had pre-empted him by asking the extradition experts which countries were particularly difficult to retrieve fugitives from.

It seemed likely that Dostál and a lady friend had driven to an airport in Germany from which they had taken a flight to the USA. The woman had been detained at New York because she did not have a visa or any other permission to enter. Dostál had the brass neck to use his Interpol ID card and had talked his way into a transit lounge.

This had now become very personal for Pilik who was telling anyone who would listen that his high office was being disrespected. He had formally requested the Taiwanese authorities to detain Dostál, and when they asked for probable cause and seemed to be dithering, he asked the Japanese to order the flight to land when it crossed their airspace.

Rajka had gone back to his office and rang the American authorities with the news that a criminal was in possession of an expired Interpol pass and on board an American flight. They had been very helpful and the plane, which had been sitting patiently waiting for its turn to take off, was instructed to taxi back to the terminal where some large gentlemen boarded it to remove a passenger.

Rajka had then telephoned the Minister to tell him what had transpired, with the result that Pilik had gone home in a very good mood and Rajka took heart from Pilik's closing remarks.

'Isn't the head of OII usually a colonel?'

'Historically he has been, but there is no obligation to make him one.'

'We must see what we can do.'

Navrátil parked the car and walked with Peiperová towards Novotná's house. As Slonský regularly remarked, Navrátil didn't really look like a policeman, but just in case anyone was suspicious he held Peiperová's hand as they walked along. It was only fifty metres or so to the door but he wanted to ensure that nobody in the house should see them pull up.

'It's on the third floor,' he said.

'There's an external fire escape at the back but I don't think we need to separate to cover that,' said Peiperová. 'If she's there she won't want to run until she knows she has to.'

They climbed the stairs, taking care not to inhale the urine-scented air in the stairwell any more than was absolutely necessary. At the third floor they paused while Navrátil produced the address and silently showed it to Peiperová, receiving nodded confirmation that they had come to the right place.

Each of the detectives held their badges at the ready as Navrátil listened at the door.

'Two female voices,' he whispered.

'Adults?'

'Sounds like it.'

'Let's knock and get it over with then.'

Navrátil did as Peiperová suggested. The door was opened by a woman of around fifty. She had chestnut brown hair tied back in a ponytail and no evidence of bruising on her face, so Navrátil concluded that this could not be Broukalová.

'Would you be Petra Novotná?' he asked.

'Yes. What is it?'

'May we come in? We'd like your help in connection with a crime we're investigating.'

Novotná was not going to budge. 'Why do you think I can help?'

'We're acting on information we've received.'

Novotná bit her lip. If that was the case bluster was only going to get her so far.

'We can sit on the stairs for days if we have to,' Peiperová added, at which Novotná held the door back and allowed them to enter.

She led the way into a room at the back of the flat, Navrátil following her while Peiperová waited by the door. This proved to be a wise precaution because as Navrátil began speaking in the sitting room, a bedroom door opened and a woman stepped out and made for the exit, walking straight into Peiperová's arms. Despite her struggles she was unable to free herself, her difficulties being enhanced by Peiperová's knowledge that her right arm was injured already. Peiperová gripped the wrist firmly and threatened to twist it, at which point Broukalová submitted to the inevitable, dropped to her knees and began to cry.

Chapter 17

Navrátil and Peiperová knew that they must not ask any questions on site, but wait until they had Broukalová in the interview room. The temptation to rush in was considerable, but they had learned from Slonský that giving an interviewee time to wonder what exactly the police knew would raise her anxiety levels and was likely to make her more malleable when the questioning began.

They telephoned to say that they were bringing Broukalová back, which led Slonský to order a celebration coffee and take a leisurely stroll to the office. Mucha was just handing over to Sergeant Salzer, which was no bad thing, because Salzer was a big, silent man who could intimidate interviewees without saying or doing anything very much except stand still and look at them. It was true that he shared Slonský's hatred of crooked police officers, more than one of whom had unaccountably fallen out of his grasp and banged their heads on walls, floors and steps over the years, but in other respects he was a stickler for the rules. For example, he knew that interviewees did not have to be offered food or drink until they had been in custody for six hours, and he therefore had the stopwatch function on his watch permanently set to five hours fifty-nine minutes to ensure that he did not inadvertently give them anything too early.

Mucha threw his coat over his shoulders and donned his cap.

'Long night ahead?' he asked Slonský.

'As long as it takes. Fortunately I've just eaten.'

'You'll be good for at least two hours then.'

'I can hang on longer than that when I smell blood. Or is it fear I can smell?'

'In this place it's probably cabbage.'

'If I tell Dumpy Anna you've disparaged her cooking you'll be for it.'

'I'm not frightened of her. Remember I've learned how to handle my wife's sister, and she can turn you into a toad with one look of her eye.'

'Is she staying with you again?'

'No,' scoffed Mucha. 'I wouldn't be going home at this time if she was there. I'd put in a few more hours unpaid.'

Broukalová preceded Peiperová up the steps to the main door and was shown to the interview room, which was a grand description temporarily assigned to Cell Three once Salzer had put a table and chairs into it.

'You two do the questioning,' Slonský instructed. 'Pretend I'm not here.'

Since he then took up a position leaning against the inside of the door it was a difficult order to follow.

'You'd better lead,' Peiperová said to Navrátil. 'You've been on this case throughout, whereas I haven't.'

Navrátil nodded and took his seat with Peiperová to his left. He turned on the tape recorder and recited the date, time and those present. 'Our interest is in the abduction and death of Viktorie Dlasková, otherwise known as Viktorie Broukalová. You know who we mean?'

'Yes,' Magdalena whispered.

'Let's start at the beginning with her kidnapping. You were working at the time in a kindergarten where Viktorie was one of the children.'

'I'd left a few weeks before. My then husband and I had been trying for a baby for a long time. I'd had tests and treatment and finally I managed to fall pregnant. I lost the baby at six months.'

'I'm very sorry,' said Navrátil, earning himself a look from Peiperová who clearly felt that this was a poor justification for stealing someone else's child.

'I got depressed,' Magdalena continued. 'I must have been difficult to live with.'

'And your marriage suffered.'

'My husband was a good man but he didn't understand. When you want a baby so badly nothing else matters. I said we could adopt but Jan wasn't keen. If he couldn't have a baby of his own blood he didn't want one just for the sake of having a baby. I did.'

She spread her hands expressively as if that explained all that had followed.

'When did you come up with the idea of kidnapping a child?'

Magdalena's tears began again. 'I don't remember exactly when Jan walked out. He went to stay with his sister — the one you met tonight. I should have been heartbroken but it seemed like the last obstacle to having a baby had been removed. I decided to start again somewhere else. I'd come to Prague — nobody knew me here and if I turned up with a baby they wouldn't know it wasn't mine. So I hired a van to take the few things I owned with me. My dad had let me drive a fork-lift truck at his work a few times when I was a teenager but I couldn't drive really and I didn't have a car. I told the van driver we'd have to drop by the kindergarten on the way to pick my child up, and directed him to the back car park. I didn't know which child it was going to be. I didn't really care, so long as I got one.'

'Didn't it occur to you that you were going to cause great pain to some other woman?' Peiperová asked.

'Of course not,' said Broukalová, 'or I wouldn't have done it.'

She gave Peiperová a look as if to convey that it was possibly the stupidest question she had ever been asked. Peiperová, for her part, felt any last shreds of sympathy for the woman opposite dissipate into the air like fairy wings. And Navrátil, who was a sensitive soul at any time, but particularly attuned to Peiperová's moods and thoughts, decided to move swiftly along because he was detecting her "Give me strength" vibes and feared she might reach across the table, shake the suspect and tell her to pull herself together. Of course, he reasoned, Peiperová is never less than entirely professional, but she has very little tolerance for what she regarded as "wet girliness".

Broukalová decided more explanation was needed. 'You're a woman. You should understand. Having babies is what we're made for.'

Peiperová was about to respond when Slonský cut in.

'I think at this stage we shouldn't get bogged down in motives and explanations. Let's stick to what you actually did. We can come back to why later.'

Broukalová nodded.

Navrátil picked up the questioning. 'So you admit that you took Viktorie Dlasková?'

There was a prolonged pause before the whispered response. 'Yes.'

'A little louder for the tape, please.'

'Yes. Yes, I took her. And I loved and cared for her.'

'So did her moth—' began Peiperová.

'How did you persuade her to come with you?' asked Navrátil.

'She and I always got on well. I had a dark blue jacket with a kitten on the pocket and when I held it open she wanted to try it on. Then I just wrapped her up in it and carried her outside. In no time she was in the van and we were on the highway to Prague.'

'And where did you plan to go when you got here?'

'I'd seen an advertisement for a women's refuge. We headed there and they helped me get set up. I found a job and they got Viktorie a place in a nursery. If I needed a babysitter one of the other women would always help just like I'd help them if they needed it.'

She glanced at Peiperová to suggest that some people might not understand the nature of that kind of sisterhood.

'And how did you meet Daniel Nágl?' Navrátil persisted, feeling it better not to invite Peiperová to reply.

'After a few months the refuge finds you a place outside. Mine was near where we've been living. We were out in a park one day and he was jogging. When he came back round the second time he said hello and we got talking. Most men are put off when you've got a child but he wasn't.'

'But it seems his interest in Viktorie wasn't entirely innocent,' Peiperová interjected.

Magdalena looked at her hands for quite a while before answering. 'No.'

Peiperová continued the questioning. 'We know what he did to her, Ms Broukalová. We have forensic evidence. We know how she suffered at his hands.'

Broukalová began to sob. 'I didn't know for a long time. I'd never have had anything to do with him if I'd even suspected…'

'But you stayed with him even after you discovered it.'

'He'd discovered she wasn't mine.'

'How?'

'I don't know. I may have said something when we'd been drinking. Or maybe Viktorie told him — she sometimes called me her other mummy, and I said she just didn't speak proper Czech yet. Anyway, he said if I shopped him he'd go straight to the police to tell him I'd stolen Viktorie.'

'So you allowed your partner to abuse a child for whom you had assumed responsibility rather than face up to what you had done?'

Slonský admired the direct line of questioning. He didn't believe in a softly, softly approach to interrogation.

'If that's how you want to put it…'

'It doesn't matter how I want to put it,' Peiperová commented, 'it's how the prosecutor sees it.'

'How long had this been going on?' Navrátil asked.

'I met him about six months after I got to Prague. We moved in together early in the New Year. I don't recall exactly when I discovered it. About three years ago Viktorie was complaining of being sore and when I checked her out I couldn't understand what had happened. I wanted to take her to the doctor but Daniel convinced me she must have sat down awkwardly and she'd soon get better if we bought some cream.

'Then a few months later it happened again, but this time Viktorie said Daddy had hurt her when they were playing. He denied it, of course, but I could see something in his eyes. I couldn't get him to admit anything but I told him firmly that if I ever knew he'd been interfering with Viktorie I'd be going straight to the police.

'Then I suppose nothing else came up for the rest of the year but one day in the following winter Daniel was looking after her while I was at work and when I was bathing her she said

Daddy had hurt her again. That's when I shouted at him and he told me he knew she wasn't mine.'

'But you didn't leave?' Peiperová persisted.

'I thought he'd been a good partner in other ways. Whatever he had, he gave us. He looked after us both. I didn't make enough money to keep Viktorie and me. I just told him that if I was going to stay, this mustn't happen again. But I can't say I really trusted him again, and when I came across some photos he'd taken of her I decided I had to get away.'

'These were explicit photographs?' Navrátil prompted.

'They were vile, horrible photographs. He said they were just pictures of her having fun but I knew otherwise. So I told the teachers at her school one Friday that Daniel and I were separating and that she wouldn't be back on the Monday.'

'Where were you going to take her?' Navrátil enquired.

'I didn't know. Anywhere I could get to. Then I thought of Petra. I don't want her brought into this — she didn't know about any of it till I turned up. We'd always been friendly, even after Jan walked out. She tried to reconcile us because she said she liked us both. So I thought if I went back home I might find someone who would help us. But I couldn't leave on Friday because I didn't have my pay and papers.'

'Your boss said she'd have given them to you early if you'd asked,' Navrátil said.

'But that would have been different, so he'd have been suspicious. It had to be a normal weekend. Usually he went out for a run on Saturday afternoon. He'd only be gone forty to fifty minutes, but I thought I could pack a bag and run to the bus and be gone with her before he got back.'

'So why didn't you go?' asked Peiperová.

'I had to leave him with her while I went to get my pay. I don't know exactly what she said, but he told me she'd been upset about leaving all her friends. "What do you mean, leaving your friends?" he asked, and she let the cat out of the bag. I suppose he was mad with me and he took it out on her.

'When I got back they were upstairs. She was face down on her bed, and he was flushed and sweating. He said she'd been upset because we were leaving and he'd been trying to keep her quiet, but I could see she'd been gasping for air and her underclothes were missing. When I saw the state of the sheets I knew what he'd been doing.

'I attacked him and he hit me back several times. In the end he got hold of my arm and twisted it so hard I thought he'd broken it. He told me to be quiet, and he'd explain how we were going to get out of this mess. We'd wait till it was dark and then we'd go down to the river and drop Viktorie in. Then we'd wait a couple of hours and then call the police saying she'd run away from home and we were worried about her. They'd find her, assume she'd drowned, and we could go back to our lives.'

'What did you say to that?' Peiperová responded.

'I told him I didn't want to spend a night under the same roof as him ever again. He said he felt the same way, but I had a choice. I stayed where he could keep an eye on me or I'd finish up the same way as Viktorie. Either way I wasn't leaving, he said.'

'But you decided you were.'

'I didn't see how he could keep me. If I could get enough of a start I could get away. It's a big country and he'd never find me.'

'So you stole his car on Sunday?' Navrátil picked up the narrative again.

Broukalová nodded. 'I thought if I could remember what Dad had taught me when I drove the fork-lift trucks I could get to a train or bus station and get away. More to the point, if I had the car he couldn't have it so it would give me a bigger start.'

'And you drove it to the main train station and caught the first train you could?'

'Yes. I didn't have enough money to get out of the country so I thought the first thing was to get out of the city. Then I'd pick up my original plan of going back home to meet up with Petra the next day.'

'Daniel didn't know about Petra?'

'He knew a bit because I'd told him about my ex-husband, but I'd never told him her address. It was in my address book, but that was always in my handbag. I didn't think he'd ever have found us there. My fear had been that he'd find Viktorie through her school, but once she'd died and I wasn't travelling with her I didn't have to worry about that. I thought I could get away and start again, and not be hurt any more.'

Navrátil looked enquiringly at Peiperová who shook her head.

'That's enough questioning for tonight. We'll have to keep you here but we'll send some food for you. We'll make our report to the prosecutor and we may have to question you again.'

Since there was no female officer at the front desk by this time Peiperová was given the job of removing anything Broukalová could use for self-harm. This included her bra, though Navrátil had never been entirely clear how you could kill yourself with one of those. He busied himself in organising a tray of food and some bedding, and completing the arrest log. By the time the two of them had finished they walked up to Slonský's office to see what he had been doing.

'It's too dark to go now,' he told them, 'but first thing tomorrow we'll take her down to the river and she can show us where she and Nágl put Viktorie in. I've organised a scenes of crime officer to come with us to gather any forensic material that may still exist. I doubt there'll still be any but you never know.'

'You'll want us in, sir?' Navrátil asked.

'Not all day, lad. I know you've got a weekend planned. Make the most of it. As you climb the tree the police will eat more and more of your private life. Anyway, aren't you two supposed to be at your mother's?'

'Yes, sir.'

'Well, take the car. You'll get there quicker that way. Then in the morning you can drive straight over to Komořany. Having come here first to collect me and Broukalová, of course. Eight o'clock suit you? The technician is meeting us at eight thirty when I call to tell him exactly where.'

'Yes, sir. Thank you, sir.'

'Not at all. Well done, the pair of you. It's a nasty, sordid case with some unpleasant people. You did well to keep your natural contempt in check.'

'I didn't do that very well, sir,' Peiperová admitted. 'I'm sorry, it was unprofessional of me.'

'The thing is, lass, that you thought Broukalová and Nágl were unusually unpleasant people. Whereas, if you'll take a tip from me, the key thing in a police officer is to believe that everyone is just as contemptible until proved otherwise. It makes dealing with their sort much easier. Now, hop off before I decide we're all going for a beer or eight.'

Mrs Navrátilová was still up when they finally arrived. This was not a surprise because although Navrátil liked to describe her as a retired lady of regular habits, she was very fond of television quiz shows and late night horror movies, particularly those of an exceptionally lurid type. On this particular Friday evening she quickly turned off a film about lesbian vampires when she heard the key in the lock, preferring to be found watching a documentary about Slovakian nuns who made and sold their own honey.

Navrátil explained that they needed to be at work on the following morning and apologised in advance if they disturbed her when leaving.

'You won't disturb me,' his mother replied. 'I'll be up at six. Always was, always will be. I'll have some breakfast ready for you both. Speaking of food, I kept some fish pie for the pair of you. It's in the warm oven.'

As they gratefully ate, Navrátil wondered if he needed to explain that his mother still followed the prohibition of meat on Fridays, being a good Catholic woman, and that he actually did the same when he could but had never seen fit to mention the fact in front of Captain Slonský, who regarded abstinence from meat as un-Czech.

'I thought Kristýna could have my room,' Navrátil explained, 'and I'll sleep on the sofa.'

'If you like,' said his mother, 'but I don't mind moving into the single bed and giving the two of you my room if you prefer.'

Peiperová had never seen Navrátil spit food across a table before. She covered the lower half of her face with her hand so he could not see her laughing.

Navrátil finally managed to hiss 'We're not married' at his mother.

'I know, but there's no harm in a cuddle. When I was a girl if you had to share a bed with a boy they put a line of pillows down the middle of the bed to keep you apart.'

'And suppose I'm overcome by passion?' Navrátil protested.

'You're bright young folks,' said his mother. 'I hope one of you would have the wit to throw the pillows away.'

Chapter 18

If Broukalová had slept at all, there was no sign of it in her haggard face. She left her breakfast untouched, which came as no surprise to Sergeant Mucha.

'To be frank, I'd be worried about her if she ate and enjoyed it,' he explained to Slonský. 'Some of those rolls are coming up for a long service award.'

'She's probably fretting about being in the back of the car with Peiperová again. They don't get on.'

'One's a young, intelligent policewoman and the other's a child abductor who has admitted disposing of a body illegally. I don't suppose they've found too much in common.'

'Broukalová thinks every woman thinks like she thinks.'

'Does she? She'd get on well with my wife's sister. They could exchange spells.'

'Peiperová doesn't have a lot of patience with women who plead their sex to explain why they do things.'

'You've noticed that too?'

'She doesn't hold with all this fluttering your eyelashes stuff in the hope that your boss will give you a helping hand up that has been the mainstay of women's progress in the Czech police force since time immemorial. She believes in getting promotion by being better than everyone else.'

'She's young. She'll learn.'

'Times may be changing though. Have you noticed that people are getting promotions based on merit these days?'

'No, who?'

'Well, me for a start. Twenty-something years as a lieutenant, and suddenly I'm a captain.'

'Yes, but you never applied.'

'I know, but it wouldn't have mattered if I had. And then look at Colonel Urban getting the Director of Police post.'

'I didn't think that had anything to do with merit. I thought you put a word in for him.'

'You overstate my influence,' said Slonský. 'Slightly.'

Navrátil had the look of a man who had spent a very uncomfortable night on an elderly sofa; or, more precisely, dividing his time between the elderly sofa and a rather older floor, onto which he had fallen at least twice. Peiperová had slept quite well once she had stopped trying to deduce anything about her boyfriend from the appurtenances of his bedroom. There was only one photograph of him in there, taken when he was about fourteen and showing him in some sort of uniform with a startlingly white shirt and shorts with creases that could have cut cheese. She moved it to the bedside table and gazed at it until she fell asleep.

In a startling development unanticipated by Slonský Peiperová had not tied her hair in its customary ponytail, but was sporting a red and blue headscarf within which her blonde hair had been bundled apparently carelessly, though the artifice in this was demonstrated to Navrátil by the knowledge that it had taken her fifteen minutes to get it as she wanted it. It was as if she wished it to be clear that Saturday was meant to be a day off.

As they drove into Komořany Slonský turned to speak to Broukalová.

'Our purpose in coming here is so that you can show us where Viktorie was put into the water. Navrátil will drive wherever you direct him, and we'll search the area for any additional clues. I need to make plain to you that you can expect a substantial prison sentence for the abduction of Viktorie. Your guilty plea, and the degree of co-operation you give us today, may go towards reducing your sentence. And while the difference between, say, fifteen years and twelve years may not seem much, try thinking how you'll feel about it eleven and a half years from now.'

Broukalová appeared unmoved, but turned to look out of the side window.

'Head right towards the train station, then once you've crossed the railway line turn next left,' she said in a low, flat voice.

Navrátil did as directed. The road became narrower and eventually it was not possible to drive any further.

'Ignore the "cars prohibited" sign, Navrátil. I bet they did,' said Slonský.

Navrátil drove a little further until the path became too narrow.

'We parked here on the right,' said Broukalová.

'Then we'll do the same,' said Slonský. 'We can walk the rest of the way with you.'

'It's not far,' Broukalová whispered.

As they climbed out of the car she indicated a gap in the bushes.

'There's a path parallel to this one that runs along the riverside. We carried Viktorie through here. Daniel couldn't get the car any closer to the water and doing it this way we could hide out of sight if anyone was taking a late night walk along the river.'

'How were you carrying her?' Slonský demanded.

'She wasn't heavy. Daniel could have carried her by himself but he wanted me to help so I'd have to share the guilt. And to stop me running off, I suppose. He carried her under the arms and I had hold of her ankles. I couldn't really use my right arm after he'd hurt it, so I made a loop out of my left arm and carried her ankles on my hip with my arm holding them against my body.'

'So you were in front?'

'Yes. Daniel barked at me to look up and down the river path before we stepped out. There was nobody there, so we ran across and put her on the ground behind that clump of greenery.'

'Navrátil, call the technicians to search there. We won't go any further than the gravel area until they're done.'

Broukalová moved closer to Peiperová so that the people using the path could not see the handcuffs that linked them. Peiperová took a step further away to re-establish the space between them.

'So you've got Viktorie on the ground. Then what?' demanded Slonský.

'Daniel said that we had to put her into the water face down because when people drown they finish up face down, so he wanted me to climb down into the water. I wouldn't do it because I thought he'd push me under once we'd put Viktorie in, so he crouched down and rolled her into the water himself.'

Slonský nodded as if this confirmed what he had already pictured in his head.

Broukalová began to cry softly. Peiperová resolutely refused to put a comforting arm around her.

'I see,' said Slonský quietly. 'And this is where you killed Daniel, isn't it?'

Broukalova's eyes opened wide, but no wider than those of Navrátil and Peiperová.

'No!' Broukalová protested. 'He took me home and I ran away the next day. He's been chasing me. He wants to kill me.'

'He's going to find that difficult,' observed Slonský, 'given that he's been lying at the bottom of the river here for a couple of weeks. Have it your way, if you want. You can protest your innocence, but when I call the divers in and they dredge him up you're going to need a really good story to explain how he drove you home after you battered his head in.'

The sobbing began. Peiperová seemed unsurprised that Broukalová might have killed her partner as if nothing that the woman could do would astonish her. Navrátil knew that his best course of action was to listen and learn, and to make the occasional note that might be needed later.

Slonský remained impassive. He just wanted the truth, and Broukalová could provide that.

'It was the forensic report on the car that made me realise what might have happened. You see, Daniel loved his car. Maybe he even loved it more than he loved you. He certainly spent a lot of time on it, polishing it, cleaning the inside, making the glass sparkle. So it seemed a little odd to me when the technicians remarked that it was missing its wheelbrace and jack. How could that happen?

'Then an idea came to me. When you lifted the body of Viktorie out of the boot you could have picked up the wheelbrace and hidden it somewhere, probably under your jacket. When Daniel bent down to push her into the water, you struck him over the head with it, and you kept doing it until you were sure he couldn't fight back. There's probably some blood spatter in those plants. If so, we'll find it.

'Then you'd need to get rid of his body, and lo and behold you had a thumping great river in front of you. He'd probably more or less fallen in as it was, but if he floated along beside Viktorie it would provoke questions and was bound to lead back to you. Much better if he went into the river and never came back up, so you looked for something heavy to weight him down, and there was the jack. It's a couple of kilos of metal, not perfect but a good start. Put some stones in his pockets and shove the jack down his pants and kick him off the bank, and you've done all you can. At any rate, it was enough to stop him bobbing straight back up. He's probably slowly moved along with the current but the divers will find him. Now, I'll ask you again, are you going to co-operate by telling us the truth?'

All eyes turned to Broukalová. She gazed helplessly from one to the other until finally she dipped her head and agreed to give a confession.

Three hours later Slonský was in his accustomed seat, Navrátil was putting the finishing touches to the documentation for the prosecutors' office and Peiperová was returning with a tray of coffee and pastries from the canteen. In the interests of gender equality she had been offered the option of writing out the statements but had allowed Navrátil to take the lead on that.

'There's something I don't understand, sir,' Navrátil began.

'There's a lot of things you don't understand, lad, and a lot of things I don't understand about you, but don't let it upset you.'

'Why didn't you tell us we were on the wrong track?'

'Because you might not have been, and then I'd have looked a real turnip if I'd told you you were wrong and I was right, wouldn't I? Better to hold my peace until I had a bit more information.' Slonský took an expansive bite of pastry. 'Strangely enough, it was you who convinced me, Navrátil.'

'Me, sir?'

'Yes, with your spirited defence of Kobr. You see, we'd all got a story in our heads that fitted the facts. Everyone was inclined to believe that he had a stash of cash somewhere waiting for him. We created a story, and then we saw the facts in the light of our story, so of course they all fitted.

'Then you came along with an ugly little fact that didn't really fit, but couldn't easily be shaken. Why would the villains actually pay a bribe when they'd got him on tape agreeing to take a bribe? Common sense said he'd never had his hands on the money.

'When you'd gone home I thought about what you'd said and realised where we'd gone wrong. Now — and I say this from the point of view of encouraging self-improvement and not to gloat over you cocking this up — it then seemed to me that we were doing the same in the case of Magdalena Broukalová. When you were questioning her you were asking questions designed to confirm the narrative we'd all cooked up, so of course she went along with it because it didn't incorporate any extra wickedness on her part. She gave you the answers you were expecting, and you accepted them because it proved your story right. Well, our story. I mustn't attribute it to you personally.'

'But I can only ask questions based upon what we know, sir.'

'Maybe, but you mustn't close off other options. In Kobr's case, you pointed to a fact we hadn't considered, and yet with Broukalová we all accepted something as fact that was purely speculative and was actually at odds with common sense.' Slonský clammed up and returned to his coffee and pastry as if he needed to explain no more.

'So what was it, sir?' asked Peiperová.

'The use of Nágl's credit card. We'd formed a picture of a man chasing a partner he'd abused. It fitted that story to assume that he'd used his card. But when you think about it, why would he use a credit card to draw out cash? It's an expensive thing to do. Surely most of us would just buy what we needed with our card? So why did he draw cash?

'And then it dawned on me. He didn't. Someone else did, and the obvious person was Broukalová. If she'd used his card for purchases the shopkeeper would have looked at the card and realised she couldn't be Daniel Nágl. But if she knows that magic number you have to type in, she can get money from his account at any teller machine.

'She drove his car to the railway station and left it there, but when you look at that video footage she isn't running to the train. She needs to get out of Prague but she hasn't yet worked out where she ought to go. So she goes to Kolín and sleeps there, thinking through her options.

'Next day she draws out some money and heads to her old home. Maybe she used the card in a ticket machine and that gave her the idea that she could draw money out of his account. But if he isn't chasing her, when all logic says he should be, the obvious explanation is that he can't chase her. And the top reason for that would be if he was dead too.'

'And the car report persuaded you that was what had happened, sir?' asked Navrátil.

'Not exactly. It was the improbability of what we were proposing. It worked for us because we have the resources of the state behind us. We can make a good fist of tracking someone down when they run off, so we were disposed to believe Nágl could find Broukalová. But when you think about it, finding a woman who could be anywhere in the country is a tall order. He can't just walk around until he spots her. Heavens, we couldn't find him for a fortnight so why should we think he could find her?

'Once she'd boarded a train she was as good as safe. She might not have believed that, but it was the case. He'd have given up on Sunday afternoon and been back at work on Monday, no doubt concocting some story about Magdalena and Viktorie having run away so that if the girl was found the finger would point at his partner, not at him. And she would have set herself up for that by telling the school that that was exactly what she and Viktorie were going to do.'

Navrátil scratched his head in perplexity.

'Careful, lad, you'll get splinters.'

'It's beyond me,' Navrátil argued. 'If it's obvious, it must be wrong because it's too simplistic. And yet it has to be where we start our enquiries. How do we ever solve crimes?'

'That's been puzzling me for some time,' Slonský conceded. 'I put it down to clean living, and enormous slices of luck. Plus a bit of hard work and keeping our brains in top notch working order.' He reached into his inside pocket and extracted two cream envelopes. 'I've been meaning to give you these for some time. I wanted to be sure you'd get them simultaneously, so this seems as good a time as any.'

He handed one to each of them.

Peiperová must have read from the bottom upwards, because she reacted first, gasping with delight and surprise.

'You've been promoted to lieutenant!' she cried.

'So have you!' came the reply.

'Why did you give us the letter addressed to the other one?' Peiperová asked.

'Because this way each of you got to celebrate the other's success instead of just your own. Congratulations to the pair of you. And now you understand why you won't be working together in the future. We don't usually have two lieutenants in a team. Dvorník will be senior lieutenant, and you'll each have a helper. You'll have to wait a bit for yours, Peiperová, so in the meantime you can give me a hand.'

'Thank you, sir,' they chorused.

'Don't thank me, thank Colonel Urban. He's the one who has the power to promote you. And he made it one of his last acts as Director of the Criminal Police to bump the pair of you up the ladder before he becomes Director of Police and is far too grand to speak to the likes of us.'

'Do we know who's replacing him here, sir?' Navrátil asked.

'No idea,' said Slonský. 'Probably someone we've never heard of and we'll have to break him in. Who knows what rubbish we'll be fobbed off with?'

Since Slonský was taking his wife Věra out for the evening they agreed to celebrate their promotions after the weekend, and rushed back to Navrátil's mother's house, pausing only for a twenty-five minute phone call in which Peiperová conveyed the glad news to her mother and father at home in Kladno. Her parents declared themselves delighted but unsurprised, because they always knew she would be a success in Prague, thus neatly drawing a veil over their previously expressed views when she was kidnapped by a criminal and held in a warehouse. Peiperová was made to promise that she would come home as soon as she could wearing her augmented uniform, in which she could be paraded around the town to draw the admiration of all her mother's friends.

Navrátil's mother was a martyr to arthritis and therefore sat to peel potatoes, holding one bowl on her lap and dropping the peeled ones into another at her feet. Peiperová offered to take over the duty while Navrátil told his mother something important. Having conveyed the information Navrátil flinched as he was attacked by seventy kilograms of newly-mobile old lady intent on a hug. He went out for a run while Peiperová and Mrs Navrátilová busied themselves in the kitchen. This went very well indeed, so much so that Mrs Navrátilová shared her secret method of making her much-acclaimed cheese straws, and when Navrátil returned his mother brought him a glass of water, seizing the opportunity to grasp him by the arm and whisper her verdict to him.

'This one's a keeper,' she said, nodding towards the kitchen where Peiperová was making a blueberry sauce. 'If you muck this up you'll have me to deal with.'

Chapter 19

Slonský had very fixed ideas when it came to soap.

He had grown up with one type of soap in the house. It was a big square-sided brick, usually green but occasionally pink, and it was used to wash anything that needed washing. His mother would rub it along shirt collars and then transfer it to the back of Slonský's neck. To his way of thinking, soap should smell of cleanliness and disinfection rather than of the flower garden. Accordingly, he continued to buy these blocks whose phenolic smell lingered for some time and convinced anyone within around ten metres that he had just come out of the shower. He even used it to wash what remained of his hair.

That Saturday evening Slonský was taking his estranged wife Věra out to celebrate her impending birthday — if only he could be sure when exactly that was — and he therefore went to town in the shower. He sang *Lady Karneval* as he scrubbed away. If Mucha's desk colleague Sergeant Vyhnal had been there he would have been able to tell Slonský it had been a big hit in 1968 and therefore was probably part of the soundtrack of Slonský's romancing of Věra. Slonský had forgotten that, just as he had forgotten some of the lyrics, though the bigger surprise to him was how hard he found it to hit the top notes these days.

Unlike many of his compatriots Slonský hated going out unshaven, and since it was around ten hours since his last shave he repeated the exercise using the same large bar of soap to provide the lather. Slonský had seen advertisements for new-fangled razors with three or four blades, but since he did not hold with so-called safety razors he stuck to the cut-throat version his father had given him in 1962. Suitably buffed up, he eschewed deodorant or body spray in favour of a liberal dousing in talc and turned his attention to a precise parting of his hair.

Věra had also made an effort. She was wearing a long-sleeved dress in blue. Since Peiperová was wont to ask what his wife had been wearing, Slonský decided he ought to define the shade of blue more closely, and came up with the description "a bit darker than Czech flag blue". He also observed that you could see through the sleeves.

It was a good thing that he had made a reservation, because the restaurant was packed when they arrived. The waiter had no difficulty in indicating their table, it being the sole unoccupied one in the centre of the floor. Having seated Věra Slonský took his own place and perused the menu.

Ordering was the easy bit. It was conversation that he had always found difficult. It would have been so much easier if Peiperová and Navrátil had been there. Peiperová was never stuck for small talk, and Navrátil was a really good listener, though how much of that was due to all the practice he got these days was hard to tell.

The problem was that there was so much he could not share about his work, and if he did not talk about work, what could he talk about? There was so little other than work in his life.

Slonský looked around the room in the hope that he would find something worth saying something about. There was a group of men in the corner who looked as if they were planning on a heavy night. To his right were four women who were soaking up wine as if they were made of blotting paper. Slonský was unsurprised to discover that they were British, and he assumed that the pink sash one was wearing proclaimed her to be a forthcoming bride. Czech women were less inclined to get drunk in public. At least the respectable ones were, but he acknowledged that times were changing. In his days on the beat he had never arrested a woman for being drunk. Nowadays it was a rare night out that didn't involve either stepping over a woman or trying to prop one up.

Věra was busily reminiscing about their courting days, but for all Slonský remembered of them she might have been making it all up. It wasn't that he was unromantic, but when she walked out he lost the best part of two years in an alcohol-derived oblivion and his memories of the time before that was now sketchy to say the least. He could remember, if pressed, the first time he saw her. They were young adults at a Communist party get-together during which he noticed a tall, blonde girl with a nice figure who was similarly attracted to the young man who couldn't be bothered to clown around with the other boys.

They met up at a few more such events which was always convenient because you allegedly needed no chaperone at a party function, though if Slonský recalled what went on behind the building correctly it seemed to him that if all the babies conceived there had been called Lenin even the dimmest party official might have suspected that they had failed in their duty of care.

The waiter removed the plates after their starter. As a concession to the refined nature of their meal Slonský was drinking beer in 300ml glasses rather than the usual half litre, which meant he had to go slower than usual if he was not intending to set up an assembly line of waiters delivering drinks like firefighters drawing water from a well.

Those idiots in the corner were looking his way again, or at least one of them was. It was a hazard of nights out in the city that there was always a chance that he would come up against someone he had once put away, so his antennae were constantly searching for potential trouble, and he was looking at it right now. However, he could not place the man, which was unusual for him. Normally he could recall everyone he had ever arrested, but he put the temporary failing down to having to concentrate at least partly on what Věra was saying.

Slonský had ordered a steak, which demanded his complete attention, and since Věra was trying to eat pasta in a ladylike fashion without splattering their neighbours with arrabbiata sauce the next course was consumed amid only desultory conversation. As the waiter swept the table with a small brush cunningly disguised, for no good reason that Slonský could imagine, as an elephant, the detective became aware of a shadow across the tablecloth. Looking up he could see the man from the table at the back but it was not Slonský he was interested in, but his wife.

'Věra? I thought it was you,' he said.

Věra glanced up and her smile froze.

'Cat got your tongue? Not pleased to see me?'

Slonský had no idea what this was about, but he knew he did not like it.

'I don't think my wife wants to talk to you,' he said.

'Wife? She's got her claws into you now, has she? When did that happen?'

'I don't think that's any of your business,' said Slonský, rising to his feet and scouting out the most convenient stretch of floor in case the visitor wanted to take an impromptu nap at the end of his fist.

The waiters seemed to have grasped what was happening and two were threading their way through the tables to intervene.

'Word to the wise,' said the man. 'Three years of my life she had, then she just slipped out and never came back. She'll do the same to you one day, mark my words.'

The waiters had each grabbed an arm.

'Let's get some fresh air, sir,' said one. 'My colleague will get your coat for you.'

Slonský watched as the man was steered out into the street and the door was closed behind him. Looking down he could see Věra dabbing her cheeks with a tissue. She did not look at him.

'I think I'd like to go home now,' she said quietly.

'Yes, that's probably best,' Slonský agreed.

On Sunday morning Slonský went into the office to borrow a car. He wanted to tell Mr Dlask and Mrs Dlasková the result of the enquiry face to face. They deserved that, rather than a phone call, he thought. He was not one to brood on disappointments so if he regretted how the previous evening had gone there was no sign in his demeanour. Stuff happens, and that was all there was to it. Compared with what the Dlasks had experienced last night's little upset was nothing.

He was pleased to find that Viktorie's parents appeared to be attempting a reconciliation, because both were in the house when he knocked.

'I thought you'd want to know what we've discovered,' he said simply, and was invited in.

'Can I offer you some coffee?' Mrs Dlasková asked.

'No, thanks. I just wanted to keep you informed.'

'We appreciate that you've driven all the way from Prague just to talk to us,' said Mr Dlask.

Dear God, that's not much to ask, thought Slonský, in the circumstances.

'The man who killed Viktorie was himself killed by his partner. She was the woman who abducted Viktorie from the kindergarten. She used to work there.'

'What was her name?' asked Mrs Dlasková.

'Magdalena Novotná. She used to be Broukalová.'

'I remember her,' Mrs Dlasková said. 'She left to have a baby.'

'She miscarried. But that doesn't justify her in stealing yours.'

'No, nothing does. At least she looked after Viktorie. Was it her husband who abused her?'

'She separated from her husband and took Viktorie to Prague where she met another man, Daniel Nágl. Nágl was the one who maltreated your daughter. According to Broukalová she couldn't tell the police because he'd discovered her secret and threatened to expose her as a child abductor. She says she came home and found Viktorie dead, and her partner demanded that she help him dispose of her body. When they went down to the riverbank she hit him over the head with a wheelbrace and killed him.'

They sat on the sofa and tried to absorb what they had just been told.

'Is she admitting it?' Mr Dlask asked.

'You can never be sure till you get to court but I think she will.'

'How long will she get?'

'Killing her husband carries a life sentence. Abducting your daughter could be anything from twelve to twenty years. The prosecutor is talking about life with a minimum of sixteen years before amnesty or parole.'

Dlask was crying. 'It's not enough,' he said. 'Not nearly enough.'

'No,' agreed Slonský, 'but it's the law.'

As he drove home Dr Novák rang to pass on the results of the diving party.

'They found him,' the pathologist said, 'though he was about fifty metres upstream from where you told us.'

'She lied about where it was, then.'

'She probably guessed there might be blood splashes, but didn't think you'd be looking for them when she told her story.'

'And were there?'

'There's not much on the greenery but there's blood in the earth. It won't be difficult to prove someone was killed there. Nágl's not in bad condition considering his skull's been cracked open and he's spent a fortnight or so underwater. Definitely recognisable, I'm pleased to say.'

Back in his office Slonský wrote up his report and printed it out. Rather than wait for Peiperová to show him how to correct it as usual, he wrote in the changes in ballpoint pen, initialling each meticulously, before walking along the corridor to leave it on Colonel Urban's secretary's desk. He wondered who would read it now that Peiperová was no longer there, or indeed whether Urban was still doing his old job now that he was getting a new one, but decided it need not concern him. His job was to report, and reporting was what he was about to do.

To his surprise the inner office was open, suggesting Colonel Urban was at his desk, so Slonský knocked on the door and walked in. Rajka looked up from the chair.

'What are you doing here?' they both said.

'I'm delivering my report on the abduction and murder,' Slonský explained.

'I heard you'd sorted it out,' said Rajka. 'I sent one of my captains up there to look into the original investigation. He's a good man. The department was a shambles eight years ago, and he doesn't think it's much better now. I'll have to deal with it.'

'Why you?'

'I'm surprised the grapevine hasn't kept you informed. With Colonel Urban moving up he's offered me his old job as Director of the Criminal Police.'

Slonský could not have been more delighted. He respected Rajka and this would mean that he was in favour with the Director of Police and the Director of Criminal Police. Life was sweet again.

'And you're accepting it?' he asked.

'I haven't said yes yet.'

'But you will,' urged Slonský.

'I think so. I enjoy what I do and it's important work, rooting out corruption and improving police standards, but the Director of Police doesn't come from that line of work. You have to be in the mainstream to have a chance of that.'

'And they'll make you a colonel too.'

'Already promised, whichever way I jump. Dr Pilik was pleased that we saved him from a lot of potential embarrassment over Dostál, so I know if I say yes I'll be appointed. And a colonel's wage would be welcome. I'll be back in uniform every day but I can put up with that.'

Slonský was smiling like a cat left alone with a bucket of cream. 'You'll be my boss,' he beamed.

Rajka stood up and walked around the desk to place a hand on Slonský's shoulder.

'You can escape that if you want,' he said.

'Why should I want?' asked Slonský.

Rajka perched on the corner of the desk. 'Someone has to replace me as head of OII. You're good at dealing with corruption. You've got a good track record of sniffing out dodgy cops. Captain Bendík is good but he's too young. He needs an experienced officer over him. And you'd get made up to major.'

'I've only been a captain four months,' Slonský observed.

'See, that's just the kind of old-fashioned thinking we need to chuck out,' Rajka answered. 'If you're the right man, it doesn't matter how long you've been a captain.'

Slonský was stunned. He had spent the best part of those four months plotting to reshape the team he worked in, he had manoeuvred his boss into the top job, and now it was all about to be taken away from him. He couldn't deny that the idea of banging up naughty policemen appealed to him, but he would miss Navrátil and Peiperová. Damn it, he'd been a loner for so long, then twenty months earlier they had forced him to take Navrátil and his life hadn't been the same since. If they'd asked him then he'd have jumped at the job, but now…?

'Can I think about it?' he asked.

'Please do,' said Rajka. 'If I can help you make your mind up, let me know.'

There's only one thing that can help me make my mind up, thought Slonský, and it comes in a tall glass.

A NOTE TO THE READER

Dear Reader,

Thank you for investing your money and time in my book.

Sometimes people ask where the ideas for stories come from, to which the honest answer is "Who knows?". However, I can identify a couple of distinct groups.

Occasionally the spur is a real life crime. Plainly the facts cannot be shamelessly lifted and used; that would be more like reportage than fiction, and unkind to the victims of the crime. There are occasions, though, when an author can look at the basic facts and ask "What if?", changing something to take the story down a different path. There is a long history of this back at least as far as Edgar Allan Poe's "*The Mystery of Marie Roget*"; for a particularly brilliant example, see John Hutton's "*29 Herriott Street*".

I often begin with a question I want to answer. *Lying and Dying*, for example, asked what happens when law and justice do not lead to the same outcome; *Slaughter and Forgetting* was concerned with how far we can trust distant memories; *Field of Death* came about when I heard the story of the ghost battery and asked myself how it could possibly be true.

A Second Death came to mind when I was reading an article about why crime goes unreported. The archetypal crime for which this is true is domestic violence; people (mainly, but not exclusively, women) may suffer many instances of abuse before it comes to notice, and this is reflected in my story, but there are other crimes for which it is true — and I started to ponder what would happen if someone could not report a crime because to do so would uncover a crime of their own.

I thought long and hard before introducing child abuse into a story. It is not a comfortable subject, but unfortunately it is something that police have to deal with. They find it just as unpleasant and upsetting as the rest of us, and I hope that I have captured this here.

If you have enjoyed this novel I'd be really grateful if you would leave a review on **Amazon** and **Goodreads**. The best salesmen for my books are readers, so please tell your friends too! I love to hear from readers, so please keep in touch through **Facebook** or **Twitter**, or leave a message on my **website**.

Všechno nejlepší!

Graham Brack

SAPERE
BOOKS

Printed in Great Britain
by Amazon

35990097R00158